SHADOW GAMES

AND OTHER SINISTER STORIES OF SHOW BUSINESS

SHADOW GAMES

AND OTHER SINISTER STORIES OF SHOW BUSINESS

ED GORMAN

SHORT, SCARY TALES PUBLICATIONS

BIRMINGHAM, ENGLAND

Shadow Games first published by Cemetery Dance Publications in 1993
"Scream Queen" first published in *Midnight Premiere* in 2007
"Riff" first published in *Postscripts* in 2004
"Such a Good Girl" first published in *Subterranean Gallery* in 1999
"Pards" first published in *The Best Western Stories of Ed Gorman* in 1992

ISBN: 978-1-909640-52-8

2016 SST Publications Trade Paperback Edition

Published by
Short, Scary Tales Publications
15 North Roundhay
Stechford
Birmingham
B33 9PE
England

www.sstpublications.co.uk

Book design by Paul Fry

Printed in the United States of America and the United Kingdom

First Edition: May 2016

10 9 8 7 6 5 4 3 2 1

For Martin H. Greenberg

A special thanks to Larry Segriff for his editorial work.

—EG

"It is hard to laugh at the need for beauty and romance, no matter how tasteless, even horrible, the results of that need are. But it is easy to sigh. Few things are sadder than the truly monstrous."

—Nathanael West, *The Day of the Locust*

My cousin Bobby Driscoll won a special Academy Award in 1949. He was a fine child actor. While this novel is in no way about him, it is about the sad ends met by some of Hollywood's most talented teenagers.

SHADOW GAMES

THE COBEY DANIELS STORY

"I know a lot of people think I'm a goody-goody because of my role on the show. Well, what's wrong with being a clean-cut, all-American teenager?"

> Cobey Daniels, interviewed in *Teen Scene*,
> August, 1984

(Reporter)   The police are saying that you pulled a knife on the waitress because she wouldn't serve you liquor. Any comments?

(Cobey)   Yeah, just one. Why don't you fuck off, you asshole?

> Cobey Daniels responding to
> KABC-TV reporter, May, 1985

Cobey: I'm an alcoholic. I can't touch the stuff. It's poison to me. Literally.

> Cobey Daniels, interviewed in
> *Rolling Stone*, "Notes from the
> Asylum," November, 1988

1985

PROLOGUE

|

JUST BEFORE THREE THAT AFTERNOON, ON A COOL
spring day in Miami, Florida, it became quite apparent that the
girl—a sixteen-year-old named Kimberly Jane Conners—possibly
was missing. Which was just what her mother had been insisting to
the officials of Windmere Mall for the past half hour.

The usual proceedings then took place.

Kimberly's name was put on the loudspeaker every five minutes
("Would Kimberly Conners please come to the mall offices right
away") and the mall security force, overweight people in starchy blue
uniforms and thick-soled shoes for comfort, were given her description and told to look hard for her.

The trouble was, her description—"five-three, one hundred
pounds, long, blonde hair, blue eyes, white blouse, designer jeans,
argyle socks, penny loafers and a pretty face"—could easily fit at least
two hundred girls who happened to be roaming around the mall just
now.

Because today was the day when the nation's hottest teen star, Cobey Daniels, the main attraction on NBC's number one sitcom, *Family Life*, was making three appearances at Windmere Mall.

He'd already done one earlier in the day, just before noon, and security had been awful: thirty-eight hundred teenage girls trampling anything in their way to get closer to the small, makeshift stage set up in the center of an open area. Mothers had gotten trampled, little brothers had gotten trampled, merely curious sales clerks had gotten trampled, and certainly security personnel—God, they only made minimum wage—had gotten trampled.

All so these crazed, hormonal, shrieking little girls could rush the stage and literally tear at the clothes of a handsome, blond, icily grinning, blue-eyed heartthrob who was lip-synching to his new number one record, "Won't You Be My Special Baby?"

In the midst of the melee, several ten- and eleven-year-old girls acquainted themselves with sexual frenzy—and liked the feeling so much that they decided to come back for more, meaning the four o'clock performance Cobey was scheduled to put on.

Somewhere in the midst of all this had been Kimberly Conners, who'd slipped away from her mother so she could get a better position near the stage.

Now, nobody had seen Kimberly for the past three-and-a-half hours and talk—whispers, really—had turned to the sonofabitch who'd come into a similar Florida mall last year and taken a three-year-old boy right from the men's room while his dad was in one of the stalls. The bastard had then driven the kid out to the Keys and molested him and then disemboweled him . . .

Kimberly's mother was trying real hard not to think about this incident. Kimberly's mother was trying to convince herself that Kimberly was here somewhere, just wandering around and spending some of the hundred dollars she'd gotten from Grammy Levin last birthday.

Around three o'clock, Mrs. Conners called her husband at work. He was an architect and always busy and occasionally hostile when he came on the phone. She didn't like to trouble him unless absolutely necessary. She considered this absolutely necessary.

She explained to him about Kimberly.

Within a minute-and-a-half, he was sliding behind the wheel of the new, blue, family Buick and heading straight for Windmere Mall.

||

In both grade and high school, Sharon Marie Bowers had been known as "Hairy Sherry" because of the undue amount of silky, black hair that covered her arms and put a faint, Hitlerian mustache on her upper lip. Her parents, who were working class, determined to spend all their money if necessary to help their only child. They heard how she sobbed at night after a day of teasing at school, and there's nothing more heartbreaking than hearing such sobbing from the child you love. There's also nothing that makes you feel more helpless.

Thus began a quest that went on for eleven years and ended in failure.

At twenty-four, Sharon Marie Bowers still had all her silky hair, though thanks to the option of long-sleeved shirts that the folks at Federal Security gave their guards, at least nobody had to gape at her arm hair.

There just wasn't much she could do about the mustache despite her best efforts with razors and a myriad of creams.

But you couldn't call Sharon Marie unhappy. True, she didn't have a boyfriend, but she did have a nice, seven-year-old Pontiac rag-top that she took out to the summer park and buffed in the summer sun, and she was newly elected captain of her credit union's bowling team, and her collection of country-western CDs kept growing. And she knew the particular pleasures of the lonely and the outcast, pets and special TV series only she seemed to like and the unexpected delight of meeting another lonely outcast and making friends.

So, despite the way she sometimes twitched and shuddered when she recalled the chant of "Hairy Sherry," and despite the fact that she needed to lose twenty or thirty pounds, and despite the fact that some of the other security guards usually got the more convenient hours, Sharon Marie Bowers was a happy woman, even when people occasionally hinted that she might be gay. Sharon Marie was rip-snortingly hetero and just waiting for this crew-cutted guy at the bowling alley to let her prove it.

She would be even happier by the time this day—April 28—had passed.

Because it was Sharon Marie Bowers who found Kimberly Jane Conners.

III

Any way you looked at it, the whole thing was pretty crazy and after about fifteen minutes Kimberly had started to realize just how crazy it was.

Just before he'd rushed through the doors that took him to the maze of back hallways that wound through the mall, Cobey Daniels had paused a moment—just a fraction of a second, really—and looked right at Kimberly.

Right at her.

With the full force of his blue eyes.

With the full force of his white-capped grin.

With the full force of his number-one-teen-idol aura.

And his eyes and his lips and his aura had said: follow me, Kimberly Jane Conners. Follow me into the hallway here and beautiful times will befall us. I promise you.

So, trance-like, she did just that.

She pushed past the screaming, jumping, jostling, pushing girls and, somehow, shoved, angled, wriggled and willed herself past the throng and into the hallway where Cobey stood waiting for her.

He didn't say anything.

He simply took her hand and led her away.

She had no idea where they were going. Obviously, Cobey had scoped this whole place out. He knew just which way a given hallway wound, and just where it ended.

His destination was a large door behind an upscale dress shop. He took her inside.

In the spill of light from the hallway, she saw a dozen shadowy mannequins. Some were only heads and shoulders. Some were full-bodied and, curiously, obscene. She'd seen a horror movie once where all these partial mannequins had beaten and strangled to death this fashion designer who had been murdering his models.

Now, their eyes stared, dead but knowingly, at Kimberly. They seemed to sense something that she didn't.

For the first time—everything had happened so quickly—Kimberly began to realize that something wasn't . . . right . . . here.

That maybe this really cool, really sexy guy here wasn't . . . right.

IV

Her name was Andrea Neely and until four years ago she had been a moderately successful swimsuit model who had dabbled in the escort business but had decided instead on getting her license to practice psychotherapy and forget modeling and professional screwing once and for all.

The first thing Andrea did was send Cobey to see a psychiatrist. Let Dr. Kostik do the heavy lifting. Andrea, who was a party friend of Cobey's agent, would just do the maintenance. The good Dr. Kostik decided quickly that Cobey was bi-polar and needed to go on heavy duty meds to keep him from indulging in the tantrums and fantasies that two PR people worked hard to keep from the press.

Just before Cobey had left on this round of mall tours she'd said, "Listen to me, Cobey. It's bad enough when you do go off your meds when you're here in LA and can get to Dr. Kostik or me right away—but when you're on the road and you're not taking your meds."

"I hate my fucking meds. They just make me feel worse."

"They keep you under control, Cobey. For your own sake. They don't let you go too far in either direction. I need you to promise me, Cobey. Everybody's worried something might happen."

"You think we'll ever fuck again?"

Cobey and his games, sometimes he could be pretty good at them.

Former swimsuit model and escort practitioner actually blushed. "That was a mistake. We never should've opened that bottle of champagne. Or smoked that weed. And anyway I know what you're doing."

"Yeah, what's that?"

"You're punishing me for reminding you to take your meds. You want to get back in control."

Cobey slumped in the comfortable leather armchair while seventeen floors down sunshine-flashing cars, trucks and motorcycles streamed toward the beach.

His smile was bleak. "That's the problem, Andi, isn't it? I always want to be in control but I never am."

V

So here's the bad part. Whenever he realizes that both Andi and Dr. Kostik are right AND THAT HE SHOULD NEVER BE OFF HIS FUCKING MEDS . . . he becomes both participant and observer.

Right now he's in this dusty dark room with all these bits and pieces of mannequins—talk about your war crime victims—and he's watching and listening to himself destroy his entire career.

"Cobey, please, just let me leave, my mom'll be real worried. And you haven't really done anything to me so there's nothing for you to worry about."

But he knows better. Nearly half an hour now and every time she starts to walk toward the door he grabs her wrist. Doesn't hurt her. But doesn't let her go, either.

"Have you heard even one word I've said to you, Kimberly? Even one?"

She's really not even pretty, just a thin little stick figure but with a little earnest face and jittery fingers that constantly pick at each other. But he knows instinctively—this is almost religious for him—that she's the one. It's the LA starlets and hangers-on you can't trust. A solemn girl like Kimberly, the instant his eyes, scanning the crowd, saw her the rest of them became a dull black and white photo. She stayed in color.

"Just please, *please* listen to me one more time, Kimberly. Then I'll let you go."

"You already said you'd let me go four times now, Cobey. That's why I'm getting scared."

"No reason to be scared. Just let me tell you again. So I'm sure you'll understand."

The observer-Cobey knows this'll all be in the *LA Times*. Maybe even front page. And Barbara Walters will interview Kimberly and her mother.

"I have the money to move you and your family—your mom and dad and your whole family to LA and to set you all up."

"Cobey—please listen to me. It's what I said before. I go to Catholic school here. I'm sixteen years old. We don't even know each other."

"That's the whole point, Kimberly. We'll all be in LA together. I'll get to know your folks so they'll know they can trust me. And then you and I can start going out. There're so many things I can show you. You won't believe some of the people you'll meet."

The observer-Cobey doesn't blame the poor girl for the terror and the disgust on her face. Thirty-some minutes of this insanity now it's a wonder she doesn't—

But she does.

Rushes to the door sobbing and screaming.

Sobbing and screaming.

And Cobey behind her—rushing to grab her—saying, "We just have to give it a chance, Kimberly. Just give it a chance."

VI

At this moment, Sharon Marie Bowers was passing by the storeroom door. And she heard Kimberly sobbing. And screaming.

From the considerable belt Sharon Marie Bowers wore around her middle dangled a jangling group of keys unmatched anywhere for sheer bulk and entanglement. But Sharon, being the type of person she was—organized, dutiful, responsible—knew just which door every key unlocked.

So, without hesitation, she called out, "I'll be right there!" to Kimberly, and quickly located the proper key.

And then she threw the door open.

Sharon Marie Bowers acted instinctively.

With great maternal elegance brought the weeping frightened girl to her with her left hand with her right she pointed her baton straight at Cobey and said, "You don't even try to move there, Mr. TV star. Otherwise I'm gonna do a lotta of damage to that pretty boy head of yours."

VII

On the six o'clock news that night, Sharon Marie Bowers was shown rushing into the hospital where young Kimberly was taken. Kimberly, being hugged by her mother, was a few steps ahead of the security guard.

The cameraperson tried to get in close for one of those weepy-creepy shots that news directors love, but Sharon Marie Bowers, being of sound mind and body, slapped the shit out of the cameraperson, and sent camera and operator heading, willy-nilly, into the hedges.

VIII

"Jesus Christ, Cobey."

"Please, Lilly. Please."

Lilly was his agent.

"She was goddamn jailbait."

"Please, Lilly. Please."

"Sixteen years old. I'm surprised you could even get her little pussy opened up."

"Please, Lilly."

"I'm getting on a goddamn plane."

"Lilly, listen, I—"

"And I'm goddamn flying out there—"

"Lilly, all I was doing was—"

"And I'm bringing David Feldman along. He's the best goddamn lawyer I know—and that's exactly what we need right now thanks to the fact that you can't keep your dick in your pants—the best goddamn lawyer I know."

The flight to Florida took six hours.

Lilly was in no better mood when she got to the police station and bailed Cobey out.

"The defendant will please rise and face the bench for sentencing."

Judge T.K. Stevenson
The People vs. Cobey Daniels
Miami, Florida
August, 1985

1988

"Lilly Carlyle would eat her young if she thought they tasted good enough."

—Unnamed producer

|

I N BEVERLY HILLS THAT SEPTEMBER, THE NEW EXERCISE guru was a lithe Korean chap who taught that you could *will* weight and cellulite away. Of course, he also put you on a diet of 834 calories a day, just in case the willing part didn't work so well. But he wore a version of a *dobro*, one of those white, belted jobs that Tae Kwon Do instructors favored, so he must have known what he was doing, right?

Anyway, the deal was this: you'd go into a small, dark room that was lit from above only by a small, rose light. In the background, soft Korean music played (or what the Korean chap said was Korean music; actually, it sounded a lot like the 101 Strings Playing Ravi Shankar's Greatest Hits); and then the Korean chap, sitting in the exact center of the floor, with all the overweight ladies around him, would start reciting long lists of presumably Korean phrases, and the overweight ladies would do their best to repeat them.

This went on for nearly half an hour, at which point the Korean chap stood and went around to each of them and touched his sharp, damp thumb to their foreheads, and said a prayer that they should shed their excess pounds. Again, he spoke what was presumably Korean, though Georgia Feldstein, a wise-ass matron Lilly liked a lot, said that sometimes the man's Korean sounded like some of the things Shemp and Moe muttered to each other in the course of a "Three Stooges" two-reeler.

The cost for all this was three hundred and fifty dollars a week and, in the first month, Lilly Carlyle lost not a single pound. She had, as always, drawn up a list of "substitutes" for the things the Korean chap had recommended for his 834-calorie diet.

And they were the usual substitutes, too: cake for bran bread; rich ice cream for Jell-O; and spare ribs for tuna fish. So what were a few more eensy, teensy calories, anyway?

The sessions with the Korean chap ran five mornings a week, which put Lilly in her office at International Talent Management just before eleven. By that time of day, she was sure to have received at least six "really urgent" phone messages from the various actors, writers and directors she represented. So what else was new?

||

It was a typical Los Angeles autumn morning. Raining like a mother.

The mayor was asking people not to hate him just because he was black. (They didn't; they hated him for many other reasons.) And there had been another freeway shooting last night. This time, thank God, nobody actually killed, just maimed a little. And a Lakers' cheerleader tearfully told KTLA-TV viewers that her decision to become a nun was not a cheap publicity gimmick just because her agent had dropped her, "the greasy little bastard."

Lilly drove her twenty-year-old, wire-wheeled Jag from the Korean chap's to the office and arrived just in time to wave goodbye to International's lone superstar, a silver-haired man Lilly had tried to sleep with one drunken night after the Oscars, only to have him turn her down.

Ricardo, the male secretary who really hated Lilly and vice-versa, lifted his azure gaze and said, sweetly, "How's the diet going, Lilly?" even though he could plainly see that, despite her very chic linen suit, she was still fifty pounds overweight.

But she was too single-minded this morning to let the little bitch set her off. She went directly to her office and closed the door.

After she had returned all the "really urgent" messages (only one out of six was really urgent, a very decent director of hers who was sweating out an AIDS test and just wanted a few kind words, which she gave him) and read the usual memos From Above urging all six International agents to try harder for big names, she poured herself a cup of coffee and walked over to the window.

The size and condition of her office bespoke Suzie O'Malley's (aka Lilly Carlyle—a name she'd taken from a bodice ripper paperback) time in Hollywood.

While the carpet was pretty good, the furnishings were dated and, if one looked closely, scuffed. The burnt orange couch, for instance, was missing a button which she'd had to cover with a burnt orange throw pillow that did not exactly match the couch itself. There was a tiny cigarette hole in the leather-like armchair that sat next to the wood-like bookcase in which Lilly kept neat stacks of the scripts she was currently schlepping around town.

Lilly hadn't sold a script in two years.

The office smelled of something that had been too long deprived of fresh air, a musty smell. Because, Lilly supposed, it was something of a musty agency—or that was its reputation, anyway. International had only one mega-star, and him they clung to with all the fervor and force possible. Nobody in the business could figure out why the guy stayed with Wade Preston and Lilly Carlyle.

Mostly, International dealt with TV stars, of the sitcom and car chase fodder variety. They'd be big three, four seasons on a hit show, and they'd get lots and lots of press (good press, if Lilly was doing her job), and then the series would fold and go into syndication and then the stars would go into a new sitcom or car chase series and it wouldn't do very well at all. And two seasons later you could catch said stars sitting inside a box and having dimpled John Davidson bounce would-be funny lines off them. That was the arc: nobody to star to nobody. Usually the round trip took seven, eight years. Hey, pal, do you know the way to San Jose?

With one exception.

Cobey Daniels.

Cobey hadn't just been big, he'd been super-big, and if he hadn't gotten in trouble with that sixteen-year-old chick in Florida—

Lilly'd had to work her considerable ass off to keep him out of the slam. As was only proper. Wade Preston, who was in love with Lilly and at least once a week asked her to marry him, had sold Lilly a size-able share of the agency several years ago.

She'd managed to maneuver Cobey into a mental hospital. The usual bit, really: perils-of-teenage-stardom, stress, fatigue, hadn't-really-been-going-to-hurt-the-girl.

The judge had gone along, God bless him.

Now, recalling all this, Lilly looked down on Sunset Boulevard.

How romantic, that name. Sunset Boulevard. She'd come to Hollywood as Suzie O'Malley from a small Ohio town, the same plot setup all those hack musical-comedy writers used in the thirties and forties and fifties.

She hadn't been a happy girl. She'd been cursed with a gorgeous face sitting atop a seriously overweight body and now she wasn't a happy woman. Twice married, twice divorced. Three abortions. She'd even tried sex with another woman once, an actress who seemed to truly believe that she was in some kind of supernatural contact with Garbo, but that hadn't done it at all. Lilly liked men; or some men, anyway.

Now she stood looking down at the wrong end of Sunset (the really successful agencies were elsewhere) on a chill, gray, rainy day, and she thought of Cobey.

She had talked to him many times lately. She had plans for him again.

He'd blown it the first time, but she was going to make certain he didn't blow it the second time.

God, she'd fought so hard for him. All those years, ever since he was a six-year-old boy.

She sighed, turning away from the window.

It was time to write the letter, time to set it all in motion again.

She went over to her computer terminal, flipped on the green-glowing machine, and waited for the small electronic dot to explode in the middle of her screen.

Then she set to work.

Doctor Robert Reeves
Chief Psychiatrist
Menlow Park Hospital
St. Louis, Missouri

Dear Doctor Reeves,

   When we spoke a year ago, you said you felt that if everything went well in the next twelve months, Cobey would be released this fall.

   I've seen Cobey four times in the past year and I speak to him at least once a week on the phone. I can honestly say he looks and sounds like the old Cobey. I believe he's ready for release and I hope you agree with me.

   I should add a cautionary note here. The Hollywood press—including the tabloids—has been eagerly awaiting his release. There's nothing they love more than finding a new angle on an old scandal. They'll bring it all up again, too—how Cobey was the most beloved teenage star of the early eighties, and what happened that day at the Florida shopping mall. Not to mention several other incidents in which he was involved.

   In light of this, I'm asking you to keep his release a secret. I have employed a Hollywood private investigative firm whose people are also trained bodyguards. A man named William Puckett will be meeting with you and arranging for Cobey's final release. He will fly with Cobey back to Los Angeles, at which point I will take over. I have already contacted a psychiatrist here so that Cobey can begin seeing him at once, three times a week.

   I appreciate your cooperation in this matter

and if you have any questions, please contact me. Cobey's release is my chief concern in life because he is the son I never had . . .

Sincerely,

Lilly Carlyle

III

Family Life had once taped one of those "serious" episodes cast with one eye on an Emmy and one eye on even greater ratings.

In this episode, Cobey's nineteen-year-old sister had a breakdown and was sent to a mental hospital.

This was the first time Cobey had ever heard of electric-shock treatments, of how they strapped you down and zapped your brain with several thousand volts of electricity. Supposedly, the shock would bring you out of your deep depression.

Cobey was seventeen at the time of the episode. For days he went around thinking of electric-shock as something like Frankenstein's monster, jagged blue bolts of electricity crisscrossing the air above the skull, the entire body convulsing. He'd also been told that in the early days of electric-shock the convulsions had been so severe that some people actually broke arms and legs; and a few even swallowed their tongues and strangled to death.

And two days before his twenty-first birthday, early in his second year at Menlow Park Hospital, Cobey received his first electric-shock treatment, which some of the patients called "riding the lightning."

The odd thing was, it wasn't so bad, not really. Cobey went into this small, white room adjacent to the big, white operating room and he read magazines and he chatted with the other patients awaiting treatments and then a slender, very pretty nurse came into the room and called Cobey's name and then led him very sweetly into an ante-room where he was given a white hospital gown and told to lie down on a gurney. Then the same very pretty nurse, talking and smiling all the time, strapped Cobey down and pushed him into the operating room.

Seen from the gurney, the room was white and vast. It smelled of various tart medicines and it was so cold that Cobey could feel goose bumps all over his arms and legs.

Everything, from Cobey's perspective, was upside down, of course.

A doctor and three nurses peered down at him, their heads forming a semicircle.

The nurses were pretty. The doctor had wide, hairy nostrils.

"Do you know what Sodium Pentothal is?" the doctor asked. He had a beard and he was young and he sort of looked like a hippie.

"Truth serum?" Cobey said.

The doctor smiled. "Well, that's its popular name. We call it Sodium Pentothal. Nurse Irene is going to give you an injection of it. All you need to do is start counting backwards from one hundred. You'll never reach ninety-six."

Cobey thought that was highly unlikely. Who couldn't count backwards from one hundred to ninety-six?

He couldn't.

He reached ninety-seven and the universe exploded. Freezing blackness—the darkness between the stars could be no colder or vaster—overwhelmed him and he ceased, at least as far as he knew, to exist.

Extinction.

He was next aware of struggling to open his eyes. Brightness pushed against his lids and a human voice rumbled something not quite understandable.

His eyes came open. He was in a sunny little room in Menlow Park Hospital. A beefy orderly in skintight white T-shirt and pants was talking to him.

There were various framed photographs that Lilly had put up on his first day here. "I want the staff to know you're somebody special, and I want you to know it, too," she'd said. The photos showed Cobey with different celebrities, including President Reagan, Michael Jackson and Morgan Fairchild. The photos tried hard to make people think that Cobey and these people were good friends.

"How you feelin', Cobey?"

When he'd first come to Menlow Park, he'd suffered what Dr. Reeves had called hysterical amnesia. He couldn't remember much, sometimes not even his own name. Following electric-shock, he'd felt pretty much the same way.

"I . . . uh . . . feel all right, I guess."

"You did good, Cobey. Real good."

"Gosh, thanks."

Cobey then started the difficult task of reconstructing the past few hours. Breakfast. Going downstairs in an elevator. A small, white room—counting backwards—and now . . .

"Cobey?" Cobey said. "That's my name?"

The man grinned. "Right. Cobey." Then he kind of punched Cobey playfully on the arm.

In all, Cobey had ten electric-shock treatments. It was felt by the staff that his spirits had improved at least slightly, and it was whispered, by the patients, that maybe the young TV star wasn't as aloof as they'd once thought, that maybe he'd just been depressed. God, if any of them had gone through what Cobey had in the back of that shopping mall . . . well, who wouldn't be depressed?

IV

On the morning he received Lilly Carlyle's letter, Dr. Robert Reeves interviewed four staffers about Cobey's recent behavior. Satisfied that the young man was indeed doing well, Reeves walked the hospital grounds looking for Cobey.

He found him on the tennis courts, playing doubles with an arsonist (his partner), a pedophile (who was also an eminent minister), and a particularly vile wife-torturer (the man's millions having kept him from a real prison).

Reeves liked to hear the *thwock* of the ball as it went back and forth across the net, the sound echoing off the green bluffs surrounding the red brick hospital which most people thought resembled a small college campus. He liked to hear patients having fun.

Between matches, Reeves went up and asked if he could speak with Cobey. Cobey said sure.

"Well, it's lunch time," Reeves said. "How about walking over to the cafeteria with me?"

V

"You know you're up for review, right, Cobey?"

"Yessir."

They walked along. Cobey smiled when he saw a plump little squirrel toting a huge acorn along the edge of the sidewalk. As they approached the main building, Cobey could smell lunch. The food here was great. He felt a wonderful sense of belonging; and then he thought, ruefully, *I really must be crazy if I want a mental hospital as my alma mater.*

"The board pretty much acts on what I say," Reeves said. He was a tall man and, in his white medical jacket, he seemed even taller. He was bald and the top of his head looked as if he Simonized it every few days.

"Yessir," Cobey said, sounding tentative. He had a hunch where this was going but he was afraid to hope that . . .

"I'm going to recommend that you be released to the custody of Lilly," Dr. Reeves said.

And then he stopped and put his hand out and Cobey shook it and thought, *oh, hell*, and threw his arms around Dr. Reeves, his head reaching the middle of the medical man's chest.

"I'm going home!" Cobey said. "I'm going home!"

"Yes, you are," Dr. Reeves said. "And a man named Puckett is going to take you there."

Lunch that day was spaghetti, a particular favorite of Cobey's.

He sat across the table from Dr. Reeves and when Reeves wasn't smiling and talking with his mouth full, Cobey was.

Warm autumn sunshine slanted through the windows, touching Cobey, painting him warm and golden, a special creature.

It was, in all respects, a wonderful day.

WILLIAM JAMES PUCKETT

|

TWO-AND-A-HALF WEEKS LATER, WILLIAM JAMES Puckett landed at Lambert International Airport in St. Louis, at which point he transferred to a Yellow Cab. He told the cabbie, a black man with an amiable face and shrewd, brown eyes, that he was headed for Menlow Park Hospital.

The driver glanced at him in the mirror again.

Patient or visitor? the black man was obviously thinking. Then he smiled. He'd clearly decided that Puckett was a visitor.

On the way out to the hospital the news came on and there was a story about Richard M. Nixon planning another European trip.

And so, naturally enough, Puckett started thinking about his days as Nixon's bodyguard.

After college, and after Nam, Puckett found himself without a job but with an uncle who'd been a Secret Service man ever since Washington wore wooden teeth. "Hell, you might like it," his uncle kept saying, so Puckett—who was broke—said why not and flew into DC and took all the tests and kissed all the asses, and what do you know?

A year later he was assigned to guarding presidential candidate Richard Nixon. He actually sort of liked the guy; which might be just a way of saying that he actually felt sorry for him because Nixon tried hard to be a regular guy, but his attempts were pathetic. Still, Puckett had never felt like a regular guy either, so despite the fact that all his people were Democrats, he developed a fondness for the sweaty little bastard.

In those days especially, guarding a national political figure was like going to war. In one spring Martin Luther King and Robert Kennedy had been killed, and so the Secret Service started treating their job like the hazardous duty gig it really was.

Before hitting a given city, you discussed which hospitals you'd take the wounded to. You packed smoke grenades and gas masks in case an assassin—or team of assassins—really got tricky. The guys in the war wagon, the car travelling just behind the candidate's vehicle, carried enough firepower to invade China, the agents packing Uzis and taping extra ammo to the ceiling. Several of the top agents, including Puckett, had been sent to Israel to train in commando tactics. Puckett had liked the Israelis and learned a lot from them.

With Nixon, Puckett would wade into a crowd, clearing the way for the candidate behind him. Puckett would immediately be assaulted by photographers and over-eager Nixon admirers. Blinded by strobes, jostled by people who were acting like stoned rock-concert crowds, Puckett kept his eyes moving constantly, looking for any sign of something wrong—a glint of sun off metal, a man reaching suspiciously inside his jacket, a woman starting to raise her arm in a curious way. If the real thing ever happened, his earpiece would burst out with *Gun left* or *Gun right* and then Puckett would be ripping his gun from its holster while the agent next to him tore open his briefcase and filled his hands with an Uzi all ready to fire.

At the end of their little sojourn, candidate Nixon had given Puckett a pair of gold cufflinks and a manly slug on the bicep.

Nixon went on to the White House and Watergate. Puckett stayed in the Service two more years and then went private.

The big international firms were just discovering the wonders of computers and a whole new world was opening up. Puckett wanted to be a part of that world.

Around this same time, his wife informed him that she'd fallen in love with the family dentist and would be leaving and taking their four-year-old daughter with them and that Puckett could see his daughter whenever he wanted and she hoped there were no hard feelings and that Puckett should not only look for a new woman but also—"to save embarrassment, Puckett, you know what I mean"—a new dentist. "Karl would just be real uncomfortable with you in his chair."

All Puckett could think about was the ancient, evil dentist drilling into Dustin Hoffman's teeth in *The Marathon Man*.

||

Menlow Park Hospital looked like a college campus, Puckett thought, filled with rolling green lawns and overhanging willows and oaks, and resplendent with lots of nubile young ladies from good, solid, Midwestern states.

He met first with Dr. Reeves, who told him that Cobey was in his care now and he hoped that Puckett was ready to assume complete responsibility. To that end, Reeves had Puckett sign several forms that made Cobey Puckett's total responsibility.

Cobey surprised him. He looked older and more tired than a teen-star had any right to. Puckett's daughter Cindy had had a long-time crush on Cobey.

They shook hands, said goodbye to Dr. Reeves, and left. Halfway down the broad front steps of the Administration building, Puckett said, "Oh, I forgot."

"Forgot?"

"Your Acme Camouflage Disguise."

"Huh?"

"This stuff here," Puckett said.

And put this lounge-lizard black wig on Cobey, and then a black *bandito* mustache—and finally slipped on a pair of black, wrap-around shades.

Cobey laughed. "God, I bet I really look like shit."

Puckett picked up one of Cobey's bags again and started walking. "You're right. You do."

|||

Turned out, Cobey wasn't real thrilled with flying. Every time they'd hit the least little bit of turbulence, Cobey would grip the arms of his seat as if he were in an electric chair and they were putting the juice to him.

And somehow, despite all the terrible things he'd heard about the kid, Puckett sort of liked him.

Given the fact that Puckett worked out of Los Angeles, many of his clients were entertainment types and, face it, they weren't the nicest people in the world.

But this kid—

Puckett either liked somebody or he didn't, and he did like this gentle, friendly, unassuming kid. Of course, every once in a while he did think of Cobey trying to strangle some sixteen-year-old girl . . . And then Puckett'd wonder if he really should like the kid. Maybe the stay at Menlow Park hadn't really changed him at all. But then he'd think that Cobey was fine as long as he didn't touch alcohol—not a drop—because the stuff turned him into a monster.

As they were travelling over Salt Lake City, Cobey got sick and had to use his bag.

When he finished, he said, "I'll bet I've got puke on my mustache, don't I?"

"You do indeed," Puckett said.

"OK if I throw the mustache away?"

"Fine with me."

"It won't ruin my disguise?"

"It may ruin your disguise, but at least you'll smell better."

Cobey sat back. "You got any kids?"

"One. A few years younger than you. Eighteen. A girl."

"You see her a lot?"

"Not as much as I should."

"That's what parents always say."

"Well, the way you say that, sort of sarcastic and all, sounds like you're finally old enough to hear the truth."

"The truth?"

"Yeah," Puckett said, "about parents."

Then he leaned over and whispered into Cobey's ear, "All parents are assholes." Cobey must have laughed for a good three minutes over that one.

As they were just sliding over the California border, Cobey said, "I really wouldn't have strangled the girl that day."

"What brought that up?"

"Just the way I caught you looking at me a few times. You've got a daughter of your own. It's natural that you'd be curious." He shook his head. "I like girls. And I respect them. While I was in the hospital, this nurse taught me about feminism and I really believe in it." He shook his head again. "I don't know what happened to me that day at the shopping mall."

"Relax, Cobey," Puckett said. "We've all done things we try not to think about."

"Even you, Puckett?"

Puckett laughed. "Especially me."

IV

Lilly was waiting with a limo at LAX.

While the uniformed driver took care of the bags, Lilly shook Puckett's hand and thanked him for doing such a good job.

"Well," Lilly said, looking at the disguised Cobey. "I guess it's time for us to go."

Cobey said, "You want to play tennis sometime, Puckett?"

Puckett smiled. "I'm afraid I'm more the bowling type." Puckett gave him the kind of manly slug-on-the-bicep that Richard Nixon had given Puckett. "But I will treat you to lunch at McDonald's sometime."

"Great!" Cobey said.

Puckett glanced at Lilly and, right off, he got the sense she wasn't crazy about Cobey's idea of seeing Puckett again.

Then they were in the limo, and gone.

V

Puckett never did keep his promise to Cobey about going to McDonald's (even as a stand-in father, he wasn't worth a shit) and, in fact, he pretty much forgot Cobey entirely, just sort of assuming, he supposed, that he'd never see the kid again.

He was wrong.

From the June 3, 1989 edition of *The National Tattler*

Is Cobey Daniels Still Alive?

Aging teen star vanishes

———

TV star Cobey Daniels, best known for his starring role in the No. 1 rated sitcom *Family Life* (1981-1985) is now the subject of an intense search by Los Angeles police. None of Cobey's friends have seen or heard from him in six weeks. Authorities and friends alike fear foul play.

Cobey was discovered at age six by Hollywood talent agent Lilly Carlyle, who took the boy from his parents and raised him herself to be a child star.

But while fame and fortune came Cobey's way, so did a series of run-ins with the law. Between the ages of 15 and 19, Cobey was arrested three times for OMVI, four times for assault and battery, and two times for possessing cocaine.

In 1985 he was convicted of statutory rape in a case involving a 16-year-old girl in a Florida shopping mall. The conviction resulted in Cobey being sent to a mental hospital for more than three years.

After his release, Cobey found work in many TV dramas, usually in minor roles. During this period, he also worked with the prestigious Hollywood Actors Playhouse. More recently, Cobey had auditioned for the leads in two different sitcom pilots.

Friends can't explain Cobey's sudden disappearance. They say that Cobey had been in fine spirits lately and had displayed none of his darker moods.

Los Angeles police continue their intensive Investigation. They would not answer any press questions, saying that the matter was still too new to speculate about.

1993

"So whatever became of Cobey Daniels? Well, all grown up, (and sobered up, too), Cobey has written and stars in a play about his travails as a teenage star. And the play is as funny, powerful, strange and haunting as anything seen on the American stage in the past decade. No mistake about it—this is Cobey Daniels' comeback vehicle."

Time Magazine
February 22, 1993

CHAPTER ONE

CHICAGO

H E HAD A TERRIBLE AND SLIGHTLY RIDICULOUS MOMENT when he couldn't remember who he was.

I am—

Shit. Nobody forgets his own name.

I am—

Damn. It was so ludicrous to forget your own—

He *had* a name. Everybody had a name. What was his? Who was he, anyway?

His eyes were still closed.

Real tough job getting them opened.

Head throbbing.

He knew what that was, of course.

He'd started drinking again.

How could he have been so stupid, anyway?

He lay there for the next few minutes, acquainting himself with the various parts of his body.

Very dry mouth. Heat: dehydration from the alcohol, he knew. Hands twitching: the shakes. Nausea travelling up from his belly and into his throat: raw sewage.

How could he have been so stupid?

He knew what alcohol did to him.

So stupid, so . . .

He fell asleep again.

When he awoke the second time, he smelled rain; chill, spring rain. He smelled night. He smelled—apple blossom. Yes, apple blossom.

Where the hell was he, anyway?

Who the hell was he, anyway?

He needed to open his eyes. He needed to stand up. He needed to find out some things.

One eye opened on to deep night.

He angled his head.

He was in a shadowy room on a bed. To his right was a window. A sheer white curtain cavorted like a dancing ghost. Through the open window he could feel the faint, chill spray of rain, the way rolling surf sometimes sprayed you from a distance.

Surf?

California.

But this wasn't California.

He wasn't sure where it was, but he was sure it wasn't California.

In the distance now, somewhere beyond the window, the steady rush of traffic.

Closer, but still faint, human voices on the street below. Laughter sharp as a gunshot; then footsteps, fading, fading in the sudden wind whipping the white curtain.

Not California.

He stretched his right leg.

Big toe touched cold, hard wood.

He opened his other eye now.

New information: to his left, a woman's dressing table with a round mirror mounted in the middle of it, the minor reflecting him lying on the rumpled bed.

He stared at himself as if staring at a stranger.

Just who the hell was he, anyway?

The bile in his throat made him want to puke right now.

He sat up straight in one abrupt, head-pounding movement.

God, his headache—

He spent the next few minutes delicately rubbing sleep from his face and trying to work up enough strength to stand up.

He thought of turning on a light. No. Right now, light, any kind of light, would be profane.

He eased himself off the bed and stood up.

For the first time, he noticed that he was naked. Freezing. Poor little dick hanging limp, cold as the rest of him.

Through a dark doorway he could see the dark square edge of a mirror. Bathroom.

He staggered forth.

The shadowy bathroom was filled with the pleasant odors of baby powder and perfume, lingering like music on the night air.

Girl, he thought.

Girl lives here.

Why am I here, then?

He peed so hard it was almost painful. He felt as if he stood there shooting a steady stream for at least ten minutes, though that was, of course, impossible.

When he finished, he leaned over the sink and looked at his dark shape in the dark mirror.

Please . . . Is it asking too much to know my own name? This isn't funny, you know. This isn't one goddamn bit funny.

Then he wondered to whom he was addressing his question. God, he supposed. Yes, God. And why not? God was supposed to help people like him. It was in the contract, wasn't it?

He left the bathroom and went to stand before the open window.

He let the sheer white curtain envelope him like smoke.

He looked to the street below. Quiet. Residential. Lone street light on the corner showing the edges of two or three well-kept brick apartment houses. Rain shone like black glass on the sidewalk and street. Wind covered his body with goose bumps again. Then, abruptly, the curtain covering him once more, he was lost inside silken whiteness, ghost inside a ghost. Safe.

The dehydration was starting to get very bad. He needed a Pepsi or something. And soon.

Where was the kitchen in this place, anyway?

He walked through the bedroom door and out into a living room that was even darker except for the window on the west wall. Muzzy street light played on the glass like dying fireflies in sweet summer gloom.

There was a small brick fireplace, two long, narrow, built-in bookcases on either side, a stylish white couch and a TV set with a twenty-one inch screen. No wind reached this room and so the air was stuffy and smelled of—

At first he didn't recognize it, but then—

Marijuana. The harsh, weedy stench of marijuana smoke. He looked at the shadowy room, studied it, but it was completely unfamiliar.

Where was he?

Who was he?

Please, God, you gotta help me. It's in the contract. Honest.

A terrible panic replaced his sarcasm. He had to fight hard against the impulse to start shrieking and then start smashing things.

And then a notion so horrible he thought he would lose control entirely: I'm in a little box, like the little boxes rats are kept in for lab experiments, and somebody is watching all this, all my misery, all my fear, and taking notes on everything I do, and sometimes He just nods when I do the expected, and sometimes He smiles when I do the unexpected.

He had to get rid of this thought—

He forced himself, despite the huge pain pounding inside his skull, to shake his head, ridding himself of the thought . . .

He studied the room some more, tried to get a sense of it. The books said culture; the white couch, more like a divan, really, said style; and the brick fireplace, apparently a working fireplace, said reasonably expensive. In many apartment buildings, fireplaces were strictly ornamental. Cost too much to keep them working. He decided to take a look at the titles in the bookcases. Maybe that way he could learn something about where he was right now . . .

He walked across the edge of a rug that was either Persian or trying hard to be Persian, and stepped over to the bookcase to the right of the fireplace.

He grabbed several books at once and then walked with them back toward the window, so he could read them in the street light.

God, he couldn't believe what he was seeing.

You're A Real Person, Too, by Dr. Stanley M. Derkum; *Why You Should Love Yourself*, by Phyllis Glanze, PhD; *Pushed Around No Longer*, by George Fenton O'Malley; *Tell Them The Lord Says To Shove It*, by Evangelist and former NFL tackle M. "Butch" Harding (with Ken Arnold).

The person who read these books had to be a past master at low self-esteem.

He shook his head again. The books had told him nothing, really.

Kitchen.

Diet Pepsi.

Maybe he could get real lucky and find some aspirin, too.

He tried licking his lips. Didn't work. Mouth too dry.

He found the kitchen through the living room and down a short hallway that sent panic through him again. The hallway was utterly dark and too narrow. All he could think of was the grave, of being buried alive and suffocated within the confines of a casket. Clawing to get free, his ripped fingernails running with blood . . .

He hurried down the hallway, to the vague gray light awaiting him there.

The kitchen was L-shaped, vinyl on the floor, fashionable black and white tiles covering much of the walls. Above a white gas range, several pots and pans were suspended from the ceiling.

He was just walking into the kitchen when the bottom of his left foot stepped into something sticky.

He looked down and saw that something had been spilled on the floor, an oozing puddle lying in the center of the vinyl.

But he kept walking. He had to drink something fast, even though he knew he would probably throw it up.

He had reached the gas range when he noticed two things. One, that the kitchen didn't seem to have a refrigerator and two, that the kitchen smelled badly. Very badly.

He stood still a moment, fighting another wave of disorientation, and then realized he was being silly.

The kitchen was L-shaped. Around the corner he'd find a refrigerator. He was sure of it.

He took a step forward and once again his foot stepped into a sticky puddle.

He had to be careful not to slip.

All he needed now was to land on his ass and break an arm or something.

At the end of the kitchen was a door with a small, lacy curtain covering the glass. Holding on to the stove for purchase, he walked to the door and looked out at an alley two floors down.

Small rows of dumpsters against the brick backside of the building on the other side. Light pole swaying in the breeze, scattering faint light everywhere like gold dust. Lonely tabby cat trundling into darkness.

He turned back from the window and for the first time stared down the small end of the L.

A large, white, square refrigerator sat there, one of those new jobs with a little plastic window and a juice dispenser built right into the door. He could hear the motor thrumming in the silence. The big machine sat in the cove of darkness like a Madonna in a grotto, expecting adoration.

He took a step forward.

This time he nearly slipped.

So sticky . . .

He had to grab on to the wall fast and even then he could feel his groin pull as he scrambled to stay upright.

All he needed was a hernia.

He felt as if he were walking through taffy, the stuff was that sticky and warm. He had a thought about what the stuff might be but rejected it immediately. Too foolish. Too paranoid.

He went over to the refrigerator and pushed back the sliding plastic door on the juice dispenser. Somebody had been thoughtful enough to leave a clean paper cup in there.

He dispensed juice, the grinding sound of the machinery irritating in the stillness.

The beverage turned out to be grape juice, probably the same Welch's grape juice he'd always liked as a kid. The coldness was wonderful, and so was the sugary taste. All the time he drank, he leaned against the refrigerator door. He didn't want to slip.

Unfortunately, after he finished the grape juice, he was still in need of a Diet Pepsi. Hard, dry need.

He stood back from the refrigerator, wrapped his fingers around the handle, and opened the door.

The odd thing was, he didn't scream or run around smashing things. He didn't lose it at all.

He just stared into the stark white refrigerator, the interior light painting his face with a color that was almost silver.

He just stared.

He'd never seen anything like it, of course.

Somebody had cut a young woman's head from her shoulders and then taken out the top three shelves of the refrigerator so the head would fit comfortably inside.

She had very blue eyes and she stared right back at him. She'd probably learned to do this, to stare right back at people, from one of those books he'd just seen, probably the *Tell Them The Lord Says To Shove It* book, which certainly seemed to advocate aggressiveness.

Just stared at him.

She'd been beautiful in a high-fashion way, all sharp cheekbones and erotic mouth and cunning little chin. She'd had long, blonde hair that was really nice somehow, even with blood splattered all over it . . .

The refrigerator was a mess.

Blood and slop from the ragged line of her neck dripped and dropped through the tines of the shelving to splatter and splash on the white bottom. A piece of bloody brain meat covered one letter on the Fruit drawer so that it read: F UIT.

And then it hit him, all of it, not knowing his name, the strange apartment, the girl's head in the refrigerator.

He turned from the refrigerator, already running even before he was all the way around, and then he went right down to the floor, skidding through the blood on his backside.

But he did not slow down.

If he couldn't run from this room, he would crawl, which was just what he did. He got on his hands and knees and walked, dog-style, out of the kitchen.

Every few moments he'd make this sick, mewling, animal noise in his throat when he realized that he was crawling through human blood and entrails, but he kept going nonetheless, out of the kitchen and down the narrow, coffin-like hallway and into the living room where he pitched himself on to the dry floor and let himself rest momentarily. He was shivering from frozen sweat and his lungs were threatening to catch fire. His headache was so severe, he wondered if it might not become a permanent condition.

He had to remember his name. Had to . . .

Then, somehow, sometime, Lilly was there, in the dreamlike darkness. How he clutched his little cock, as if somebody were about to cut it off. Where had Lilly come from, anyway?

She got him clothed and on his feet and led him to the kitchen door. He was crying all the time but she told him to stop; please, Cobey, stop. *But did you look inside the fucking refrigerator? Yes, I did, Cobey*—but everything will be fine. I promise you, Cobey, everything will be fine.

He followed her out to the fire escape.

The night was very cold. It seemed vast and filled with menace.

She went back and checked the door, making sure it was locked. She wore gloves.

Then she preceded him down the fire escape.

Even though she walked on tiptoes, she moved quickly, holding tight to the thin metal railing.

They had to be very, very quiet.

On the ground, she took his hand and they began walking quickly down the alley.

God, she was so strong.

He could barely keep up. He wanted to puke/piss/scream/bleed/ die. Had he killed that girl or what?

They went down to the end of the alley and over half a block. The rental car she drove sat there, waiting.

Once they were inside and pulling away from the curb, she said, "You're going to feel better now. I know you will. We'll go to my hotel and I'll get you some food."

But all he could think was how alien everything looked to him. He was on the wrong planet, desperately in search of his real home.

When they had gone six quick, dark blocks, he started sobbing so hard she had to stop the car and take him in her arms and cuddle him like an infant.

CHAPTER TWO

THREE DAYS LATER

1

THERE WERE A LOT OF MISCONCEPTIONS ABOUT SUR-
veillance. For one thing, you didn't usually just pull up in front of
a guy's house and park there. The guy might not be aware of you,
but his neighbors likely were, and the first thing they'd do after seeing
you was call the cops and report some strange man sitting out at the
curb. A cop car would soon pull up—and, even if the cops went along
with your story, your cover was blown. By that time, the guy you were
staking out would have had plenty of time to get out the back door.

So, the first thing a smart, contemporary, respectable private
investigator did was call the cops, tell them that he was about to conduct a surveillance (without giving any exact reasons why), and then
off he went to do his work unhindered by neighbors or police cruisers.

This was just one of the many things that real-life private eyes did
that fictional private eyes didn't do. Puckett often spoke about the dif-
ferences between real and fictional on a variety of radio talk shows in

the LA area—never TV because he didn't want his face shown—and he'd developed a real following because of his gentle humor.

His listeners especially liked it when Puckett talked about operatives for a big, international agency, such as he was, who relied on mainframe computers instead of guns and shoe leather to do much of their work.

As Puckett frequently said, before he began to investigate anybody, he spent a few hours at a computer terminal learning such things as where the man was born, what sort of education he'd had, any notable sports or interests he indulged NESTFORM, and any information available on ex-wives or lovers. In addition, he also checked out the man's financial background thoroughly, any liens, lawsuits, bankruptcies, etc.

Puckett's next step was to go to the man's house and check through his garbage. You could find marvelous things in garbage and it often told fascinating tales. Thus armed with all this information, Puckett set about the serious, formal phase of the investigation, which usually meant interviewing friends of the man.

Listeners loved it.

The vampire hour had come. He called it that because, with darkness, they would appear, the freaks and geeks and victims and observers of the night. They would be furtive, little old ladies robbed by gangs of twelve-year-olds for a few dollars; half-naked dancers of many sexes enjoying the noisy, incandescent kiss of the disco spotlight; a farmer from Iowa coming out of his third-rate hotel to find that his two-year-old Dodge had been stripped clean of everything valuable; the junkie so desperate for a fix he decides to share a needle despite seeing the way his friend died of AIDS last year; a priest in a runaway shelter counseling a fourteen-year-old Michigan girl to at least call her parents and tell them she is all right; an S&M participant feeling the first lash of the whip ripping his flesh as his scream of pleasure and fulfillment sings on the air; a little girl hearing the brawl between her mother and drunken father, whispering frantic prayers that her mother won't be beaten as badly as she was last time; a very angry black youth sticking up a liquor store owned by a very angry Korean man, both so filled with hatred and rage they can barely contain it.

This was Chicago, but it could just as well have been Los Angeles or Detroit or Miami . . .

This was night, and sometimes Puckett thought he should go back to the old family farm in Maine and live out his life there. No vampires there, except maybe for those in Stephen King's books.

He was contemplating all these things—he was a great, if useless, contemplator, was Puckett—when a familiar name came on the radio talk show he'd been vaguely listening to.

"Our guest tonight is Anne Addison, one of the best-known non-fiction writers in the United States. Anne is in Chicago doing an interview with Cobey Daniels, the former teen-star whose new play is dazzling everybody who sees it. Good evening, Anne, and welcome to our studios."

"Good evening, Ron. I'm pleased to be here. Thanks for asking me."

"Why don't we talk a little bit about how you prepare for an interview, and then we'll take some calls from our listeners?"

Puckett tried hard not to be seduced by that soft, intelligent, but completely unaffected voice of hers. He tried to concentrate on his surveillance job and he glanced determinedly up the hill at the dark outline of the apartment house.

He had left Los Angeles yesterday because the man he'd been tailing was originally from Chicago and consequently—and unbeknownst to his wife—kept a place here.

The Ardmore was a big playpen for wealthy adults. In this case, the toys were three swimming pools, a physical training room that would rival the most sophisticated gym, tennis courts, squash courts, a jogging path and a "social" room so splashy and upscale that very good rock bands often showed up for a set or two. The Ardmore was constructed of unfinished wood and sprawled over a hillside that pitched perilously toward a raw, jagged ravine below. There were enough floodlights on the ground to make you think there was maybe a movie premiere going on here tonight.

Puckett was here because of a geezer named Fenwick, a round, bald, sunburned man who had impulsively deserted his wife of forty years for the receptionist he'd hired six months ago. Said receptionist had previously been an aerobics instructor, a flight attendant and a runway model for several second-tier department stores. She had also put most of her hard-earned money back into her one and only product, which was herself. Puckett had discovered that she'd had plastic surgery on her breasts, her nose, her chin and her bottom.

Mrs. Fenwick, or Mildred, as she insisted Puckett call her, was actually a very nice, rich, older woman who just wanted some photos of her husband making a fool of himself—on the dance floor, poolside with his considerable belly hanging over his swimming trunks, or in the lobby of a French restaurant where the girl on his arm would look very much like his daughter, and a slightly whorey one at that. Mildred Fenwick was convinced that once her husband saw how ridiculous he looked in such photos, he would come to his senses and return home.

Puckett didn't necessarily believe that the aging American male was all that sensible, but he wasn't being paid for his beliefs. He was being paid to tail Fenwick, and get photos of him in as many contexts as possible. And that's how Puckett, good gumshoe that he was, came to be in Chicago tonight.

"I'm a real fan of your writing."

"Thank you," Anne said to the caller.

"Do you have any opinions about where Cobey Daniels disappeared for that nine month period?"

Several years ago, Cobey had vanished. Utterly. A nationwide manhunt ensued. But no Cobey. Then one day he simply showed up again. He would never talk about where he'd been or what he'd done. Ever.

"I'm afraid I don't know any more about it than you do," Anne said.

Hearing her voice again, Puckett couldn't help himself. He picked up the hefty Chicago phone book on the seat next to him, looked up the number of the station where Anne was, and then called the place and left a phone number for her to call—and the name of the hotel where he was staying. The receptionist treated him about the way he'd expected—as an unholy masher.

Twenty minutes later, Puckett's replacement showed up—the agency, thank God, had a working agreement with a Chicago investigative agency—and Puckett went and found himself a Hardee's drive-up. He did not exactly have gourmet tastes . . .

2

Around eleven, Puckett decided Anne was neither going to call or show up, so he took off his trousers and watched the second half of Jay Leno in his shorts.

He also spent a lot more time than he wanted to thinking about Anne Addison.

Two years ago, after the magazine she was writing for assigned her to interview a private detective, she spent a week with Puckett on the job. She was a bright, fetching woman with coppery hair, little-girl freckles and one of those great, odd smiles that seemed to contain both joy and sorrow.

Their relationship lasted much longer than either of them planned, ending one night when she smashed up a good share of his living room after he told her, as gently as possible, that she was an alcoholic. She called him arrogant, smug and uncaring, all the things most alcoholics call people who try to point out the obvious.

Puckett still felt sorry for her, of course. She was a thirty-one-year-old woman who'd endured an abusive first marriage and, four years earlier, had seen her five-year-old son dash out into the street and be struck by a car. Donny had died six days later, having never emerged from the darkness of his coma.

So Anne drank: at first just to kill the pain, but then out of habit and, finally, out of overwhelming need. By the time Puckett had first met her, she had two distinct problems: the loss of her son and her alcoholism . . .

Puckett had phoned her many times following their terrible, violent argument in his apartment but it had done no good. She wouldn't return any of his calls. He'd even written her twice. She wrote RETURN TO SENDER on the front of the envelopes and mailed them back. He wanted to know how she was doing. He cared about her, more than he imagined he might. Hell, he'd been half-assed in love with her when they'd had the shootout that night. If they'd kept on seeing each other . . .

Toward the end, things had gotten pretty crazy, her drinking taking more and more of her sanity, her anger becoming more frequent and more strange . . . until one night in the parking lot of a cocktail lounge, trying to steer her into his car, Puckett had watched as Anne raised a gin bottle she'd stolen from the lounge—and smashed Puckett's windshield in, shattering both safety glass and bottle as she did so.

As he tried again to grab her, she startled him by pushing the jagged edge of the gin bottle right in his face.

"You want me to cut you up, you sonofabitch?" she'd screamed. "Then keep your fucking hands off me!"

She spent the next day calling to apologize for the night before, but by then Puckett knew that their relationship was quickly and grimly coming to a close . . .

Not long after that he told her she was an alcoholic. That was the last time they'd gotten together.

But now, as he thought about Anne, the worst of the memories faded. And he thought, instead, of her little-girl laugh, of her gentleness after lovemaking, of the sad, yet dignified way she dealt with troubles when she wasn't drinking . . .

It was good to think of her again, sweet and tender to remember the clean scent of her as she stepped from the shower . . . and the quick, melancholy brilliance of her smile.

The phone rang.

He grabbed it immediately, knowing with a rush of exhilaration who it would be.

"God. I couldn't believe it when I got out of the studio and saw the note from you," she said. "Why're you in Chicago?"

"Work."

"Figures. You still haven't learned how to relax, have you?"

He laughed. "I guess not."

"Are you decent?"

"Depends on who's asking."

"I am. I'm downstairs in the lobby."

Three minutes and seven floors later, she knocked on the door. As he opened the door, he caught himself sniffing the air and felt ashamed of himself. He was already assuming she was drunk.

"Hi, Puckett."

"Hi, Anne."

"Surprised to see me?"

"Very."

She wore a Dodgers T-shirt under a rust-colored suede car coat. Her white jeans hugged her neat little bottom and her long, slender legs very nicely.

"I've missed you, Puckett."

"Ditto."

She laughed. "Same old 'ditto' routine, huh?" Then she was in his arms.

Neither of them made a move to kiss; they just stood there in the doorway, holding each other, as if they weren't quite sure if they were lovers or just friends.

She sure felt good, Puckett thought. He'd always been comfortable with her sexually because they liked the same things and liked sex at about the same rate. But it was more than that, of course. He knew, now, just how lonely for her he'd really been.

He closed his eyes and just held her, liking the familiar smells of her, too, the baby shampoo in the hair, the sweet, subtle perfume, the warm, clean aroma of her flesh.

"This is really nice," she said.

"This is better than nice. It's great."

She giggled. "I just wish we didn't have to go and ruin it all by closing the door."

God—he'd actually forgotten all about standing in the doorway.

He led her inside the pleasant but unremarkable room with its pleasant but unremarkable furniture and its pleasant but unremarkable atmosphere.

Then he just stood there staring at her, a dumb, love-smitten junior at his first high school prom.

Anne Addison had come back into his life.

◆ ◆ ◆

3

The name of the treatment center was St. Francis Xavier and the name of the priest there, himself a recovering alcoholic, was Father Doheny. Anne had stayed there four months, until she had just about run out of insurance money. At least twice a week she'd started to call Puckett, but always stopped at the last moment because her memory of trashing his living room was too acute. She'd done many things in her drinking years that embarrassed her, but none as much as that. So she hadn't called.

After she got out of the treatment center, she went home and stayed in her apartment for a full month without leaving or even calling anybody. She was afraid to go out, afraid she wouldn't be strong enough to pass by a bar without going inside and ruining her five months of sobriety.

Then an editor called one day and gave her a freelance assignment, an interview with a European director staying in Malibu. Anne specialized in serious journalism about the film industry.

The interview was a real trial. Besides the fact that the director spent almost their entire time together trying to seduce her, she watched as he consumed nearly two bottles of wine. This was the closest she'd come to alcohol since leaving the treatment center.

The tangy smell of the wine frightened her. He offered her a glass. Not wanting to go into her drinking problem, she declined without elaboration. But he kept offering. Finally, she saw her hand reach out and her fingers touch the stem of the glass. Her whole body shook. She would take one glass, just one glass, but no more. But then—and here was where she started believing in Father Doheny's guardian angels again—something stopped her at the last moment. She said no.

The director looked crestfallen. His best and last seduction ploy had failed. She completed the interview and got out of there and it was now eleven months, three weeks and four days since she'd last had a drink.

She leaned over and tapped her knuckles on the top of Puckett's forehead. "Knock on wood that I never take another drink again."

Puckett felt the way he had when he saw the first *Rocky* picture. Nothing was more inspiring than real people overcoming great obstacles. He wanted to stand up and cheer. Figuring that that might be a little embarrassing, he settled for leaning over and kissing her tenderly on the mouth. "I'm really proud of you."

"Thanks. I've been dreaming about this for months. Telling you that I was sober, I mean. And then tonight a good excuse fell into my lap."

He held up his can of Diet 7-Up. "Want one?"

"Please."

He stood up and walked to the bathroom where he had some cans of Diet 7-Up stashed in a stylish Styrofoam ice bucket.

"You want a plastic glass?" he called from the bathroom.

"Gee, Puckett, after all the dates we had drinking out of cans, why spoil our record now?"

"I guess you've got a point there," he smiled.

He came out and handed her her very own can and then sat down on the couch next to her. He'd hit the "mute" button and now David Letterman babbled silently.

"Didn't you interview Cobey Daniels once before?" he said, remembering the reason she'd given on the talk show for being in Chicago.

"I wrote a long piece about him just after—" She hesitated. "Just after Donny was killed."

He reached over and took her long, narrow hand in his blunt, wide one.

She went on, "I suppose, in some way, I used him as a substitute for my son. Remember all the trouble he got in? The time he stole the car and the Highway Patrol chased him across half the state? The time he was arrested for possession of drugs? And that time in the mall with the underage girl?"

He nodded. "Right. Not that anybody ever got the story straight. She said he was trying to strangle her and he said he was just playing and—" He shrugged. "Anyway, that security guard came in and broke it up before anything happened."

She sighed. "That was Cobey. But look at him now."

"I've got to admit, he seems to have done the impossible. That one-man show of his is doing very well." Like many people on the periphery of show biz, Puckett read the trades to keep up with the news. Because he worked so many celebrity cases, the trades—*Daily Variety* especially—were an important part of his job.

"Most child stars never make a comeback, but people are talking a Tony award when Cobey finally brings the show into New York."

She took her hand from his. "Anyway, a week ago I got an assignment to do an update on Cobey for a very big magazine. The editor wants me to dig into his background and make it a really major piece. She has a whole file of stuff on Cobey that she's never been able to use." She sipped her 7-Up and then said, "Say, I'm going to see his show tomorrow night. Why don't you go with me?"

"That'd be great. I'd enjoy seeing it."

"And you can protect me from Lilly Carlyle."

"His manager?"

"Right. She hated me back then and she still hates me. Cobey and I developed a very intense relationship during the two weeks I was doing my research and she was very—jealous. I don't know any other way to put it. She really hassled me. My last day on the set, she ordered me off and then slapped me across the mouth before I even had time to turn around."

He thought back. "Yeah, you know what her nickname is? The Iron Maiden. A very tough lady. And mean when the occasion warrants."

"And incredibly possessive of Cobey. Do you know that he lived with her from the time he was six? She took him from his parents and just sent them checks." She laughed. "So I figure you can handle Lilly while I sneak off and interview Cobey."

"Gee, thanks. Lilly is my kind of woman, all right."

And then the silence fell. It was inevitable, both of them being essentially reticent types.

"You kind of nervous, Puckett?"

"Yeah. Are you?"

She nodded.

The silence again.

"I don't want to make love tonight, Puckett."

"All right."

"I'm sorry if that hurts your feelings. Or your pride."

"I'll survive."

"I feel a whole lot of things. Confusing things. Contradictory things."

"I understand."

"You look so sad."

"I'm just kind of confused, too."

"You are?" she said.

He nodded.

"I guess we could always sort of compromise," she said.

"Huh?"

"And just sort of hold each other and sleep together and not make love."

"Do you think we're adult enough to actually do that?"

"I know I am—but I don't know about you."

"Wise ass."

And then she was in his arms again.

4

It wasn't easy, but somehow they did not actually make love. It was sort of like high school. First he got to first base, and then he got to second base, and then, just when he started sliding into third, she said, soft and unseen in the darkness, "Please, Puckett. For both our sakes. Let's wait, all right?"

She was well worth waiting for, Anne Addison.

5

Sometime in the middle of the night, it began to rain. Wind blew beads of water against the window so hard they sounded like BBs. Behind the drawn white curtains, jagged daggers of silver lightning played across the sky, and thunder rumbled ominously in the distance.

The storm had awakened them both.

They lay naked in each other's arms beneath the warm covers. They felt snug and safe and happy as children.

"I've missed you, Puckett," she said.

She didn't need to say anything else.

CHAPTER THREE

1

THEY SPENT THE NEXT DAY VISITING PLACES ON A LIST A friend of Puckett's had given him a while back—lunch at Rocky's on the Navy Pier where they had white codfish sandwiches—then taking a tour of the Elks National Memorial Building with its huge rotunda, 100 feet tall and made of marble; then the Adler Planetarium; and finally a stop at Topper's Recordtown, where they saw such goodies as original 45s by such artists as Elvis, Chuck Berry and the Beatles.

And where, in a stack labeled "TV tie-ins," Puckett found a 45 with a sleeve that showed a young Cobey Daniels in crew-neck sweater and Beatle haircut grinning right out at you. The name of the song was "I'm Your Baby, Yes I Am!" and it was billed as "TV's No 1 Star Now Sings America's No 1 Hit!" Cobey had had several hits.

Anne was busy looking at albums, but when she came by again, Puckett waggled the record at her and said, "Who's this?"

"Who's who?" she said, taking the record and looking at it and smiling. "God, look how young he is."

They spent another twenty minutes in the store. The place was nirvana for nostalgia buffs. So many memories . . . so many eras . . . so many huge stars who were now utterly forgotten . . . and all the dance songs . . . "The Stroll" . . . "The Mashed Potato" . . . "The Twist" . . . "The Frug."

Puckett almost blushed, recalling that he'd clumsily tried to dance each and every one of them, desperately trying to please this or that girl . . .

Anne ended up buying a Connie Francis soundtrack album, *Where The Boys Are.*

"My sister took me to this when I was eight," Anne said as they walked up to the cash register. "I still remember feeling sorry for Connie Francis."

"Feeling sorry for her? Why? She was a huge star," Puckett said, puzzled.

"Yes, but in the movies she was surrounded by all these gorgeous starlets—and face it, Connie wasn't any beauty."

He leaned over and kissed her chastely on the cheek. Feeling sorry for Connie Francis . . . God!

2

While Puckett and Anne were sightseeing, a police detective named Cozzens was trying to gulp down the last of his submarine sandwich before speaking into the telephone receiver he'd picked up.

"'lo."

"Detective Cozzens?"

"Ummmhmmm."

"I beg your pardon?"

There. One last lumpy, bumpy swallow and the rest of the sandwich—wedge of salami, wedge of turkey, onions, hamburger dills, lettuce, catsup, mustard—managed to get sucked down into his esophagus and into the roiling cauldron that was his stomach.

He was already reaching in his desk drawer for some Pepto-Bismol.

"Sorry. I was just finishing my lunch."

"Oh." Hesitation. "This is Mrs. Swallows again, Detective. From North Carolina?"

"Right, Mrs. Swallows. I remember you."

"It's been three days."

"No word from her at all?"

"Nothing. And I tried her friends at the clinic several times. She hasn't called in there, either."

"How about other friends?"

"I tried those, too. At least, the ones Beth mentioned in her letters."

So maybe there was trouble, Cozzens thought glumly. *If it was his daughter involved, he'd probably assume the worst, too.*

"You can do something now, Detective Cozzens?" There was just a hint of anger in the woman's voice. The law in Chicago dictated that if an adult is reported missing, seventy-two hours must pass before the police can act on the report.

"Now I can do something, Mrs. Swallows," he agreed.

"You'll go out to her apartment house?"

"This afternoon, Mrs. Swallows. Soon as I can, in fact."

"I'm trying to be optimistic," she said.

"I know it's difficult, Mrs. Swallows, but there could be a very logical explanation for this."

"I suppose you're right."

"There's always the possibility that she met somebody and went somewhere with him."

"She'd call first."

"You're sure of that?"

Mrs. Swallows sounded irritated again. "I don't have any illusions about my daughter being an angel, Detective Cozzens, but she is very, very responsible. She'd never miss work without calling in, and she'd call me, too. She knows how I worry."

"I've got your phone number here, Mrs. Swallows. I'll let you know what I find out. In the meantime—"

"—in the meantime, I'm praying."

"That's a good idea, Mrs. Swallows. A very good idea."

After he hung up, Cozzens sat staring out at the squad room, realizing he hadn't been very good with Mrs. Swallows. He should have been more consoling. Hell, if it was his daughter missing, he'd be ten times more hysterical than Mrs. Swallows.

His phone rang again and, as he grabbed for the receiver, he looked out at the squad room.

It was usually empty in the early afternoon, three long if ragged rows of desks and telephones and typewriters resembling a stage set with nobody to man them. That had been one of his early discouragements about detective status. You spent a lot of time alone. When he'd worn a uniform, he spent most of his time with a partner. He'd had an especially good one, a woman named Sharon Rosenthal.

A lone bar of dusty, golden sunlight streamed through the window, illuminating the surface of Detective Cozzens' desk. The exact color and texture and quality of the sunlight made him recall, momentarily, his days back in Catholic school, sitting in the back of the classroom, chin cupped in his hand, daydreaming. He'd been a great daydreamer; hell, still was. He'd wanted to be, in those days, a pirate, an airplane pilot, a football hero and, most especially, a really neat guy like his hero, Roy Rogers.

But then he grew up and found that he wasn't any of these things. He was just this little, stubby bastard with a wife and two kids living in Chicago. Roy would never have settled for that; sometimes, Cozzens wondered why he had.

"'lo."

"Mitch?"

His wife. Or, to be exact, his soon-to-be-ex-wife.

"Hi."

"Did you see Dr. Sondegard this morning?" Karen asked.

"Yup."

"How did it go?"

He tried to keep from being bitter but it didn't work. "Well, as usual, we decided that I should take total responsibility for our marriage failing."

She sighed. "That hardly sounds like Dr. Sondegard."

"Well, maybe I over-interpreted his remarks, but after he managed to sneak in the fact that I'm not tender or sensitive, that I didn't spend enough time with our daughters when they were growing up, and that I've never really tried to satisfy your needs in bed—Well, hell, maybe he was trying to pay me a compliment and I just didn't know it."

A long silence on the other end. Then, "I have a date tonight, Mitch."

Now there was silence on his end.

"I don't want a repeat of last week. You had no right to—"

He managed to speak, finally, but when he did he sounded weak, almost sick. "I'm sorry I haven't been a better husband, Karen. And I—I'm sorry about last week."

Karen and his daughters had taken an apartment in Evanston. He was permitted to visit the girls twice a week. Edie, the youngest, had mentioned to him that her mother had a date last Thursday night. Cozzens managed to show up the same time as the guy, hating the fucker on sight, slick and polished, a total goddamn crowd-pleaser, making Cozzens feel like something that had just crawled out from under a maggot-encrusted rock.

It had been a horrible scene, her date with his frozen-in-place smile, Karen with fury in her beautiful dark eyes, the girls—twelve and fourteen—trying to steer Dad into the living room, away from the intruder. He hadn't said anything, or hinted at any violence, but his mere presence there had been wrong, as the good, gray Dr. Sondegard the marriage counselor had told him this morning.

"I don't want a repeat of last week," she said again.

"You don't have to worry, Karen."

But she couldn't let it go. He heard years of her pent-up rage—and years of his own failures—in her voice. "I was so goddamn mad, Mitch—"

The rest of it, he tuned out.

He started thinking about the Swallows girl. Moved up here a year ago, right after graduating from the University of North Carolina, and had a future bright with promise and seemingly filled with fun, and then—

"It's getting serious, Mitch, and I don't want anything to jeopardize it."

But he'd been tuned out. "Serious?"

"God, Mitch, you don't *listen* to me. You never did. I start talking and your mind wanders—which shows just how much respect for me you really have." She sighed. "I said that things are getting serious between Robert and me."

"I see."

"And that I don't want anything to spoil it."

"How do the girls like him?"

"That's not a fair question, Mitch, and you know it."

Now years of his own anger and frustration were back. "They told me that he's a real showboat and they don't like him at all."

"They feel guilty, Mitch. You know what Dr. Sondegard says. If they said anything nice about Robert, they'd feel disloyal to you."

He felt sick suddenly—raving, violently sick—of himself, of Karen. But mostly of himself.

He thought of her the autumn day he'd met her at the University of Illinois—so fucking gorgeous. She never should have let him even get close to her she was so fucking gorgeous. He thought of her that autumn day, so shiny and fine and new, radiating not only great beauty but also great hope and great promise. How had all those wonderful early years led to this inching, hesitant, painful conversation today? Maybe the pods had taken them over, as in *Invasion of the Body Snatchers*, and they weren't really the Karen and Mitch who'd met that day by the victory bell.

Then he started crying. No big, dramatic sobs, just sad, angry, quiet, male tears, and he didn't want her to know it and so he said, "Give my love to the girls," before she could say anything.

And then he hung up.

And he got the hell out of the squad room.

Dealing with a maybe-dead girl suddenly seemed a lot easier than dealing with a living soon-to-be-ex-wife . . .

3

The Swallows girl lived in a two-story apartment house in the Lincoln Park area, one of the many old greystones that had had a facelift in the past ten years, in this case a cedar shake façade. Given the number of Volvos parked along the curb, and the number of mothers with strollers moving along the sidewalks, it was easy for Detective Cozzens to surmise that this was a neighborhood for young and very successful professionals and their families.

He got out of the car and stood for a moment touching the small of his back. It hurt. Ten years ago he'd suffered a problem with a disc and his back hadn't been right since. Sitting for any long period of time gave him special trouble. And cops frequently sat for long periods of time. He went up to the apartment house.

He was used to vestibules that smelled. In some neighborhoods, they frequently reeked of food. In others, they reeked of drugs and the feces the junkies had left behind while squatting in the vestibule shadows. But this place, wide and sunny and bright, had no odor at all. There was a long row of mailboxes on the left wall, two or three silver boxes for the milkman on the right wall, and a steep staircase covered with a spotless rubber runner.

He walked past the staircase, to the rear of the first floor. The last apartment on the left bore a discreet sign, MANAGER.

He knocked once and waited.

On the other side of the door, he could hear an announcer identify the radio station now playing as WFMT. He spoke with great care and dignity. He then announced that listeners would now be treated to Vivaldi. Detective Cozzens felt ashamed of himself. To him, Vivaldi sounded like a shortstop the Cubs had deep-sixed a few years back.

The door opened. A small man in a tan cardigan sweater, a white shirt, a red bow tie, dark trousers and a fussy little pair of rimless glasses stood looking up at Cozzens. With his white hair and prim mouth, he looked like Cozzens' old Latin teacher back in Catholic school.

"Afternoon," the man said. The Vivaldi was loud behind him so he had to shout a bit.

"Afternoon." Cozzens showed him all the ID he was supposed to.

"I thought that had been taken care of."

"What had been taken care of?"

"You know. Jenny's boyfriend."

"Jenny's boyfriend?" Cozzens was bewildered.

The man leaned forward, looked around the hall a moment as if somebody might be listening, and then said, "I still think it was him who smashed my kitchen window. You know, because I called you fellows when he parked in that spot again."

"What spot?"

"You know. In the back. Right in front of the fire exit. If somebody had to get out of there—" For the first time, the man seemed to take real stock of Cozzens. "You're not the fellow, are you?"

"I guess not."

"Officer was out here the other day. Trying to help me with a tenant whose boyfriend got mad because I called the police on him. Next morning, I found my kitchen window smashed in. I think it was him, her boyfriend."

"Well, I hope you get it all straightened out, Mr.—?"

"Mr. Kemper. Albert Kemper. I'm the super. I used to teach English, but after my wife died—" He shrugged. "Well, I don't have to tell you how the Chicago school system is these days. I got scared to go to school, if you can imagine that. A teacher scared to go to school."

"Yessir," Cozzens said, "I can imagine that."

Kemper shrugged again. "So I quit. Just went in one day—this was right after one of my students pulled a knife, and it was one hell of a knife, let me tell you, pulled a knife on another boy right in my classroom and—"

"And you quit."

"Absolutely right. I quit."

Cozzens prided himself on his patience. At least he had until he'd met Albert here. The way the guy jabbered on . . . But then Cozzens thought of what Albert Kemper had just said. Wife died. Meaning terminal loneliness. No wonder the old guy talked so much.

"I'm looking for a young woman named Swallows."

"You mean the girl in 18-C?"

Cozzens nodded.

"Very nice girl," Kemper said. "Very nice."

"Have you seen her in the past three or four days?" Kemper raised watery blue eyes and looked at a point on the ceiling above Cozzens' head.

"Guess I haven't," Kemper said.

"Her mother is getting worried."

"Well, between us, her mother is the type."

"The type?"

"Worrier. The girl met a nice boy last year and went off on a long skiing weekend with him to Wisconsin, way the hell up in the hills. Perfectly fine as far as I'm concerned—I mean, I'd just as soon that all these kids would get married, but I don't want to be some disapproving old fart who begrudges the young having a good time—anyway, that mother of hers called me every single day the girl was gone. I knew where she was, of course, but I wasn't going to tell her mother. She doesn't seem very up-to-date, if you know what I mean."

Cozzens would sure hate to get stuck in an elevator with this old coot. The guy would talk him to death. Cozzens could imagine himself on his knees, pleading for mercy as Albert here kept yammering.

"Mr. Kemper?"

"Huh?"

Albert Kemper had been in the middle of starting up with a new topic but Cozzens interrupted him.

"I don't have a search warrant."

"You don't?"

"No. So legally I can't go up to her apartment and look around."

"You think something's wrong?"

"Getting a search warrant would be a lot of hassle—and even then I'm not sure I could get one. But you could help me."

"I could?"

"As the super, you could take the responsibility for letting me into her apartment."

"I could?"

"And then you could stand there and watch me look around the place."

"And I wouldn't get in trouble?"

"Not as long as you're the super."

"You think something's wrong, don't you?"

"That isn't the point, Mr. Kemper. Her mother thinks something's wrong and—"

"—but like I told you, her mother's a—"

"—worrier. Yes, Mr. Kemper, I remember you telling me that, but why don't we go up and have a look? If you'd like to, I mean."

Kemper straightened his bow tie and said, "I'll bet that woman's been pestering the hell out of you, hasn't she?"

Cozzens let Kemper precede him up the stairs. Kemper left his apartment door open so everybody could share in the wonders of Vivaldi.

4

Somebody had been killed in here, and recently.

The odor told Cozzens that, as did the faint discoloration at several points on the hardwood floor.

The sunlight tried to brighten things up. So did the bird song through one of the partially raised windows. The neat, trim furnishings—tasteful in a trendy off-white way—lent the living room a brisk sense of life, and it was easy enough to imagine a nice young woman moving through these sunny rooms, whistling as she dusted or munching on a bright red apple as she snuggled up on the divan and read a novel.

"You want me to go along with you?" Kemper said.

"If you wouldn't mind."

"Something's wrong here, isn't it?"

"What makes you say that, Mr. Kemper?"

"I guess I believe in what my students call 'vibes.' You know, when you instinctively sense something."

"And you instinctively sense something?"

"Yes. Yes, unfortunately, I do."

"So do I," Cozzens said, and moved from the doorway into the apartment proper.

There were two closets in the living room. Cozzens checked them both. They were full but orderly, one smelling of moth balls, the other of dust. In the latter closet, he found examples of things that said the Swallows girl probably got a great deal of exercise. There was a tennis racquet, a softball bat, a pair of white ice skates and a grass-stained volleyball.

While Cozzens did this, Kemper, ever the English prof, checked out her bookcases. "She's even brighter than I thought."

"How's that?"

"Henry James."

"Oh, yes, Henry James," Cozzens said, remembering a literature course at the University of Illinois in which he'd had to slog through a novel by Henry James. He'd liked Jack London, Ernest Hemingway, F. Scott Fitzgerald and Willa Cather, but he'd never developed a taste for Henry James. He'd always supposed this marked him as a peasant for sure.

"Of course, she's got a lot of trash here, too, a lot of self-esteem books and things like that. *Tell Them The Lord Says To Shove It.* My God."

Cozzens said, "Why don't we try the bedroom?"

"Detective Cozzens?" Kemper said.

"Yes?"

"I don't know how I'll handle it if we find—Well, if something happened here. I mean, you're used to it, I suppose, but—"

"That's a myth, Mr. Kemper."

"A myth?"

"About cops being used to it."

"Really?"

"Nobody ever gets used to it, Mr. Kemper." Cozzens offered a sad smile. "Being good professionals, we just have to pretend we do."

Cozzens went into the bedroom.

Kemper stood in the doorway, watching him.

The room was small and sun-splashed. A very sweet scent of sachet lay agreeably on the air. The motif was pink and almost aggressively girlish, as if the Swallows woman were trying to recapture her lost teen years. On the neatly made bed, three plump teddy bears sat watching Cozzens with bright button eyes. Between a wicker chaise lounge and a rocking chair sat a huge teddy bear, one as big as most four-year-olds. He had a jolly smile but curiously melancholy eyes.

"My stomach is in knots," Kemper said from the doorway. "I'm afraid . . ." He was much less talkative up here than he'd been downstairs.

He let his voice trail off.

There were also two closets in this room, one containing good but not expensive clothes, the other holding skiing gear on which she'd obviously spent a good deal of money.

Cozzens closed the door.

"I guess that leaves the bathroom and the kitchen," Kemper said. His voice was shaking. He obviously sensed they were getting closer to finding something he dreaded.

Cozzens led the way into the bathroom.

He took one look at it and saw that it had been cleaned recently. There was a residue of scrubbing compound on the curving white bowl of the sink. In the sprightly yellow waste can next to it, he found an empty container of Windex and Lysol liquid disinfectant. There was also a rolled lump of dirty rags. The discoloration on them looked all too familiar to Cozzens.

He was careful not to touch anything.

The bathroom was small, tiled in mint green, with opaque sliding shower doors on the tub and two different cabinets on the wall.

It smelled of disinfectant, water and, faintly, of the mildew that always accrues in rooms where water is used frequently without benefit of sunlight to dry it.

He took a pencil and used it to slide back one of the doors on the tub.

A gray bath mat lay on the ribbed floor of the tub. A brown container of Vidal Sassoon shampoo stood in one corner. A festive yellow bottle of discount conditioner stood in the other.

The tub had been thoroughly cleaned. Suspiciously so.

Not even when Cozzens got down on a knee and looked carefully at the floor of the tub did he see so much as a single hair.

Cozzens stood up.

"I guess that leaves the kitchen," Kemper said, still clinging to his familiar position in the doorway of the bathroom.

When Cozzens turned to look at him, he saw that fear had given the aging Kemper the look of a frightened little boy.

"You don't have to go with me to the kitchen, Mr. Kemper."

"I've gone everyplace else. I may as well."

Cozzens studied him a moment.

To judge Kemper by the book, he was behaving suspiciously. By rights, he should even be a suspect in case something had happened to the Swallows woman.

But somehow Cozzens didn't think so. Here was a gentle, civilized little man for whom violence was an abstraction, something he mostly read about and heard about. Now, he was confronting it in his own life, and it was terrifying him.

They went into the kitchen, Cozzens leading the way as usual.

The scent of blood was overwhelming here, even though none could be seen, even though somebody had scrubbed the hell out of this room.

The kitchen was done in black and white tiles with two small aluminum sinks side-by-side. Continuing around the corner of the L-shaped kitchen, he saw a nice, big, imposing refrigerator with a juice dispenser built into the door. There were also two closets, one on either side of the refrigerator.

Cozzens opened the door of the closet on the right.

Propped up against the back of the closet was the naked body of a young white female.

Her head had been chopped off, leaving only a raw, scabbed, bloody hole in the center of her shoulders.

"You found something, didn't you, Detective Cozzens?" Kemper said from behind him.

"Right. I found something, Mr. Kemper."

"It's pretty bad, isn't it?"

"It's very bad, Mr. Kemper. You should stay back."

"Sometimes I hate the world we live in. The things people do to each other."

"So do I, Mr. Kemper," Cozzens said, and quietly closed the closet door.

He looked at the refrigerator.

He had this hunch, this cop-hunch, was all, figuring he knew where he'd find the head that had been severed from the body.

He stood staring at the refrigerator, gulping down bile. He didn't turn around to speak.

"Mr. Kemper?"

"Yes?"

"Why don't you go wait in the living room?"

"You think there's something in the refrigerator?"

"I'm afraid there probably is."

"I don't understand. If you found something in the closet, then what could possibly be in the—"

"Just go in the living room, Mr. Kemper."

"All right. I mean, if you want me to."

"I want you to."

"If there's anything I can do, you just holler."

"I'll just holler."

"I'll be in the living room, then."

"Thank you, Mr. Kemper."

Kemper went away, size seven feet padding softly back toward the sunlight and bird song.

Leaving Cozzens here to take out his clean, white handkerchief and move his hand toward the handle that would open the big, softly thrumming machine.

He opened the door and stared right at the Swallows woman.

All the blood and other goop was covered lightly with silver frost. Somebody had turned the cold up to high to cut down on the smell. There was even frost on the edges of her false eyelashes.

The curious thing was, even now he could see that she'd been a nice-looking woman. A fine, high forehead that bespoke intelligence, large blue eyes, a patrician nose and a full, slightly heavy mouth that suggested sensuality. Her hair was blonde and shoulder-length. She'd probably had many boyfriends.

He closed the door and went back to the living room. Kemper was staring at her books again.

When he heard Cozzens coming into the room, he said, "You look pale, Detective Cozzens."

"I feel pale, Mr. Kemper."

"Bad?"

"Beyond bad, Mr. Kemper." Cozzens nodded to the hallway. "Let's close things up here for now. I'd like to go downstairs and use your phone, if you don't mind."

"Are you going to tell me about it?"

"Maybe in a few minutes, Mr. Kemper."

"I guess you fellows really never do get used to it, do you?"

"No," Cozzens said. "No, I guess we never do."

They closed up the apartment and went downstairs and Cozzens used Kemper's phone to call all the appropriate people.

CHAPTER FOUR

1

ORTY YEARS AGO, BACK IN THE DAYS WHEN NAMES such as Hecht and MacArthur and Algren and Sandburg had been a source of pride to every literate Chicagoan, the Template Theater had been a very special place. Tennessee Williams had tried out several of his more successful one-act plays here. Olivier, on tour, had stopped by to see an old friend and had been talked into giving a reading. Several New York theater critics—in those halcyon days when NYC still had several theater critics—pronounced the place a "Midwestern Mecca."

Alas, those days were long gone, as Puckett and Anne learned when they walked into the place three hours after finishing an early dinner. The interior was scuffed and dusty, the small lobby area even displayed a few pieces of graffiti which had stubbornly resisted scrubbing. The theater itself was chilly, the seats squawked and squeaked from lack of care, and the stage lighting could most charitably be described as "adequate."

The crowd almost made up for this. To judge by all the minks on the ladies and the fancy Armani suits on the men, this was the opening night of a long-awaited Broadway blockbuster. The crowd chattered and chittered and laughed as if they were on display for the cameras of *Time* magazine and *Entertainment Tonight*.

Once they were seated, Anne said, "Look at the crowd."

"I am. I can't believe it."

"They must really want to see the show. To come to a place like this."

Puckett, who'd done a little reading about the Template Theater, felt a certain amount of pity for the shabby old place.

"Helen Hayes performed here," he said.

"She did?"

He nodded. "And Arthur Miller first tried a one-act version of *Death of a Salesman* here."

"That's incredible."

Puckett made a sour face. "And, unfortunately, nobody seems to give a damn. Not the way they've let everything go to hell."

A few years ago there had been serious talk about refurbishing this place. No longer. The recession had taken care of that. When you have five thousand people waiting in a single, unending line for three hundred minimum wage jobs, a city has other things to worry about than taking care of some once-proud old warhorse of a local theater.

Puckett understood this. But it didn't make looking around at this sad, dignified, relic of a theater any easier.

The play started twenty minutes later and, right from the start, Puckett saw why critics liked it so much.

Cobey narrated the entire play from stage right, frequently stepping into scenes center stage. In this respect, it was very much like *Our Town*. The play detailed, with great, sour humor and bawdy glee, the travails of a child TV star. The script was merciless on TV execs and their minions—and just as merciless on minimally talented children who let their modest ability go to their heads. And Cobey certainly hadn't spared himself.

In the guise of Randy, the dictionary meaning of which was not lost on Puckett, Cobey showed himself to be quite a jerk. Here he literally threw money at a pregnant girl who said she was carrying his child; there he got a scene-hogging co-star fired; here he sat in a small living room with his parents and listened with obvious and vast indifference as his father told him that he was dying of cancer. Cobey was deep into contract negotiations and didn't have time for such trifles as worrying about his old man; there he seduced a very young girl, in a scene that eerily paralleled the troubles he'd had in that Florida shopping mall.

All this was rendered in dialogue, off-stage narration, and even a few biting and very melancholy songs. And Cobey had written every bit of it. There could be no doubt about his talent as either writer or actor.

Many critics had applauded the risks Cobey had taken with his own character, and Puckett agreed completely with them. Randy was a despicable character in virtually every respect . . . and yet . . . and yet there was a sorrow and curious humor about him that rose from the ashes of his pettiness and egotism and made him . . . almost likeable.

Almost.

It was this tension, this unexpected candor, that was so thrilling to watch. The play ran one hour and thirty-seven minutes without an intermission, and, when it was over, the audience was immediately on its feet. Cobey took eight curtain calls.

Even half an hour after the play ended, backstage was jammed with people of every kind—reporters, celebrity-gawkers, spouses of the cast, stage hands, and actors appreciating all the attention they were getting—that little universe of wannabes and hangers-on and minor stars that make up every professional stage production.

In front of Cobey's dressing room stood Lilly Carlyle and a handsome, white-haired man Puckett recognized immediately as Wade Preston, the majority owner of International Talent Management.

Puckett and Anne went over, Puckett not being sure that Lilly would remember him from their brief visit the long-ago day he'd brought Cobey back from the asylum in St. Louis.

But she remembered him at once. "Wade, this is the private investigator who helped us with Cobey that time."

Puckett and Preston shook hands. "Is it all right to say that you were one of my heroes?" Puckett asked and smiled.

"I'm just gratified to know that at least some of the kids who grew up watching my movies went to work for the right side of the law," Preston said. "Unfortunately, I get a lot of prison mail from my little buckaroos. Seems not all of them trod the path of right and justice." His last words mocked themselves—a 1950's movie-and TV-star now mocking some of his old and very corny dialogue. Puckett liked the guy and, idiotic as it seemed, was thrilled to meet him.

Things didn't go so well with Lilly and Anne. She said, "And this, Wade, is Anne Addison, who wrote that very heavy-handed psycho-analytic article about Cobey that time. For *Movie Talk*, remember? I nearly had to get an injunction to force her to leave him alone."

Even in the shadows of the small hallway they were standing in, Puckett could see Anne blush.

Puckett started to say something but Preston said it for him.

"Now, Lilly, we're all here to celebrate the fine things that are happening to Cobey these days. Let's not let past history spoil the night. I'm sure that Ms. Addison's intentions were honorable."

And with that, he gently touched Anne's elbow and smiled at her. "Thanks for coming this evening, Anne."

She nodded, obviously thankful that he had so skillfully changed the moment into a pleasant one.

Puckett made note of the good cop-bad cop routine for which International was famous. With his handsome, Roman senator head and courtly bearing, Wade Preston of the dark suits and brilliant white shirts, shining gold cufflinks and honest blue eyes—Wade Preston could never be anything except the good cop.

The bad cop role was left to Lilly Carlyle who, industry gossip had it, relished the part. Usually it worked opposite tonight's sequence. Usually, Preston tried to talk an uncooperative client into doing the proper thing. Sweet talk, that is. Using words such as right and honor and best intentions. And if that failed, then plump but beautiful Lilly in her $3,000 Rodeo Drive suits came at you. And the words she used were far different. Motherfucker. Asshole. Never work in this town again. And with a few cocksuckers and rip-your-balls-off thrown in for good measure.

"You're here to see Cobey, I take it?" Preston said.

"Just to say hi, see how things are going," Anne said, speaking directly to Preston and not even looking at Lilly. "I want to ask him if he'd let me do a piece on him. The magazine contacted your office, Ms. Carlyle, several times. But we got no answer."

Preston did not look happy. "Which magazine is it, my dear?"

"*Pinnacle.*"

"And Lilly didn't get back to you?"

Preston looked most unhappy. He shot a nasty little glance at Lilly and then turned his attention back to Anne. "*Pinnacle* is a very important magazine in our industry."

"It's probably the best," Puckett said.

"And we'd be very happy to have Cobey be in it," Preston soothed. "But, really, the decision is his." He shot his sleeve and consulted his watch. "Lilly and I have a dinner engagement and we're going to be late if we hang around here anymore. Why don't you give our best to Cobey—and then ask him yourself about the article?"

Anne smiled, obviously pleased at the turn this conversation had taken.

Lilly glared at her, not even trying to hide her displeasure.

"Good night, Ms. Addison."

"Good night, Mr. Preston. It was really nice to meet you." Anne laughed. "I wanted to say the same thing Puckett did. I grew up watching your movies, and your TV series, too. I had this terrible crush on you for years."

Preston tapped a finger to his forehead. "Music to a former matinee-idol's ego." He nodded to Puckett. "Good night, Puckett. Nice to meet you."

The two men shook hands again.

Lilly Carlyle got in one more good glare and then left on Preston's arm.

"I don't think Lilly's going to invite you to her next birthday party," Puckett said.

"Good," Anne laughed. "Because I wouldn't go, anyway."

After the photographers, after the two wealthy Chicago matrons, after a college drama instructor and his three very cute coeds, after the two overweight leaders of Cobey's Chicago fan club . . . after all these people, Puckett and Anne finally got to see Cobey . . .

They walked into his dressing room and there he sat, Diet Pepsi in one hand, cigarette in the other, a very good-looking young man in a dark V-neck sweater, jeans, and white Reeboks.

When he saw who Anne was—when she really registered on his mind—a curious expression filled Cobey's eyes and he jumped up from his chair.

But then Cobey stopped himself, looking over at Puckett. It was obvious that, at first, Cobey didn't recognize Puckett, even though the man looked familiar somehow.

Puckett said, "I did some work for your manager, Lilly, a few years ago."

"Sure!" Cobey said suddenly. "The trip from St. Louis."

"Right."

Cobey stuck out his hand. His grin seemed real. "How are you, anyway, Puckett?"

"Doing fine. Do you remember Anne?"

"Of course," Cobey said and moved over, as if in a receiving line, to shake her hand, too.

Puckett sensed something right then, but he wasn't sure what. Just some kind of jolt that passed from Anne to Cobey as they shook hands . . . a sense that was reinforced by the strange way they stared at each other.

Then Anne laughed. "I wondered if you'd let me do a follow-up article on you?"

"Hell, yes, I will. I was very happy with that first one."

They looked at each other another long moment and then Cobey laughed and said, "How about a Diet Pepsi for either of you?"

They both accepted.

Cobey took two icy cans from a small brown refrigerator next to his closet door. He handed them each a Diet Pepsi and then invited them to sit down.

The dressing room was more like a spare room where odds and ends of furniture had been stored. Only the round, theatrical mirror with light bulbs encircling it bespoke show business. On the long dressing table stood several vases of dead flowers with tiny white note cards taped to each vase—the remains of opening night well-wishing.

"So how about you?" Puckett asked. "How've you been, Cobey?"

The grin again. He'd been a handsome kid and now he was a handsome young man. Especially when he grinned that Cobey grin. "Fantastic. I know that sounds gushy as hell, but it's true. You've heard that two of the networks are talking to us about new shows for the fall?"

"Congratulations, Cobey," Anne said.

"And there's talk about HBO taping this show and running it as a special."

"Things are starting to roll again for you," Puckett said.

Cobey hoisted his Diet Pepsi. "As long as I stay on the wagon, I'm fine."

He was just about to toast his guests when there was a knock at his door and a very pretty, very shy young woman said, "I saw the Dragon Lady leaving so I thought it'd be safe to come in."

Cobey laughed, jumped up and walked over to slide his arm around the woman. "Veronica Hobbs, this is Anne Addison and Mr. Puckett."

Veronica Hobbs nodded quietly to them. She was, Puckett guessed, in her very early twenties, blonde and pale, like a beauty from Poe, perhaps, possessing an ethereal quality that only made her gentle beauty more mysterious. In the proper light, those shadowed eyes would be a deep green. And if she ever smiled, there would be as much pain as pleasure in that smile. She wore a simple, green, woolen jumper that flattered her slender but attractive body.

"'The Dragon Lady' Veronica was referring to is Lilly," Cobey said. "They're not exactly what you'd call the best of friends."

"She hates me," Veronica said simply. "She wants Cobey for herself."

There was no humor in her remark and Cobey looked uncomfortable. He guided Veronica over to the last empty chair, got her seated and got her a Diet Pepsi.

"Anne Addison . . ." Veronica said. "Now I remember. You wrote an article about Cobey."

"Yes."

"That's the best thing ever written about him."

"Thank you."

"You're still writing, I hope?"

"Writing about Cobey again, in fact."

"I'm surprised you haven't written a book by now," Veronica said to Anne.

"Well, I'm trying to put one together—the best of my pieces on movie-and TV-stars over the years. Even a lot of the things I had to do under pen names."

"Why did you use a pen name?"

"Usually because I had more than one article in the issue and the editor didn't want my name appearing twice. I'm making decent money now, but when I was just starting out I really had to write a lot."

"God, I wish I could write," Veronica said. "I'm twenty-two years old and I don't have any talent at all. For anything."

"C'mon, now," Cobey said, gently kidding her. "Don't get into this." He leaned over and put his hand fondly on Veronica's shoulder. "This is a woman who was a piano prodigy and paints well enough to have her work hung in several New York galleries . . . but she says she doesn't have any talent."

"I'm a dabbler," Veronica said. "I'm not a professional the way Anne is or you are."

Puckett could certainly understand Cobey's fascination with the young woman. She was even prettier when you watched her close up. And her self-deprecation was so sincere and painful, it was fetching. You wanted to put your arm around her and protect her.

"I know how you feel," Puckett said. "I'm the same way, Veronica. I'm constantly surrounded by really talented people, but there isn't a damn thing I can do."

"By the way," Cobey said, "Puckett is a cop. A private one these days. And one of the best paid in Los Angeles. So he must be doing something right." Cobey clapped his hands together as if he were leading a hoe down. "But, c'mon, people. Let's stop all this self-deprecation and really dish somebody."

Anne giggled. "Now that's more like it, Cobey. Let's really do a number on somebody."

"Have you heard the gerbil story?" Cobey said.

"That old chestnut?" Anne laughed. "You can do better than that."

"But apparently it's true. He really *did* put a gerbil up his—into his behind," Cobey said.

"I'd like to take his defense," Puckett said. "I don't think that ever happened. I think it's one of those stories that some malicious twit started that took on a life of its own."

"You know the guy?" Cobey said.

Puckett shrugged. "I did some work for him and got to know him a little bit. And I don't believe that gerbil story at all."

The man they were discussing was one of the screen's hunkiest hunks. He was also a man whose sex life the gossips never tired of whispering about.

"All right, then," Cobey said, "did you hear the one about Dirk Fleming? The new guy on *Precinct 19*?"

And then they were off. Story followed story; laugh followed laugh. Puckett felt guilty about even listening to tales like these. There was a nastiness to gossip that always started to wear on him—a cruelty that too many people seemed to relish.

Somewhere in the middle of all this, Veronica suggested that the four of them have dinner the following evening at a restaurant Cobey had wanted to try. Anne accepted without asking Puckett. But what was he going to say? "No, I'd rather not?"

Puckett was finishing his Diet Pepsi when he looked up and saw a familiar figure in the doorway. Cobey's old friend and enemy—and now director—Richard Boyle.

"There's an interviewer here from the *Trib*, Cobey," he said. "Wants to do a piece on the show. You want me to handle it alone?"

Cobey smiled at the other man. But it was an icy smile. "Unless you plan to stab me in the back."

Boyle had the dark good looks of a 1940's leading man. His own smile was just as thin and empty as Cobey's. He wore a green suede car coat, white shirt and black trousers. His curly hair was fashionably mussed. "I've got a vested interest in this show, Cobey, remember? I'm the director."

And with that, he was gone.

When the doorway was empty again, Cobey looked at Puckett and said, "We've basically hated each other since his acting days, Boyle and I."

Puckett wanted to ask him why he'd hire a director he hated, but decided it wouldn't be polite.

"Well, now," Anne said, obviously sensing the mood in the room. "We were planning dinner for tomorrow night, I believe."

"That's perfect," Veronica said. "The theater is dark tomorrow night."

They finished making their plans, when and where.

Puckett and Anne stood up. There were handshakes and hugs and a promise from Anne that she'd call Cobey tomorrow to set up an appointment. And a promise right back that he'd be glad to hear from her and would consult his schedule before she called. Veronica had sweet little hugs for both Anne and Puckett and, in return, they had sweet little hugs for her, too.

"I'm really looking forward to tomorrow night," Veronica said.

Then they were gone, Puckett and Anne, out into the spring night, the theater long darkened, the streets empty. They found a cab stand around the corner.

As they were approaching a Yellow taxi, Anne said, "I really got the sense that Cobey and Boyle hated each other, didn't you?"

Puckett smiled. "I take it that's one of the first questions you're going to ask Cobey. About Boyle, I mean."

She laughed. "Absolutely."

2

An hour-and-a-half later, they were in Puckett's bed. She was reading a collection of Joan Didion's essays, he was going through a stack of old magazines she'd brought over at his request, magazines that contained a lot of her early material, when she had to write so much that she used pen names: Mary Swanwick, Evelyn Day, Phoebe Case, Serena Davidson.

"This is really great stuff," Puckett said every few pages. "Especially the piece on rip-off acting schools in Hollywood. I don't imagine that made you a lot of friends."

"Well, when you get done reading them all, tell me which three you like best. My agent said I should only put three of the early pieces in there—the rest of the book will be more current articles."

He told her which three he liked best. At least so far. They went back to reading.

After a time, she said, "I'm feeling pretty comfortable tonight. How about you?"

He looked over at her. "Feeling not only comfortable, but very peaceful. And nice."

"You want to try making love?"

"I suppose you could talk me into it."

So she talked him into it.

CHAPTER FIVE

1

THE FOLLOWING EVENING, JUST BEFORE SEVEN o'clock, Detective Cozzens, trying to forget that his wife was out with Robert again, entered a nightclub called "The Spandau Ballet." It was one of those places where you found a lot of young doctors and young lawyers, and splendid young women eager to marry same.

On his way in, Cozzens watched two very long-legged young women in sparkling mini-dresses hold coats over their heads and run the quarter block to the front door of the place, splashing and laughing as they ran through the slanting rain that banged off car roofs, turned gutters into rushing overflows, and soaked the few patches of city grass you found here and there.

Cozzens got out, pulled up the collar of his Mike Hammer—the name one of the homicide wags had given Cozzens' classic trench coat—and then strolled to the front of the place. His fedora—if he was going to catch hell for his trench coat, why not catch a lot of hell and wear a fedora, too?—was perfect for rain; the stuff just rolled off the snap-brim edge of the thing.

The nightclub was an oasis of light and noise in the vast gloom. The rain gave a watercolor cast to the purple neon sign atop the front door, and bounced like silver beads off the sidewalk. Even without the door open, Cozzens could smell cigarette smoke and human heat. Even out here, the noise of the dance music was deafening.

He went inside, and immediately felt like a spy from another species. Not only was everybody younger, everybody was also better looking, men and women alike, better poised and infinitely more self-absorbed, which was a great defensive posture for pushing on through life.

"Help you?" asked the bouncer. He resembled a Bears fullback of several seasons ago, the nose smashed in a cigarette ad sort of way, the Armani double-breasted suit that somehow only made his hulking shoulders and wide, white fists all the more menacing.

Cozzens showed him his badge.

The bouncer simply nodded, seeming neither impressed nor intimidated.

Cozzens showed him the photo of Beth Swallows which he'd taken from the apartment. He had spent most of the day interviewing people in the apartment house where the Swallows girl had lived. One of the tenants had told him that Beth sometimes came here.

"Hey," he said. "Beth."

"Right. Know her?"

"Know her real good." Then he grinned. "Not that way. I mean, she's a nice chick."

"In here a lot?"

"Yeah. A lot."

They were both shouting over the din of the music. The lobby area was small and carpeted and featured paintings of record stars painted in garish, stylized tones. There was a hat check window where a skinny girl with pink hair and cocaine-dead eyes watched Cozzens with what appeared to be both interest and fear—must have seen him flash the metal—and a small alcove that led to the restrooms. Two very slick young men were just emerging from MEN's, both of them giving out with little marijuana coughs as they walked toward the dance floor.

"Anybody here know her especially well?"

"Marcie."

"She here right now?"

The bouncer nodded. "Oh, by the way, I'm his brother Bob. Mike was the fullback. That's why people always stare at me." He touched a massive finger to his nose. "We even got our noses busted the same way." He laughed. "Our old man's fist." Then he started away, throwing, "Be right back," over his shoulder.

Cozzens could only catch glimpses of the people on the dance floor. The strobe light never showed you more than flashes of arms or legs, breasts or hips. As he stood watching, he felt again that he was a spy from some other species. His species was too old and too chunky and too inhibited to ever dance around that way, or break the drug laws so casually, or risk AIDS by constantly picking up new lovers.

No, his species was better at going home alone and eating cheese sandwiches and catching the tail end of a venerable John Wayne movie and then lying awake all night wondering what love words that slick sonofabitch was whispering to the not-yet-ex-wife at that very moment . . .

"This is Marcie."

She had one of those black, ersatz-Bunny costumes on, with the fishnet stockings and the low-cut front and the high-cut crotch that could have gotten you arrested as recently as 1958.

"Hi, Marcie. My name's Cozzens."

"It's about Beth?"

"Right."

"God, something happened, didn't it?"

"Is there somewhere we could talk?"

"You didn't answer my question."

She had a pleasant if not pretty face, one already a little too fleshy at thirty or so, and very frightened brown eyes. She had a sullen, nervous and overmuch mouth.

"Is there somewhere we could talk in private?"

Marcie looked at the bouncer.

"Brad's gone," the bouncer said. "Use his office."

Marcie led the way in.

The office continued the shadowy motif of the nightclub itself. A single lamp on the corner of the oak desk lit the small, box-like room. There were two filing cabinets that matched the desk, a leather couch and matching armchair, and enough posters of the same semi-nude famous model to enshrine the lady.

"No other lamp in here?"

"He likes it dark. He—he brings girls back here."

"I see."

"He isn't married or anything," Marcie said. "I mean, it's all right."

He sat on the edge of the clean and orderly desk and she sat on the edge of the leather armchair. She had very nice legs and small hands that were folded almost prayerfully on the tops of her knees.

"Marcie, I don't know your last name."

"She's dead, isn't she?"

"Now you're the one not answering the question."

"Tolbert. Marcie Tolbert. She's dead, isn't she?"

"Yes."

"Oh, God."

He waited a moment before he spoke again. He felt odd in a room this dark, as if he were a child playing hide-and-go-seek or something.

"Somebody murdered her."

"God." Then, "Will you tell me about it?"

"I'm not sure you'll want to know."

"She was my best friend."

He sighed. "All right." And then told her. He didn't tell her all of it, and he didn't tell it in any detail, but she did get the part about Beth's head being in the refrigerator.

"Is this a joke?" she said, angry.

"No joke."

"Who the fuck would do something like that?"

"A very sick person."

"Jesus." Still angry. "I don't fucking believe it. And I'm not going to apologize for using the 'F' word, either."

Not going to apologize for using the "F" word. He'd always remember that.

"Was she depressed lately?"

"Kind of, I guess."

"Do you know why?"

She shrugged with her nice, skinny shoulders. "She was having some trouble with her boyfriend."

"What kind of trouble?"

"You know, the usual. He wasn't in a place where he could really make a commitment and she wanted to start seeing other people— she really got hurt when she was in college and she didn't want to set herself up for that again—so she felt she could protect herself if she could keep dating."

"So she dated other people."

"Oh, once in a while; but you know how that goes."

"Tell me."

"Well, you know, you go out with them, but even if they're nice looking and a lot of fun, your mind isn't really there."

"I see." And he did see. He'd had several dates just like that himself lately. The good Dr. Sondegard had recommended it.

"They try very hard to be nice and you try very hard to be nice— but somehow you can't quit thinking about the person you're in love with and so then, eventually, your date starts picking up on this and he gets just as distant as you are—he gets hurt, too—and so the whole night is ruined."

"Did her boyfriend know that she was dating other people?"

She nodded. "He followed them."

"You know that for a fact?"

"Yes. She saw him. Once, he was following them down the street and she turned around and told him to leave her alone."

"What did he do?"

"He threatened to punch out her date."

"Did he?"

She shook her head. In the deep shadow of the room, she looked five years younger than she was. He tried not to notice his occasional pass at an erection. Then he realized he should be happy about it. He hadn't thought of having sex in months.

"No, he finally just walked away."

"So they argued a lot?"

"All the time."

"Did he ever hurt her physically that you know of?"

"She told me that he slapped her once. And I believed her. She wasn't the kind of girl who exaggerated things much."

"Did she ever try to break the relationship off?"

"Several times."

"But it didn't work?"

"I don't think she really wanted it to end."

"I see."

"She—"

She stopped herself.

"You were going to say something, Marcie," he probed gently.

"I don't know that it matters. Not now."

"I'd appreciate it if you'd tell me."

She looked up at him. "You're not like a cop at all. You're nice."

He smiled. "I'll pass that compliment along to my fellow officers."

But her sense of play was quickly gone. "I'm afraid I'm going to throw up. I can't stop thinking of what you told me about Beth."

She brought her small hands to her small face and started crying softly.

He got up and took a clean white handkerchief from his back pocket and gave it to her. He had another clean white handkerchief in his other back pocket. In his line of business, you went through a lot of clean white handkerchiefs.

Sometimes you felt like using them yourself . . .

"Thank you," she said between sobs.

He let her go.

He sat on the edge of the desk and looked around and wished again that he hadn't been such a jerk and driven by his old house tonight; and then he sat there and looked around and wished he had a date tonight, even a bad one. Despite her grief, Marcie's presence reminded him of how lonely he was.

"Thank you," she said when the worst of it was over.

"You can keep it. Compliments of the City of Chicago."

She smiled politely and balled the handkerchief up in her small fist.

"I need to know his name, her boyfriend."

And then she told him.

She was the fifth person he'd interviewed today and they'd all told pretty much the same story—very angry, sometimes violent relationship between Beth and her boyfriend—and they'd all used the same name.

A few minutes later, he walked her out to the front of the place again.

She looked shaky, and scared.

He slid his arm around her waist and gave her a little peck on the cheek. He knew that this was highly unprofessional conduct, but at the moment, he didn't give a rat's ass.

He took one more look at all the pretty people out there on the dance floor. Beth Swallows had once been one of them.

She might be alive today if she hadn't been one of them, if she'd been some other kind of young woman, one disposed to quieter and more lasting pleasures. But there he went being a priest again. He hated that side of him, the stem priest side of him, just as his wife and both his daughters hated it. Who was he to judge anybody?

Cozzens nodded good night to the bouncer and left the smoke and roar and rage of the nightclub behind, out into the chill, silver rain, his Mike Hammer and his fedora keeping him good and dry as he walked slowly back to his car.

2

Puckett and Anne met Cobey and Veronica outside the restaurant. It was a quarter after eight, and the rain was little more than a mist, though the temperature had fallen eight degrees since late afternoon.

The restaurant decor reminded Puckett, as it was supposed to, of the bar in *Casablanca*. Easy to imagine international spies sitting at the various small tables, paying only a modicum of attention to the eight piece orchestra, and never even looking at the dance floor, which was populated by older men in dinner jackets and matrons in pastel-colored organdie gowns. There was even an upright piano—but it was unlikely that the pianist's name was Sam. The man, true to the times, was Japanese.

Many of the customers even cooperated by smoking cigarettes, which was no doubt bad for their lungs but great for the atmosphere.

After being seated, served drinks and given time to look over their menus, Anne said, "This is really a nice place."

The other three agreed.

Cobey said, "I picked it because of the food, though. They're supposed to have great steaks."

"Steak for me, then," Puckett said. "Now I don't have to pore over the menu." He laughed. "That's why I like McDonald's. None of these big decisions."

Just before the food came, a small woman dressed like a nightclub singer of the forties stood at a microphone in a baby blue spotlight and sang a medley of WWII favorites, including beautiful versions of "I'll Be Seeing You" and "The White Cliffs of Dover." She then did a brief Cole Porter medley and left the floor to hearty applause.

"She was great." Anne exclaimed.

"She sure was," Cobey said. Then frowned. "That's one thing you realize when you get out and about."

Veronica made a face. "What's that? How many pretty girls there are?" She'd tried to make her remark a joke, but there was a nasty edge to it.

Puckett stared at her briefly. He'd already turned Veronica into a cliché. The beautiful, dutiful girlfriend of a celebrity—long-suffering, accustomed to sharing him with others. But he saw now that he'd been wrong. Veronica was a lot more complicated than he'd first imagined.

"No," Cobey said. From his tense expression, he'd obviously taken Veronica's remark seriously, too. "I was going to say that when you get out and about, you realize how many talented people there are. And how few of them ever get discovered." He poured Diet Pepsi from the can into his glass and raised the glass in a toast. "We call this 'Alcoholic's Delight' at our AA meetings. So here's an 'Alcoholic's Delight' toast to talent—wherever it is. May it long endure."

Anne nodded. "You know Charles Grodin, the actor? He wrote a book about acting and he made the same point. He said that he was successful just because he'd hung in there all those years, determined to make it. But he said that a lot of actors he worked with, people he said were a lot more talented than he is, dropped out because they couldn't take all the rejection or they had families to feed."

Dinner came and it was just as good as Cobey had promised.

Toward the end of the meal, the girl singer came back, shimmering in her tight, blue gown, her blonde hair giving her a Veronica Lake type of sultry beauty.

This time, she chose songs from later in the decade and into the early fifties, just before rock-and-roll took over the record business forevermore. She did "Red Sails in the Sunset," and "Nature Boy," and "Tennessee Waltz" and "Three Coins in the Fountain," and charmed the asses off, everybody listening to her, including one young busboy who was so obviously entranced by her beauty that he stared at her with beatific lust.

There were only two people in the nightclub not paying any attention to the singer. One was the maitre d', a stuffy Polish fellow who hoped that his black tuxedo gave him a continental look, and a kind of dumpy man in a dramatic trench coat who was showing the maitre d' his identification.

"You're a policeman?" the man whispered.

"Cozzens," the man whispered back. "Now where is he? His hotel told me he was here."

The maitre d' frowned. It was not often that the restaurant entertained bona fide TV stars. They finally got one—and one no less a personage than Cobey Daniels, who was about to get another network TV show—and what happens?

A frigging cop, all dressed up like Mike Hammer, comes in and wants to spoil everything.

And just why would a Chicago cop be interested in Cobey Daniels, anyway?

But what choice did the maitre d' have?

He raised a plump hand and pointed it to the east wall of the place and said, "There."

"Thank you," Cozzens whispered back.

And set off to talk to Cobey Daniels.

At first, Cobey saw the guy only peripherally, too busy drinking in the chanteuse to pay any attention to anybody else.

Veronica had rightly suspected that Cobey was becoming seriously enamored of the girl singer. He was trying to get a better look at the way her breasts moved beneath the sequined gown, of the gentle but erotic way her mouth widened when she reached for a high note, of the tender but sexy way her hands moved in the spotlit darkness. It was a marijuana dream of lust . . .

Until he saw the guy moving toward the table, that is, and then it all ended, because Cobey had had enough trouble with cops over the years to spot one immediately. For one thing, only a real cop could get away with wearing a dork-o-rama trench coat like that . . .

And for another—

For another . . . Cobey had never been made to face what happened in Beth's apartment five nights earlier . . .

Images: brutally severed head inside refrigerator, blood pooling on the floor. Images: Cobey at trial . . . DA parading all of Cobey's sins past the jury . . . including that incident with the sixteen-year-old girl in Florida.

Images: Cobey in reeking, steamy shower room . . . two beefy, naked queens moving toward him, shark grins on their faces . . . ready to divide the spoils.

Cobey started to get up from his seat just as the trench coat arrived . . .

◆ ◆ ◆

Puckett made him right off, too. Cop. More specifically, detective.

Coming here. Now.

Puckett saw the way Cobey writhed in his seat. Scared.

Puckett wondered what Cobey had to be scared about.

And, just then, the girl singer ended her performance. This time, the ovation was so generous it probably got the club owner to double the singer's money.

Lights came up. Red-jacketed waiters scooted about.

The detective came over and said, "Evening, everybody. My name's Cozzens and I'm with the Chicago police."

"My name's Puckett," Puckett said, putting out his hand. The men shook.

And then Cozzens turned to Cobey. "My kids grew up watching you."

Cobey tried to appear interested and flattered, but the sick look of fear in his eyes dominated his face.

"Cobey," said Cozzens, "I'm really sorry to ask you this, but do you think you and I could go over to the bar there and have a little talk?"

"About what?" Cobey asked. His voice was trembling.

"Well, your name came up in a case I'm working on, and . . ." He shrugged. "Well, I'd just like to spend a few minutes talking to you."

Cobey looked at Puckett. "You think it's all right?"

"It's all right, Cobey, as long as you understand that you don't have to answer anything you don't feel like answering, and that you're entitled to an attorney any time you want one."

Cozzens nodded. "Well put, Mr. Puckett. Very well put."

Cobey glanced at Veronica. He might have been a prisoner about to take that last walk to the electric chair.

"All right," Cobey said, gulping and standing up. In his dark suit and white shirt, he resembled a young and successful business man. He looked even more so standing next to the disheveled Cozzens.

"We'll be right back," Cozzens said.

He led the way to the bar, but they hadn't taken six steps before Cozzens slid a fatherly arm around Cobey's shoulder.

"God." Veronica said. Tears stood in her eyes.

"He'll be all right," Puckett said, wondering at the depth of her reaction.

"I need to go to the powder room," Anne said, trying to cool it. "Care to come with me, Veronica?"

Veronica nodded and then asked Puckett, "Doesn't that detective have to tell Cobey what's going on?"

"That's probably what he's doing right now," Puckett replied, soothingly.

Veronica's tears were becoming more evident. "They're *always* picking on him just because he got in trouble a few times."

Anne took Veronica's hand and led her off toward the back of the restaurant.

Puckett sat there and sipped his scotch and water. Every minute or so, he'd glance at the bar to see what was going on.

Cobey and Cozzens sat on bar stools next to each other. Even from here, Puckett could see that Cobey was drinking his Alcoholic's Delight, his Diet Pepsi. He admired the kid for waging the battle. It was a bitch.

From up near the bar he heard some loud and sudden shouts.

He turned, just in time to see Cobey push Cozzens from his stool and into the bar.

In moments, Cobey was running from the bar, across the dance floor and into the kitchen doors.

Cozzens was up and following him now, shouting for Cobey to stop.

But Cobey wasn't about to stop.

He pushed and shoved his way through a small crowd standing in front of the back door.

Shouts went out. The back door opened—and then slammed shut.

"He got away!" somebody shouted.

Puckett watched as the bartender handed a phone over to Cozzens. Puckett knew just what the detective would be doing. Putting an APB out on Cobey.

What the hell was going on here, anyway?

By now, Cobey was long gone, lost in the maze of rainy Chicago streets.

Ten minutes later, Puckett and Cozzens stood at the restaurant bar, sipping their drinks and talking.

Anne and Veronica stood close to them so they could hear, and when Cozzens mentioned a young woman named "Beth," Puckett noticed a curious look on Veronica's face—she'd recognized the name.

"She was beheaded?" Puckett said.

"I think that's the word you're looking for," Cozzens said, allowing himself a wry little smile. "I'll spare you the details of what she looked like."

"But why question Cobey? What's he got to do with it?" Puckett asked.

Cozzens looked anxiously at Veronica. "He was, uh, involved with this woman."

Puckett expected some kind of protest from Veronica. None came.

"Several people told me that, including her best friend," Cozzens said. "And Cobey and the Swallows woman argued. A lot. And pretty violently, from everything I've been able to piece together."

Puckett saw that Cozzens hadn't had much choice but to ask Cobey some questions—and to seriously consider him a suspect.

Quietly, Veronica said, "I know Cobey, Detective Cozzens. I know him and I love him—and I just know he couldn't have done what you said."

Cozzens finished his drink and brought his glass down a little harder than necessary on the bar. "Then he shouldn't have run, Veronica. He sure as hell didn't do himself any favors."

Cozzens put his hand out and Puckett shook it.

"I appreciate the help, Puckett."

"I just hope Cobey turns himself in before something else happens," Puckett said, frowning.

"Believe it or not," Cozzens responded, "so do I. I don't want to see him—" He was aware of Veronica watching and listening carefully. He paused. "I want everything to work out well for everybody concerned."

And with that, Cozzens nodded and left the restaurant. The diners were settling down again after all the commotion.

"I think I'll call a cab and go back to my hotel," Veronica said quietly. "I'm pretty tired after all this." Her wan smile was sorrowful to see.

"One thing, Veronica," Puckett said.

"What's that?"

"If he calls you, don't help him in any way. Convince him to turn himself in. That's the only way."

She nodded, kissed Anne on the cheek, and walked to the front of the restaurant.

"Poor Veronica," Anne said.

Puckett grunted. "Poor Cobey, too. He's in one hell of a lot of trouble."

CHAPTER SIX

1

WHILE HE WAS STILL AT THE TOP, COBEY FELL IN WITH a mannered and self-described "existential" group of actors who spent most of their time discussing Jack Kerouac; who they were presently bopping; and why any actor who was successful was innately a piece of shit—no offense, Mr. Teen Idol, Mr. Nielsen Top 10, Mr. Billboard-with-a-bullet-burning-up-the-charts.

All this was back in the early eighties. The Group studio was in North Hollywood (where else?) and was run by a very old gay man who continually hinted that he'd once had some kind of sexual experience with James Dean. Uh-huh. In between acting lessons in which everybody learned to be tortured in the manner of the late Montgomery Clift, Cobey and his more experienced (and courageous) friends picked up girls and had wine parties, watched hours of bad movies and howled, and rolled drunks and had plenty of cash in their pockets.

Cavanaugh was the name of the kid who taught Cobey how to roll drunks. Cavanaugh had three rules: a) Always wear dark clothes; b) Always wear a mask; and c) Always roll prosperous drunks.

Cavanaugh and his group mostly worked parking lots in Beverly Hills and Malibu because you saw a lot of drunks there, and drunks in such places always had lots of cash, or at least lots of credit cards that could easily be sold to a fence.

At the time, Cobey didn't need the money, but he did need the kicks. He enjoyed rolling drunks far more than he wanted to admit to himself. The danger was what appealed to him. His new favorite word was existential and if rolling drunks wasn't existential, what was?

Before going out for a night of battering high-class winos, Cobey got very upset. Once or twice he even barfed. Once he called Cavanaugh and told him he just couldn't go through with it anymore. Cavanaugh—whose biggest claim to fame was a three-week stint on *Family Life* as a bratty cousin—of course called him a pussy and said Cobey was going whether he liked it or not, Cavanaugh being the boss and Cobey not being jack shit.

Cobey went—and scored nearly six hundred dollars and a MasterCard Gold and felt good about himself and the world.

Unfortunately, all this had an unhappy ending. Cavanaugh himself went out drunk one night to roll drunks and tried to score on some chubby little bald guy who turned out to be a black belt in Tae Kwon Do and, what with one thing and another, Cavanaugh's neck was broken and he died lying right next to a new red Ferrari. The chubby little bald guy had not been a pussy after all.

This incident inspired Cobey to go straight. He gave up the Actors' Group and he gave up all his friends who said that anybody who was successful was innately a piece of shit and he went back to Lilly, with whom he'd had one of his twice annual fallings-out, and said get me some more record work, I want to go into the studio again. Which she did el pronto, the network having been asking for a new record for years (in Cobey's defense, it wasn't any fun having record critics maul everything you did).

Now, all these years later, Cobey was back to rolling drunks.

When he'd fled the restaurant after his run-in with that cop, Cobey hadn't even had time to take his jacket, and he'd made the mistake of leaving his wallet in his jacket.

He'd spent two hours running through alleys, tripping, falling down, swearing, crying, pissing his pants, wanting to give himself up, terrified to give himself up, trying to tell himself that he really hadn't killed Beth Swallows, but realizing that he very well may have killed Beth Swallows. He knew what he was like when booze got to him—and God knows he'd had enough booze that night—and so all he could do was run. And keep running.

He sort of thought of himself as Richard Kimble, *The Fugitive*, one of his all-time favorite shows. In fact, that was just how he saw life, as a sweaty run through the jungle, dark forces on his tail at all times.

But actually being a fugitive had proved to be not so romantic or existential at all.

In reality, being a fugitive, especially one without any money, meant trying to find a restroom to use; trying not to be noticed as he walked around; scurrying, but not scurrying so fast that he attracted attention, whenever he saw a cop car; and looking for a place to get out of the silver, slanting rain when it started coming down around midnight.

Which was when Cobey had remembered Cavanaugh and rolling drunks.

He prayed to whatever gods there were that the drunk he picked on wasn't some kind of Marine commando disguised as a priest or something. Just give him a good old overweight insurance agent from Skokie, somebody in a brown suit from Sears, wearing lace-up Hush Puppies.

He had found a block of restaurants and lurked in the shadows of the alley running behind. Now he didn't feel like Richard Kimble, he felt like Darren McGavin on *The Night Stalker*. Freezing. Nose running. Rats nearby gnawing their way through the garbage. Feeling almost numbingly sorry for himself. *I didn't do it. Or did I?*

Mostly couples had come out, chunky, middle-aged, middle-class couples, high and silly on a few middle-aged drinks, getting into Buicks and Oldsmobiles and Audis. Wrong sort of people.

Finally, around one, Cobey getting bolder, and more desperate, he crouched behind this dumpster and saw the guy he'd been waiting for.

Mr. Peepers. No fooling. No more than 5' 3" tops. No more than 135 pounds tops. Walking like a tipsy ballerina. Probably a drama teacher in some high school.

There was a God after all.

The guy had even been considerate enough to park his one-tone Chevrolet at the wee end of the shadowy lot, just where Cobey waited to spring.

The guy got the key in the door and then nearly pitched over backwards. He was really bagged.

Cobey jumped.

And felt exhilarated. Existential. There was no other way to put it. He was a goddamned existential drunk-roller. It might sound pretentious, but . . .

Cobey started to reach out . . .

Started to grab the guy by the overcoat collar . . .

Tried to keep the little bastard from falling over backwards and cracking his skull on the pavement . . .

When the guy, who was still somehow upright, started—and this was just plain effing unbelievable—when the little guy, still on his feet, his key still plugged into the car door, started *snoring*.

He was out on his feet.

Was this a mugger's dream, or what?

Cobey leaned against the little guy so he wouldn't fall over backwards, and then started going through the little guy's pockets.

In moments, Cobey was the happy possessor of a wallet chockfull of credit cards and maybe two hundred dollars in crisp, green twenties.

And the guy was still snoring.

Cobey got the car opened and put the guy in behind the wheel as if he was going to start this baby up and tear off toward the Dan Ryan, but then his head flopped back against the seat and he started snoring loud and wet again and he was somewhere outside the known solar system.

After taking the credit cards and the money, Cobey started to put the guy's wallet back in the overcoat, but then he noticed the color photograph of the guy with his wife and two cute little daughters. He felt sorry he had to mug a guy who was probably as nice as this one—but nobody had ever said that being existential was easy.

He closed the car door and hoped the guy didn't freeze his ass off. And then Cobey started running, running.

2

He found an all-night drug store and bought some Lady Clairol rinse, a good pair of scissors, two different kinds of sunglasses, a blue vinyl bombardier jacket with some plastic lining designed to look like down, two pairs of underwear and socks, an Ed McBain paperback and a carton of Lucky Strikes.

Five blocks east, on a deserted corner where the traffic light flashed yellow and lonely on the rain-slicked street, he found a motel, just the kind of place Norman Bates would really go for. The newest car in the lot was a 1982 Ford, and that had its back window smashed out, cardboard filling the hole.

The desk clerk was sleeping. The lobby smelled of rain and piss and wine. The desk clerk jumped, startled to life and said, "Help you?" With his rimless glasses, pockmarked face and pinched, feral mouth, he looked like a composite photo of every serial killer Cobey had ever seen.

"I need a room."

The clerk looked him up and down. "You got a bag?"

Cobey hoisted his sack. "Sack."

"Oh," the clerk nodded, "right." Apparently, lots of people checked in here with big paper sacks.

The room was the sort of place you went to die, a tiny cell with a tiny bed, a white sink discolored with rust, a TV with the channel selector missing and a pair of pliers to turn the little dealie, a cracked mirror, a carpet scuffed and worn clear through to the poured concrete floor, and a bureau with two drawers, one of which contained one of the most vile porno magazines Cobey had ever seen, color photos of two naked, black, four-hundred-pound women doing each other and, later, taking turns with this dildo with some kind of African totem on it. Oh, yeah, and the toilet didn't flush very well, either. Two dark brown turds floated in it to greet him.

Cobey turned off the light and got beneath the covers. The sheets stank of sweat and jism. He didn't care. He just wanted to sleep. He was tired of trying to make sense of things. Things made no sense at all.

Finally, fitfully, he slept . . .

3

By the time Anne came awake in the morning, Puckett was not only up but dressed and opening the door for the bellhop who wheeled in a breakfast of scrambled eggs, bacon, toast and two large pots of coffee—Puckett was a caffeine junkie. And the day itself was just as invigorating, one of those sudden spring days in the Midwest that hit the high eighties. It was already seventy-six degrees and sunny.

While Anne was in taking a shower, Puckett called the Los Angeles office of his investigation service. Since it was only seven o'clock there, Puckett left a message for an operative named Kevin McCoy. A former assistant to a gossip columnist, McCoy was the best "backgrounder" on the staff—meaning that with his computer and phone skills, he was able to learn more than any other six operatives pounding the pavement. Or had been, anyway.

A year ago, McCoy had told everybody at the office that he had AIDS. He had lost a lot of strength in the ensuing months and was now working out of his apartment and phoning in for messages . . .

After hanging up, Puckett read a few more of Anne's pen-name articles. They were first-rate, all of them.

When Anne came out of the bathroom, her copper hair was dark with water and her white terry cloth robe was almost blinding in the sunlight.

Over breakfast, she said, "You sure you want to get involved?"

Puckett smiled. "Cobey needs all the help he can get, and you're forgetting that I used to be a cop myself—I know how their minds work. They've already got Cobey convicted."

"How about the case you were working on?"

"I've already arranged for somebody else to tail my wandering husband."

He finished his coffee, stood up, went over and kissed her on her freckled cheek and said, "He really does need some help. I want to talk to the people around him. See what they know."

She took his hand and held it tight to her cheek. She felt soft and warm, and he felt a desire that was a mixture of sweet affection and rampaging lust.

"I know you're right, Puckett," she said. "It's just that I won't have much time to spend with you."

"I'll keep checking in."

"Promise?"

"Promise."

Then he got out while he still could.

4

When Cobey got up, the first thing he did was take out the Lady Clairol and rinse his hair several times until it was a deep black, far different from his usual blond look. Then he took a shower, cold water being the only type offered, so cold that his balls shrank up and he shivered as he toweled off.

Then he put on the sad, cheap, vinyl jacket and the dark glasses and then he kind of assumed (good old Actors' Group method training coming in handy here) the punk stance of a Slavic kid from the inner city, nowhere near as cool as his black counterparts, just some blown-out high school dropout hanging out in pool halls and comic book stores busting his ass for nickel-and-dime day labor jobs, and maybe thinking vaguely of joining the Army if he could get them to give him one of those equivalency tests.

There. Cobey had created a new persona for himself. He packed up all his stuff and shoved it into the paper sack and left the room. He'd rather sleep in an effing alley than in this place again.

He left the motel and started walking. It was sunny and warm and he wasn't quite sure where he was. All he knew was that there were a lot of dead and dying factories around him, rusted monuments to the good old days when a lunch bucket life had had dignity and meaning, the same kind of lunch bucket life Cobey's father, a factory worker, had enjoyed. But now . . .

He found this tiny-ass tavern where the sign advertised Blatz beer (what a name, Blatz, it sounded like a fart) and, incredibly enough, breakfast and lunch and where, incredibly enough, the breakfast was good, if you didn't mind a few cockroaches running back and forth on the bar. He had four eggs over-easy and tried not to notice as the six old guys across from him, drinking Blatz in mugs and chain-smoking cigarettes, watched him with a mixture of curiosity and contempt. They weren't sure where this kid fitted in—shit, he left his sunglasses on even inside this dingy place— they just knew he didn't fit in here. He ate fast and left fast.

He was thankful for the sunlight.

He spent the next hour-and-a-half walking.

The sun started getting warm and the surroundings started getting pretty. Old Victorians, newly refurbished, Yuppie land. After where he'd spent last night and just had breakfast, he was jubilant at seeing cliché Yuppie mothers transporting their cliché Yuppie children around in their cliché Jeeps and vans.

He found a small shopping center with a clean, sunny restaurant and he bought a *Tribune* and went in there and had himself a second breakfast, this one without the cockroaches. All the people looked smart and clean and attractive. He didn't ever want to go back to last night's motel, and he wondered now if he hadn't taken some kind of Rod Serling diversion from reality last night and checked into some other dimension, some motel hell for real.

The Chicago police were playing it very coy for the newspaper people.

They admitted that, yes, Cobey Daniels had abruptly left a meeting in which a Detective Cozzens had been asking the young star questions about the woman's head discovered in a refrigerator, but the Chicago police were in no way trying to intimate that he was a bona fide suspect. They just wished ole Cobey would give them a call and then maybe they could all go out and have burgers or something.

Right, you bastards, he thought. *You'd put my ass in jail and then plant me in the electric chair about a week later.*

Somewhere in the middle of his fourth cup of coffee, he decided to give it another try. He'd tried it last night but then he'd gotten scared and given up.

Now, feeling better, feeling more confident, some food in his belly and a pretty decent disguise hiding his real identity, he got up and paid his bill and asked the waitress for some extra change. Then he went out to the center of the mall where there was this long line of pay phones and he went over and looked up the right number.

He called and asked for Mr. Puckett's room and then he waited.

He waited a long time. The phone rang maybe twelve times. Nobody home. He hung up.

He had to talk to Puckett, *had* to. Puckett was his only hope.

He looked out at the mall, all the happy women shopping, and he wondered with sudden bitterness and high, pure terror, how the hell he'd ever gotten here.

He was a former teenage TV star, he wasn't any killer.

Or was he?

He fled the mall, going God-only-knew-where.

5

Wade Preston had spent the past week trying to get out of it, but in the end, he relented and said he'd show up to meet his fan club, as they'd requested, at eleven AM sharp. On the way over, he thought of excuses he might use to leave his fan club early.

He smiled bitterly to himself. A few days ago he'd given Anne Addison a key to his yacht on the off chance that she'd use it some night. That would be a good excuse to leave—a beautiful woman waiting for him on his boat.

These fans probably didn't think the Marshal ever got his ashes hauled, the dumb bastards.

They were the usual geeks and freaks—and Wade Preston, the last of the cowboy heroes, had to force a smile when he saw the pack of them moving toward him in the lobby of the suburban hotel.

The one in front, the one who had the full cowboy outfit on—including brown leatherette chaps and a silver belt buckle the size of a hubcap and this huge, six-pointed town marshal badge on the breast of his leatherette vest—this guy had to weigh in at four hundred pounds, including all twenty-seven of his chins, and he of course was the spokesman for the whole group.

"Happy sunsets, Marshal!" the man cried across the lobby.

A dapper young man in a blue lawyer's suit, hundred dollar razor cut, and mean, blue gaze was waiting for a bellhop to take his bags upstairs. He smirked at the geeks, and his sneer said it all too well: how pathetic all this sort of thing was—THE WADE PRESTON FAN CLUB, CHICAGO CHAPTER, as read the sign one of the geeks carried—and then he was joined by a pretty, young girl whom he was probably bopping. She sneered in much the same way he had. Grown people carrying on this way. My *God*.

The Starlight Hotel and Lounge was out near Skokie, and at eleven in the morning the lounge was mostly occupied by salespeople. In the old days, it would have been mostly men here, but now that Xerox and IBM and the big pharmaceuticals hired fifty percent women, Happy Hour places like this rang with female laughter, the women just as hard and frantic and vulgar as their male counterparts. One more reason Wade Preston was against libbers, as he still called them. Why would women—clearly the superior of the two sexes—want to be like stupid, boorish men?

"Marshal Drake, it sure is good to meet you," said the fat man as he grabbed for Preston's hand.

"Why not just call me Wade?" Preston said, blushing. "That's my real name. 'Marshal Drake' was just in the show."

The guy looked crushed. "Uh, sure," he said. "Sure."

Then the others encircled him.

Thank God only one of them was fully in costume. The others wore just bits and pieces, Stetsons or tinny little badges or western string ties over their plaid, working class shirts.

A skinny woman with badly discolored teeth leaned in and planted a big, wet, smacking kiss right on his cheek. "I've wanted to do that for twenty-five years!" she said.

The others giggled and applauded and patted both the woman and Wade Preston on the back.

"I'm Keeny!" she cried. "I'm the secretary of the Chicago Chapter of the Wade Preston Fan Club."

Keeny. God, even their names were strange.

Preston forced another smile. "How nice for you."

The pretty girl serving as hostess for the lounge glanced over from her post. She gave Preston a look of some sympathy, obviously seeing that Preston thought all this was just as pathetic as she did. They were members of the same club, the pretty girl and Preston—the club of good looking people whose appearance was negotiable currency in virtually any country.

Preston had only recently started doing these fan club gigs because the word in Hollywood was that westerns—after the success of Eastwood's *The Unforgiven*—were getting hot again. Wade Preston owned seven years of *Town Marshal* (full color and an impressive lineup of guest stars) and he planned to make several million syndicating them to local stations.

And this, alas, meant promoting the series and turning up at these fan club functions again, something he'd refused to do for the past fifteen years. It was one thing to send all the geeks and freaks a nice little tax-deductible semi-annual newsletter, and put in an appearance at the Western Jamboree of former western stars (most of whom were fairies and drunks or both), and always sign the glossies the fans sent in and mail them back at his own expense.

But now here he was, actually meeting the bastards. Seeing them in all their sad shabbiness.

"You ready to go in . . . Wade?" Keeny or Kenny or Kitty or what-ever-the-fuck-her-name-was said.

"Go in?"

She nodded with her white cowboy hat with the name Marshal Drake spelled out in spangles on the front. "We rented a room special for this afternoon. I mean, we all chipped in."

And it was then that the woman in a wheelchair produced from beneath the blanket covering her lap a cap pistol and began firing it into the air.

A handsome couple in the lobby jerked about, startled, at the sound of the cap pistol. At first, they looked terrified—face it, in our society today, most of us know that violence can come anyplace, any-time—and then, seeing the geeks and freaks gathered like puppies around Wade Preston, they frowned with great, theatrical displeasure.

And it was then that the door to the private conference room opened and the theme from *Town Marshal* blared forth on a warbling sound track.

And the old broad in the wheelchair let go with the cap pistol again.

And the woman with the discolored teeth started planting big, wet, sloppy kisses all over his face again.

And one of the men in the background, one of the men who hadn't spoken before, said in the terrible, trembling voice of the stut-terer, "W-we s-sure I-love y-you Marshal D-Drake!"

And then he was pushed forward into the room where the *Town Marshal* soundtrack continued to warble ("He's the man with the gun/the man who won't run/Town Marshal/Town Marshal").

The old broad took two more quick shots just before they got him inside and closed the door.

Preston squared his shoulders and put a manly grin on his face. He'd agreed to give them an hour, but he was damn sure going to leave sooner if he could.

CHAPTER SEVEN

Cobey's Tapes
In re: Wade Preston

The thing was, how I came to find out about what Wade Preston was really up to, was total fucking convoluted coincidence, the kind that story editors chew writers' asses off for (and I should know, having tried to sell scripts to those faggot bastards when I first got out of the asylum).

Total coincidence.

As in: The year is 1989. I've been out for about a year, and I'm doing the strip. Sunset Strip, of course, and by "doing" I am talking all the reds and blues and yellows and uppers and downers and sideways I can get my sweaty little hands on . . . because the night before, on CBS, there's this TV movie and in it, with a two-line part, is Tim Flowers.

TIM-FUCKING-FLOWERS!

The same kid, six years earlier, I bumped out of the No 1 slot as America's cuddliest-cutest teenage TV star.

His show had been off the air less than four years . . . and this following a *seven year* run at the top . . . and the best gig he can find is two lines on a TV movie?

At least I didn't drink.

I don't give myself much credit for anything . . . but at least I didn't drink.

I just got up and turned off the TV and sat in the dark for a long, long time.

Someday, sooner than later, I was going to be Tim Flowers. Two lines on a TV movie . . . and then maybe a life-long gig at some Porsche dealership along with two or three other well-kept has-beans, all those upper class bitches finger fucking themselves on the way home from flirting at the dealership . . .

Sometime around midnight—and I'm not proud of this, believe me—I called Mindy. The fag hag with all the underground connections . . .

Back in the days of radicalism, Mindy once hid out for an entire year two campus SDSers who were wanted by the federales for blowing up a science department back in the Midwest.

After radicalism, Mindy settled her sights on groupiedom and fag hagdom and you never knew who you'd see at Mindy's little house in Coldwater Canyon, her father being able to supply her with plenty of jack, owning as he does the second largest investment banking company in the world.

Anyway, I needed Mindy's blend of sex (not with Mindy, of course, but with one of her minions—Mindy's Minions, pretty good, huh?), one of those hot, crazed little Sunset street girls that she never seemed to run out of . . . one of her Minions . . . and lots of her red/blue/yellow mind-blowers . . . and lots of her good grub. Mindy can cook her considerable ass off.

A retreat at Mindy's spa is what I needed . . . and since the flesh is weak . . . it's exactly what I ordered up, too.

And, at first, it was nice.

When I got there, it was already like three o'clock in the AM. The Whole Sick Crew was there—the people may change but the roles they play are the same. This was Mindy's version of the Ark, I guess: two of everything—a lesbian couple; a gay couple; two bikers with two biker chicks with the four of them wearing matching leather outfits; two punk-type musicians from the same band, one with a safety pin in his nose and the other with one glass eye; and two of Mindy's own girlfriends, the wan and severely beautiful Barnard or Smith types that Mindy always goes for—having never been allowed to be a member of this particular club, Mindy seems in equal parts to lust after and loathe these girls . . .

And there was some kind of 1968 rave-up going on . . . the music ear-splittingly high . . . and running to the likes of Jefferson Airplane and Cream and, the only stuff I liked, some chunky, funky music from Credence Clearwater for lowborn white niggers such as myself . . .

And everybody's reminiscing about peace marches and draft card burning and what a pig Nixon was and how one of them once dropped some acid into this cop's Pepsi without him knowing . . . and this wedding ceremony one dewy dawn when everybody (bridegroom-minister-all-the-guests) stood buck ass naked in the splendiferous morn with this flute and guitar music making even the forest animals get groovy . . . and how this was a fucking racist-homophobic-male-chauvinist-capitalist-pig society and maybe Charlie Manson was a fucking psycho but at least his heart was in the right place . . .

And on and on and on.

A circle jerk for an entire generation.

And, finally, the reds and blues having kicked in, I went searching through the back bedrooms—I'd had enough of the tears and rage and pride of the Woodstock generation. You never knew what you'd find. Not at Mindy's, you didn't.

And I lucked out.

There was this street chick sleeping in a single bed. I say street chick, because the first thing I did was check through her clothes to see if she was a narc. There was a famous incident at Mindy's where this narc had had so much acid that he'd gone over to the other side.

I say street chick, because her jeans and her GRATEFUL DEAD T-shirt and little white bikini underwear were all filthy, especially the latter.

I went out and came back a few minutes later and when she woke up—stoned as shit—she said in this groggy voice, "What're you doin?"

And I said, "You'll see."

And what I was doing, of course, there with my small bowl of hot water and bar of Dove soap and clean, nubby washcloth and clean, nubby towel—what I was doing was giving her a sponge bath, cleaning up that sweet little face and sweet little breasts and that sweet little Midwestern pussy of hers.

And when I was finished—I do believe that at this exact moment she had slipped back into a state of unconsciousness—when I was finished, I slipped my finger inside her and started trying to get her wet.

By the time I was on top of her and inside, her eyes were open and she said, "Wow! You're Cobey!"

And I grinned, and then we really wailed on that sweet little Midwestern snatch of hers.

And the rest of the next twelve hours sort of went the same way. There were one or two other street chicks in and out (or, rather, I was in and out of them) and I was doing fine, but then early afternoon somebody had a bottle of wine and—

That's how it started. I remember the first drink and the feeling that I had this stuff whipped now. That drinking would never control me again, etc., etc., etc., all the standard bullshit rationalizations for falling off the wagon again.

. . . and suddenly it's night and I'm back in the bedroom with this other street chick when I suddenly realize that Mindy is in the bed too and we're both doing up this chickie and—

And my dick goes dead. Like somebody pulled the plug or something. No more Mr. Erection.

Which happens not with drugs (for some reason) but happens all the time with booze (for some reason).

So I more or less get dressed and wander out into the living room where (somehow) the '60's party is going strong and now we're hearing the mandatory Beatles and the mandatory Stones.

And one of the gay guys says something I can't quite hear and I give him a little shove (and don't tell me I'm homophobic because so many people think I'm gay that I identify with gay anger and gay pride and all those things—true facts—and no this guy was just a bleeping asshole is why I shoved him).

And I know it's starting now.

All that effing rage.

And the gay guy's boyfriend shoves me right back.

And then all of a sudden I'm in the kitchen and everybody's standing around me and Mindy's there and she's daubing at my forehead with a washcloth that she keeps dipping into this bowl of warm water.

And I hear her say, "I don't think there's a concussion. He just got knocked out is all."

And people keep peering down into my face (as if I'm seeing them through one of those distorting fish-eye lenses) and staring into my eyes and looking real concerned.

And saying, "Well, I'm sorry I pushed him, Mindy, but he had no reason to shove Jace that way."

And saying, "I knew as soon as I saw him drinking that he'd turn asshole on us. He always does."

And saying, "Give him a ride somewhere. We were having a nice time before he came."

And—

And—

And—

Sometime around ten o'clock that night, I woke up in the back booth of this little bar just off the bad end of Sunset.

I felt my forehead. There was a bump and a scab right in the middle of it. My white shirt had blood all over it, which is why, I guessed, I'd decided to keep my red James Dean jacket zipped up to the top.

And across from me in the booth was a small, nervous, ferrety girl. I had no idea who she was.

"You know where we are?"

"Huh-uh," I said.

"You know who I am?"

"Huh-uh."

She smiled with bad teeth. "I didn't figure you would."

I had just become aware of how loud the effing band up on stage was. I looked to my left and saw all these couples out on a dance floor, every sort of person you could want, from punks with rooster haircuts the color of cotton candy to one or two tight-ass yuppies in suit jackets.

The place was crazed. Deafening music. People shouting above it to be heard. The air filled with the smells of booze, drugs, cigarettes.

"I let you come in my mouth," the girl said. She was Keokuk, Iowa or Jasper, Wyoming. Had to be with those grubby hippie clothes ten years out of date and that scared, hungry look in her eyes. "I never let nobody do that before."

"Then I guess I should say thank you."

"My sister said she knew a girl who choked on this guy's come once. Choked to death."

We had our heads tilted together in the middle of the booth's table so we could hear.

"You said you'd let me stay with you," she said.

"I did, huh?"

"I figured you was lying."

I grinned. "I was."

"You fucker." And all of a sudden she started crying.

And when I reached across the booth and put my hand on her shoulder, she lashed out and slapped me very hard across the face and then she jumped up and was gone.

Vanished.

And then I was outside and stumbling along Sunset. Gritty as the air was, it was better than the air inside that disco.

All the hangover downs were with me: dehydration, shakes, terrible gnawing fear that I'd done something horrible I was purposely forgetting. (Cut a throat? Suck a dick? Fuck some eight-year-old daughter of some groupie mom, at the mom's request, the way another teen idol had once done?)

Then it started to rain and all the geeks and freaks along the Strip started looking for shelter. I wondered where my car was. I wondered how I'd gotten here. I wondered how much cash I had on me.

And then I saw Wade Preston's big-ass bronze Caddy convertible parked out in front of this once-fashionable restaurant and I knew just how I'd relieve myself of my frenzy and weariness and nightmares.

While good old Wade was inside packing away the steak— Wade being one of those guys who thinks all the warnings about cholesterol are bullshit—while Wade was in there, I'd slip into his back seat and take a nap.

And when he woke me up, he could give me a ride to my place. What's a manager for, anyway?

It took me two minutes to jimmy the lock and thirty seconds to fall asleep.

"You cocksucker."

"It's business, Jerry. If you were in my position, you'd do the same thing."

"Wonder how all those kiddies out there in TV land would like it if they knew that Wade Preston was a fucking blackmailer?"

"Wonder how all the ladies out there in movie land would like to know that their favorite leading man likes to gobble the knob every chance he gets?"

"You're scum, Wade. You're fucking scum."

"Call it what you want to, Jerry. I never would have put that private detective on you if you hadn't tried to nullify your contract with my agency."

Deep night. Caddy hurtling along beside the ocean. I can smell the water through the open window.

Apparently, when I went to sleep, I fell down between the seats and Wade didn't notice me.

Neck hurt. Had to piss bad. Megaton headache.

"I'm leaving your agency anyway, Wade. Pictures or no pictures."

I knew who was speaking. Wade's only super-big client. Jerry Parker. Hunky leading man just now making his way into father-figure roles, the graying hair helping instead of hurting him.

Big guy, Jerry. Bad temper, too. And Wade was obviously pushing it, Jerry being the kind of guy who would feed you a knuckle sandwich any time the itch took him.

Wade said, "Then leave the agency, Jerry. But you know the price. Several magazines and several newspapers get some photos of you and your new boyfriend in some very undignified poses."

"You fucker." Jerry said.

And then silence.

And then night air.

And then moonshine.

And then the tide rolling in.

As the Caddy barrel-assed along a narrow road above the ocean. Rough road—smooth road—rough road. Tires humming.

"So which is it going to be?" Wade said.

Car rolled to a stop. Jerry got out. Interior light went on. Apparently he was so engrossed in his rage that he still didn't notice me.

"You've got me, Wade, and you know it. But someday—"

And with that, he slammed the door.

Interior light went off.

Retreating footsteps.

Wade: "Faggot."

And then the car was rolling again.

And then I coughed.

Brakes slammed on.

Wade came up over the back of the seat with this big, silver-plated Magnum in his hand. Pointed it straight down at me.

"What the hell're you doing back there?"

"Wade, I—"

But he didn't give me a chance to talk.

He hit me on the side of the head with the barrel of the Magnum and he said, "If you ever repeat what you heard, you bastard, I'll fucking kill you with my own hands, you understand?"

I understood . . .

As I said, this happened several years ago. Wade must've gotten some pretty good shots of old Jerry because Jerry just signed a multi-million dollar, three-pie deal with Paramount . . . and guess who the agent was? None other than good old Wade Preston.

And I, of course, have used my secret knowledge on Wade every time he's tried to put the screws to me.

Cut him off, he says to Lilly.

And when Lilly tells me this, I just step into a phone booth a la Superman and call Wade and remind him of that little ride I took in the back seat of the Caddy that long-ago Malibu midnight . . .

And I get what I want.

But has Wade finally tired of me?

Is it Wade who cut off Beth's head and put it in her refrigerator?

God knows, he hates me enough to do it . . .

CHAPTER EIGHT

1

WADE PRESTON'S YACHT WAS OSTENTATIOUS EVEN by the standards of the other big, white sailing ships lining the harbor.

Puckett reached it just after lunchtime. Everybody in the area was quietly celebrating the fine, warm, spring day—women in bikinis and tank tops; shirtless men in jeans rolled up to the knees; and one beautiful, yipping, Border Collie who kept jumping eagerly between the deck of his master's boat and the dock.

Preston was dressed formally in white shirt, blue double-breasted jacket and white ducks. He obviously enjoyed the role of the ship's captain.

"Care for a little liquid refreshment, Mr. Puckett? I'm about to have a gin and tonic."

"Not right now. Thanks."

Preston shot him a matinee idol grin. "A man of decorum and propriety. I'm impressed." He nodded to the cabin and below deck. "Be right back."

While he waited, Puckett looked over Lake Michigan. He'd grown up reading Jack London's South Sea tales and he'd long dreamed of a life at sea. Then he spoiled the dream by spending a whiskied week in a Fiji island bar while outside it poured cold and ceaseless rain. No wonder the place had such a high suicide rate.

"Why don't we go sit down?" Preston said when he returned with his drink.

They took deck chairs. As they were seating themselves, a red motorboat flashed by towing a voluptuous blonde in a string bikini. The boat blatted its horn. The blonde smiled and waved with the fetching self-importance of a beauty contest winner.

"I just got a call from Lilly," Preston said. "She said both of us should be expecting to see you. Cobey being wanted by the police, I mean, and you being a detective and all."

"She say anything else?"

"Oh, nothing earth-shaking. Just that you were a dumb, goddamn asshole and nosy, motherfucking, arrogant prick."

"I knew she liked me."

Preston laughed. "Some people in Hollywood consider it a badge of honor to be hated by Lilly Carlyle. I have the goddamn luck to be in love with her."

Preston had switched tones from ironic to melancholy right there at the last, and he'd startled Puckett.

"It's true," Preston said. "I'm not just emoting the way some actors do because they like to hear themselves talk. I actually love her." He sipped his drink and looked out at the blonde on the water skis coming round again. "I've been after her to marry me for twenty years now and she's turned me down every time I propose. Isn't that the shits?"

He had some more gin and tonic and when he brought his glass down Puckett realized that the man was quietly drunk.

"How about Cobey?"

"What about Cobey?" Preston said, sounding guarded now.

"Well, I'm told that Lilly has spent most of her time with him these past twenty years or so."

Preston smiled. "You're fishing, aren't you, Puckett? And you've picked a good place to do it—off a yacht, I mean. You want to know if I decapitated that girl to blame it on Cobey, don't you? I mean, I guess it's no secret that I hate that little fairy."

"Fairy?"

"Oh, not homosexual, exactly. But not very manly, either."

Puckett couldn't resist. "Weren't you a disc jockey in Buffalo, New York before you became a movie cowboy?"

"So I was, Puckett. But even back in Buffalo, I had two cast iron balls I could call my own."

Puckett had no trouble believing that.

The water skier now had a friend, a dark-haired friend who was, if anything, even more outlandishly voluptuous than the blonde.

The speedboat blatted its horn again.

The women waved.

Preston gave them a tight, hip little salute.

"Goddamned AIDS, anyway," Preston said.

"AIDS?"

"Hell, yes, AIDS. In the old days, I would've had those two on board this yacht so fast you wouldn't have believed it. And I'd have screwed their brains out, too, one right after the other." He sat back in his chair. There was a real melancholy about him now. "I'm not boasting, either. No cock-of-the-walk bullshit, I mean. I'm telling the truth."

"I'm sure you are. But what about your undying love for Lilly?"

"Don't mock me, Puckett. I hate being mocked. The truth is, I do feel undying love for Lilly, but since she has never accepted any of my marriage proposals, I've never felt any great obligation to be faithful."

The soft afternoon air smelled of sunlight and water. Nearby, the two water skiers were laughing. They sounded as innocent and exultant as little girls.

Puckett said, "How about Cobey?"

"How about Cobey what?"

"Do you think he could have killed the Swallows woman?"

"Hell, yes, I do. Lilly probably told you he isn't capable of something like this, but . . . Did she tell you about the time he killed my dog?"

Puckett shook his head.

"It was a couple of years ago. Lilly had been indulging him, as usual, ever since he got out of the asylum. He was into the agency for well over two hundred thousand dollars—he had to live in Malibu, he had to have a Maserati, he just knew he'd have a new series in no time, all the bullshit you hear from people on the way down—and one day I just said enough is enough. No more toys, no more loans for Cobey Daniels.

"I told Lilly that he should go find a regular, nine-to-five job, unthinkable as the idea sounded. There was a PR firm looking for somebody at that time, and Cobey would have been perfect. Shit, the kid was twenty-six, and he hadn't worked steadily in over five years. Anything he had coming from *Family Life* syndication money he'd already borrowed against—from us and two or three banks.

"Anyway, Cobey found out that I'd cut him off—he'd forced Lilly into telling him—and next day my Irish Setter, a goddamn dog I loved like a son and I'm not just being corny—next day I find Prince dead out in my back yard. Somebody had shot him with a high-powered rifle from up in the hills to the west of my place."

"And you think it was Cobey?"

"Who the hell else would it have been? Lilly?" He scowled. "Of course it was Cobey."

"Did the police investigate?"

"Yeah, for what it was worth. They didn't find out dick."

"Did you confront Cobey?"

"I tried, but you know how Lilly is about him." Preston frowned. "She never had any children, Lilly didn't, and I know she probably doesn't strike you as a Betty Crocker kind of woman, but I think she's got this need to mother somebody. And that was Cobey. She took him in when he was a little kid and virtually became his mother. But I'm sure you know that story. Anyway, no way would Lilly let me give that little fairy what I should have. I had to make a choice—Lilly or Cobey. And I chose Lilly."

A yacht went by. A white-haired man, who looked not unlike Wade Preston, waved. Preston waved back. "I grew up around here. Oak Park. That's why I keep a yacht here. Like to see all my old friends." The matinee-idol grin again. "It's fun to play the role of movie star to the locals."

Puckett looked out on the blue water. A yacht would be nice. Just himself and Anne. Going nowhere slowly and loving the hell out of it.

"Cobey disappeared for several months," Puckett said, bringing his attention back to Preston.

"Yes, I remember. Lilly was a lot of fun to be around while he was gone—as you can imagine."

"Do you have any idea where he might have been all those months?"

"Sorry, Puckett, I don't. Seems to me he just couldn't face the fact that, like most child stars, he'd run out of time and out of luck. He was a has-been. It's a bitch, but it's how the business works.

"I mean, I had to give up the spurs and saddle when I was forty-two. Nobody wanted me anymore. Now there's a cable network that's talking about rerunning the last three years of my series and, if that happens, then my career may take off all over again, and I'll make a little jack doing all the fan shows and conventions for over-the-hill cowboys. In fact, I just got done putting in an appearance with one of my local fan clubs. God, those pathetic bastards make me shudder."

He was actor pure and simple, Puckett thought. Ask him a question about anybody or anything and somehow he can immediately turn the conversation back to himself.

"Now," Preston said, "I'm going to kick you off this yacht of mine and maybe go water skiing with the girls out there."

Puckett smiled. "I guess AIDS really has cramped your style."

Preston patted his belly. "Well, at least I've got a lot of memories. Poor bastards starting out today could be dead by the time they're old enough to have any memories."

Preston put out his hand. Puckett shook it.

On his way back to his rental car, Puckett saw at least twenty women in bikinis. He thought of Anne and tried not to feel unabashed lust. He really didn't want to be a guy like Preston. The man was in equal parts amusing and sad; sad in the rough and bluff way only a middle-aged man can be.

CHAPTER NINE

1

AT 2:35 THAT AFTERNOON, PUCKETT WAS IN THE LOBBY of the hotel where Veronica Hobbs was staying. He had invited her to come down and meet him in a nearby restaurant, and he put an edge on his voice so that she'd know it was more than a mere "invitation."

While he waited for her, he sat in a comfortable armchair in the lobby watching sales representatives hurry in and out. They were all, men and women alike, stuffed inside suits fresh out of dry cleaning bags; splashed and splotched with deodorant, after-shave (called perfume for the women), hair spray and a variety of confections to make their breath smell pleasant.

Their eyes were narrow and dark from too little sleep; and their arms weary from toting suitcases, briefcases and massive presentation cases. Their stomachs would still be hurting from last night's too spicy meal, their bowels constricted from too little fiber, and their mouths raw from too much liquor.

To raise their bodies from the dead this morning, they had required caffeine, nicotine and a certain amount of pro forma bitching—the effing bed was too soft, the effing plane landed so effing late last night, the effing client's a real asshole and probably'll only give me five minutes max anyway.

This small army of sales representatives would keep on selling until it dropped, until its endless supply of replacements topped the hill and took its place. Ancient Greece had had its peddlers, and so would the far, starry planets that mankind ultimately settled on . . .

Puckett knew a lot about sales reps because that's what his father had been—thirty-seven years with General Electric, opening new markets on the wholesale level—until all the anxiety, all the bad, rushed meals, all the Pall Malls, all the Booths Gin, all the thousand-deaths-you-died-every-single-day-on-the-road had taken their toll and the doctor said stomach cancer and there were Puckett and his mother on opposite sides of the white, starchy hospital bed, holding the old man's trembling hands and trying not to notice how often he cried though he tried hard not to.

And then, scarcely three weeks after it had been diagnosed, he was gone, utterly, utterly gone, so much unsaid between Puckett and his old man, so much undone, that even in a hotel lobby on a bright, after-the-rain, spring afternoon, Puckett couldn't help but get tears in his own eyes because even though the old man was nearly twelve years dead, Puckett thought of him every single day of the year, and realized all over again how much he loved him and missed him.

"Hi."

He looked up. Veronica stood there. She wore a yellow spring blouse and designer jeans. Her blonde hair shone from washing. She should have looked very pretty. Instead, she looked exhausted and terrified.

"Hi," he said, standing up.

"I'm ready if you are."

"Good," he said.

The restaurant was packed with Loop workers taking refuge from the long and frantic day. While the setting itself was nothing special—overly familiar framed photos of "Chicago, City on the Make," as the late novelist, Nelson Algren, had referred to it; vinyl covered booths; and the sort of indoor-outdoor carpeting that seemed to be born dirty—the food was great.

Puckett had a burger, fries and a malt. He was doing his standard Salute to Cholesterol.

"God, you're so thin," Veronica said. "How do you do it?"

He smiled. "The anxiety diet. It works great."

She smiled, too. "Apparently."

He waited until they were finished eating before getting into anything serious.

"I need to talk to you."

His tone startled her, and she looked at him with real apprehension. "About Cobey?"

"About you and Cobey. And Beth Swallows."

"About Beth Swallows?"

"Last night, when we were talking to Cozzens, I got the sense that you knew her."

"Knew her? Of course not."

He felt she was lying. He wondered why. "Any lies you tell will only hurt Cobey. Unless that's exactly what you want to do."

"Why would I hurt Cobey?"

He shook his head. "Why don't you just tell me the truth, Veronica?"

"You mind if I smoke?"

"If that'll help, fine."

She took a pack of cigarettes from her purse and lit one with a small, delicately crafted, gold lighter. Such splendid design for something that helped give you lung cancer . . .

She dropped her gaze a moment. He had the sense she was composing herself.

She said, "Do you think I might have killed her?"

"It's a possibility."

"Cut her head off that way?"

"Insane people are capable of anything."

"You think I'm insane?"

"If you'd killed her, you were, at least, insane at the time. And that kind of insanity would have given you enormous strength."

"Then you're saying I could be the killer?"

He sighed. "Veronica, I'm not saying anything. I'm asking. I want to help Cobey. He may be the killer, for all I know at this point. But I want to find out what really happened."

"I didn't kill her."

"Good."

"But I suppose that guilty people always say that, don't they? That they're innocent, I mean?"

"Usually."

She nodded. She looked very sad now. "He's never been very good at being faithful."

"I'm sorry, Veronica."

"I mean, the strange thing is, I think he honestly tries to be."

He just watched her. She seemed on the verge of tears. "So, anyway, I just started following him one day." She gave him a quick, forlorn smile. "You would have been proud of me. I bought new clothes so that he wouldn't recognize me, and I bought this big, floppy hat and these huge, Joan Crawford kind of sunglasses, and I waited in the lobby of his hotel. When he came out, I—" The quick, forlorn smile again. "It's actually a lot of fun, isn't it?"

"What is?"

"Following people around."

"Not always. I knew an investigator who decided to follow his best friend around and then spring all these photos on him at his next birthday party. Unfortunately, the man went right to the investigator's house and spent all afternoon in the investigator's bedroom with the investigator's wife. I don't think that would be fun."

"I suppose that should be a funny story, but it's actually very sad," Veronica said.

"Yes, it is, actually."

She tilted her coffee cup toward her and peered into it, as if it were a tea cup and she was trying to read her fortune in the leaves.

"There's one difference," she said. And looked up at him. "Between the private investigator and me, I mean."

"Oh?"

"I knew what I was going to find."

"You mean, you knew you'd find that Cobey was being unfaithful?"

"Right. But even more than that. I knew who he was going to be with, too."

"You knew about Beth Swallows?"

"Yes."

"How?"

She hesitated again, but only briefly. "Did you ever read any of the biographies about John Lennon?"

He shook his head.

"Well, a few of his biographers insist that Yoko Ono saw to it that John started having a sexual relationship with their very pretty secretary because this way John would take care of his need to wander, and Yoko would be in control of the entire situation. She told the secretary that she wanted this to happen. But then John started falling in love with the secretary and Yoko was furious."

"You're saying that you set up the Swallows girl with Cobey?"

"Yes."

He sat there and stared at her and realized, in a terrible way, what one of his old bosses at the Secret Service had always told him: that we really don't know each other, that treachery often hides in what appears to be innocence.

What Veronica had just described was something from the darkest of Restoration comedies, yet still she sat there, prim and lovely in her slightly wan way, looking no more manipulative than she had a few moments ago.

"You think that's pretty sick?" she asked.

"I try not to judge people, Veronica. I guess because I don't think I can hold up to much judgment myself."

"He was starting to roam again. I could feel it."

He sat there and let her talk.

"He really needs to be loved and sought after. The more conquests he has, the more secure he is. A lot of men are that way—though somehow I don't think you are—and they spend their whole lives cheating on their wives. Do you ever read James Dickey, the poet?"

He shook his head.

"He wrote this great poem about adultery in this cheap motel, about how at the moment of orgasm both people are able to hold off all thought of getting old and dying—just for that one moment. And then they go about their lives and they start getting overwhelmed by everything again, how their bodies are starting to get old, how the street is always filled with fresh, new faces to take their place—and how their spouses somehow aren't enough to make them feel young and purposeful and in control again. So they grab the first woman they can find—a woman who is married and looking for the same thing, even if she doesn't know it—and they rush off to a sleazy motel and are reborn again in their orgasms. If that makes sense."

"Too much sense, really."

"Well, Cobey's like that. Only with Cobey it's even worse because he not only wants to feel immortal, he also wants to feel famous and beloved—like Cobey Daniels, number one TV star of the decade."

He signaled for another pot of coffee. "How did you meet Beth Swallows?"

"Sometimes, when Cobey made up some excuse about needing to do something with his play that night—when he was actually sneaking off with somebody else—I'd go to this nightclub and I'd see Beth there. She was very beautiful and very smart and very unlike the sort of women you meet in nightclubs."

"How so?"

Veronica laughed. "Well, for one thing, she knew who James Dickey was." She reached across and patted his hand. "Sorry, I couldn't resist that." She cleared her throat and went on. "She'd gone out with this doctor for almost her entire senior year at college before she found out he was married. She was crushed. After graduation, she moved here, and didn't go out for months until she started coming to this nightclub. She knew a lot about classical music and painting and books and what she called 'the consolation of philosophy' and I guess that's why we got to be friends. Both being quiet and everything, I mean."

"How did your plan for Cobey come about?"

"It just sort of evolved. Beth and I saw each other two or three times a week and I told her all the trouble I was having with Cobey. And, by coincidence, I was reading Albert Goldman's biography of John Lennon and—well, that's where the idea came from, anyway."

"What was her reaction when you told her your plan?"

"She thought I was kidding."

"But she gradually got used to the idea?"

"Right."

"And finally she said yes?"

"Right."

"So how did you arrange for her to meet Cobey?"

"She went backstage after the show one night and told Cobey that she was a very big fan of his. I could see right away that he was instantly smitten. She was very beautiful. *Very* beautiful."

He wondered if he detected a trace of bitterness in her voice.

"He started sneaking off and seeing her."

"How often?"

"Once or twice a week, at first."

"But things heated up?"

"Very much so. To the point that . . ." She stopped herself.

"How were you and Beth getting along by this point?"

"You still think I killed her, don't you?"

"I'd just like an answer to my question. Nothing more."

"Well, you'll probably find out, anyway."

"Find out what?"

"I went to Beth's one night and we had a terrible argument. She told me that she'd fallen in love with Cobey and that he'd fallen in love with her. I couldn't believe it. I felt completely betrayed. I—I slapped her, and then started trashing her apartment. I just lost it completely. I couldn't help myself."

"But you didn't slap her more than once?"

"No."

"How much did Cobey know about all this?"

"Nothing that I know of."

"You didn't tell him, and she didn't either?"

She laughed harshly. "We both wanted to protect our positions. If Cobey found out that we'd both been manipulating him—well, he'd probably find himself a new girl entirely."

She smiled sadly. "Do you hate me?"

"No. No, I don't."

"I really do love him. That's why I got Beth to—to help me. But I sense you don't understand that."

"I'm trying to. Sometimes I'm more old-fashioned than I want to be."

She reached over and touched his hand again. It was a tiny hand, and he thought of his daughter.

"I'm so scared for him," she said.

"So am I. So am I, Veronica."

"I'm glad we talked, Mr. Puckett."

He paid the check and walked her back to her hotel in the sunny, warm, April afternoon.

CHAPTER TEN

Cobey's Tapes
In re: Veronica

I suppose I should begin with the time when we were up in the mountains, in that little cabin we'd rented for a four-day weekend, and we learned that Veronica had forgotten to bring her medication along—we'd decided on this weekender very suddenly.

This was about six months after I'd been released from the hospital in St. Louis—which is where I'd met my fellow nutcase Veronica—and when I still had to sneak around to see her. God, how Lilly hated her.

Veronica wasn't Lilly's first choice to hate, though, that honor belonging to a thirty-six-year-old red-haired school teacher who was in the bughouse when I first got sent there. She was being treated for depression, and thus shared the electric-shock table with me. Before I met Veronica, this woman and I would sneak out of our rooms at night and fuck in the stairwells until the muscle boys in the white T-shirts and white ducks caught us one night and told the good gray doctor who in turn told Lilly who, of course, got hysterical and told me that some night she was going to sneak into my room with a pair of scissors and cut my cock off right at the root, blood spurting everywhere like a geyser, and we'd see then who was sticking his cock into places it didn't belong. Lilly, selfish cunt that she is, didn't care that Kathryn, the school teacher, was a fine, sweet, gentle-sad woman whom I happened to really care about despite the simple, crude way it looked, us humping our asses off in stairwells. Kathryn ended up, at Lilly's insistence, in a far, far building where I never had the chance to see or talk to her again.

But I was telling you about Lilly and Veronica, who I met a month-and-a-half after sweet Kathryn's banishment . . .

First, I think Lilly was jealous of Veronica's looks. Plump Lilly has been trying to lose weight ever since she wrenched me from my parents when I was six. Who could unsettle a fat person more than a pale, slender, blonde-haired girl with grave, enormous eyes and a voice that rarely rose above a whisper?

Second, I think that Lilly learned about Veronica having one of her wealthy father's accountants fly in that weekend and tell me how, financially, anyway, I could start to pull away from Lilly.

Third, Lilly was concerned about her investment in me. What if I came to my senses and saw my Hollywood lifestyle for what it was—pain and bullshit, hardly worth the trouble? What if I settled down and married Veronica, and we went off to live in Virginia or someplace, and I dropped out of the acting scene altogether?

Anyway, that long weekend in the mountains, Veronica and I were hiding out from Lilly, who had private detectives follow us constantly.

It was a perfect weekend—until we realized that Veronica, in our rush to get out of LA, had left her medication behind.

Veronica was dependent on her pills. She had been diagnosed with a kind of schizophrenia that rendered her virtually dysfunctional if she wasn't constantly taking her medication.

I said I'd sneak back to her apartment and get the stuff, but she said no—and she was probably right—that this would just give Lilly's private eyes one more chance to locate and follow us.

For the first day and a half, everything went fine. There had been great, grim rains in the mountains that week, causing mudslides, wiping out some of the older and narrower roads, flooding the tumbling mountain creeks.

But when the rains stopped, it was perfect weather for taking small hikes up into the piney hills, looking out across the mountains, walking down small trails where every few minutes you'd glimpse a mountain sheep or a pronghorn antelope, or see an odd, colorful bird that looked as exotic as something you'd see in South America.

We ate well, sharing the cooking duties on the little gas stove that came with the cabin, making long, leisurely love and listening to a lot of classical music in an effort to lend me, at least, a little bit of culture.

And then it happened. I wasn't even aware of it until it was too late . . .

We'd made love and had fallen asleep to the sound of chill midnight rain soaking the cabin roof and walls. Snuggled deep, snuggled together, enjoying sleep.

My first impression was that I was having an especially vivid dream, the kind that is difficult to distinguish from reality sometimes.

There was a woman above me on the bed. She had a long butcher knife in her hand and was holding it up, as if she were about to plunge it into me. She was crying out my name and screaming, "You bastard! You bastard!"

And then she brought the knife down and stabbed me.

At the exact moment that I cried out in pain—at that exact moment—my mind shifted into reality mode.

This was not a dream. Veronica was kneeling beside me on the bed and she was still crying and screaming. She had just stabbed me.

And she was about to stab me again—

I rolled to the right, off the bed, landing with head-thumping pain on the floor.

And now I started some screaming of my own.

"What're you doing? Why're you doing this, Veronica?"

Not for a long time, not until she'd hurled the bloody knife into a far corner, not until she'd stopped whimpering, not until I realized how badly she needed her medication, did I calm down enough to feel the pain in my shoulder.

The knife hadn't gone deep, but it had cut wide enough to really run the blood. I grabbed a dish towel and clamped it over the wound. In a few minutes, the entire towel was soaked.

Sometime later, I stumbled out into the rain with my car keys. I drove into the nearest town and found an old doctor who took me into his parlor and sewed me up, all the while staring at my face. He smelled of booze and cigars and sweaty sleep. And when he walked, his old house slippers went slap, slap, slap. "You're that kid, aren't you?" he said.

"Kid?"

"The TV kid."

"Oh, yeah. Him." A little bit of boyish grin. "I'm not, actually. But I'm told I look a lot like him."

He finished and asked, "What do you want me to tell the law?"

"The law?"

"Hell, yes, the law. I've got to report a wound like this."

"Why?"

"Why? Because somebody obviously stabbed you. And that's a felony. At least in these parts."

Fortunately, I'd brought a lot of cash along. I gave him three hundred of it.

Without exactly looking at it, he rolled it up and stuffed it into the pocket of his faded flannel bathrobe.

"You get a lot of nookie?"

"Huh?"

"Nookie. You know, pussy." When I didn't say anything, he said, "You're the TV kid, all right, and don't tell me different. That's why I asked you about the nookie."

The guy was bald, at least as old as my grandfather. He had pinched little eyes behind pinched little eyeglasses, and every few minutes passed enough gas to start his own utility company. And he was using the word "nookie." There was something obscene about it.

"All those little sluts with those mini-skirts—I'll bet you get a lot of 'em, don't you?"

He followed me to the door with his deranged conversation, grinning, farting, insinuating.

I went out into the cold rain and drove fast back to the cabin.

The lights were off. When I got inside, I found her hunched over the toilet bowl, vomiting.

I got her dressed and into the car. She alternately raved—talking about things that made no sense, not to me anyway—and sobbed, begging me to forgive her for what she'd done.

Halfway back to LA, she said, hunched over there against the passenger door, "I followed you one night to Van Nuys when you said you were rehearsing. I know about that girl you're seeing."

I turned and looked at her. So beautiful—and now—so unfathomable in her schizophrenia. Some other species entirely there in the dim green glow of dashboard light and the pang and patter of rain on the roof.

"Veronica, she didn't mean anything to me."

"You betrayed me, Cobey."

"You're looking at it the wrong way. Honest to God you are."

"No, I'm not, Cobey. I'm looking at it in the only way I can. You betrayed me . . ."

She got better, of course, once she'd had twelve hours of the medication. We stayed in her apartment for two full days, never leaving, watching old, late night movies and fucking our brains out and eating what we felt like and going on these crazed laughing binges about nothing at all. And I apologized in this kind of non-stop way because I could see how badly I'd hurt her and could see that she felt a little better and more reassured each time I did it.

Of course, two nights later I saw the same Van Nuys girl again, this Arthur Murray dance instructress who, for some reason, really liked to take it in the ass and who gave blow jobs that brought me right to the brink of insanity . . .

The knife wound eventually became nothing more than a ragged snake of puckered flesh—the old pervert who'd sewn me up had done a lousy job, actually—and the Van Nuys girl gave way to a Bel Air girl who'd gone to convent school—Scout's Honor—and then she gave way to . . .

During it all, Veronica was the constant, however. The only time we had difficulties was when one of the girls on the side began to claim a little too much of my attention . . . I think Veronica got suspicious, at these times, times when I always seemed distracted by something . . .

But when the Swallows girl was killed and I started thinking about who might have done it . . .

It didn't take me long to conjure up an image of Veronica above me with that butcher knife that night . . .

Driving it down into me . . .
All that rage . . .
All that sense of betrayal . . .
Veronica . . .

CHAPTER ELEVEN

1

LATE AFTERNOON. CHICAGO SKY A BLEEDING RED. SILhouetted office building black against golden disk of early moon.

In bed. Lightly sweating from lovemaking. Anne's head in the crook of his arm.

"Puckett? Are you going to tell me you love me?"

"Sometime."

"Like when?"

"Like now."

2

She had recognized him. The bitch waitress had recognized him.

Cobey sat in a small diner near Union Station. After failing to reach Puckett earlier, he'd mostly wandered about, losing himself in the crowds, and had ended up here. At this point in the early evening, the place was packed with people who had just walked over from the Amtrak station and people who were waiting to go over to the Amtrak station. They were generally older people, wearing the thread-bare clothes of the working class, and the threadbare smiles of the American traveler, frustrated at every turn. They talked among them-selves about the Southern Route train to California being delayed by six hours. The place smelled of coffee and chili and cigarettes.

Cobey had been thinking about Amtrak—going up through the snowy mountain peaks, looking down into the rocky gorges and the shining silver bands of river—when he noticed the girl's attention.

She could at least have had the decency to be pretty.

Instead, she was anorexic, pimply, sweaty and furtive-looking. Her white polyester uniform was soiled.

She had been jamming glasses under the Coke fountain and watching him all the while. Watching him closely. Knowing exactly who he was.

He set his chili dog back down, unable to eat.

He wasn't sure what to do.

Even though he'd been recognized, should he jump up and take off running?

A chunky man in a white T-shirt and soiled white pants came out from the kitchen. He had broad, meaty shoulders and broad, meaty arms, on the left of which was a faded anchor tattoo. Homage, no doubt, to his uncle Popeye.

The man, bald and sweating, passed by the pimply girl at the Coke fountain. It appeared he goosed her because just then he grinned and her pelvis jerked forward and a tiny, momentary frown soured her mouth.

Then she leaned back and started whispering something to him.

At first, as she spoke, the man's eye contact went nowhere in par-ticular. He just seemed to be staring off into space as he listened.

But gradually his eyes began working around the restaurant and, ultimately, they stopped when they reached Cobey.

Now the man knew who Cobey was, too.

The girl said a few more words. The man's gaze became even more intent.

The man looked at the front door and then the rear door through which he'd come.

There were only two ways out of this place.

Cobey stood up.

The man visibly tensed.

Cobey looked frantically at the front door.

The man was already leaving the side of the girl and coming around the edge of the counter.

He moved fast and sure, the man did, fast and sure.

Cobey turned and started working his way through the crowd of old folks in front of the door.

He pushed hard. An old lady muttered something nasty to him.

Cobey kept pushing. Had to make it to the front door.

"Hey!"

No mistaking who the voice belonged to. The voice above all the conversations. Above the din from the kitchen in back. Even above the jukebox, Whitney Houston's voice almost as pretty as her face.

"Hey! Don't let him outta here!"

Cobey lunged, having no choice now, pushing through the final knot of old folks, despite all their cursing and complaining, and finally getting a hand on the door handle.

"Hey! Stop!"

The street: dusk, heavy rumbling traffic noise, the smells of the train station, heat and oil and a century of age.

"You sonofabitch! I said stop!"

The man diving through the door, almost falling forward he was moving so fast.

And then Cobey starting to run.

Down the block, against a red light—horns honking; cursing—up a sidewalk where faces appeared and disappeared like blips on a radar screen—black man with gold tooth, white man with big nose, black woman with white turban, sweet-faced white woman pushing a stroller—he ran.

And so did the man behind him.

He was good and fast, especially for a man his age, which had to be around fifty, and his size, which had to go two-, two-twenty.

Cobey kept running.

More honking. More shouting. More faces appearing and disappearing.

Cobey saw an alley, old, ragged bricks for the floor, an endless number of dumpsters for decoration, and took it.

By now, he was starting to feel the strain. Even though he exercised every day, the stress of all this was murderous, his breath coming in great, hot, sobbing heaves, his legs starting to feel like impossibly heavy dead weights that he had to keep picking up . . . picking up . . . picking up.

He wasn't even aware of falling down.

The toe of his shoe caught on one of the ragged bricks and he was tossed downward.

He heard his own voice, the sudden voice of a child afraid to be injured, on the warm, sunny air and felt the searing heat of his lungs and felt his bladder crying out to be emptied and—

And then he was thrown face downward.

And then, hearing the heavy *slap-slap-slap* of the man's shoes, Cobey turned to see the man just entering the alley now, coming straight down the narrow brick aisle between the dumpsters and the garbage cans and the back door stoops and all the wandering, homeless cats and dogs who had stopped whatever they were doing to watch the human drama unfolding before them.

Obviously, the man was heartened by what he saw, Cobey there flat on the ground, a perfect target. His hands became wide fists. He was about done with all this sissy running. Now he could get into what real men got into, which was the violence of retribution, of punishment.

This was going to be a lot of fucking fun. Some punk TV star who chopped some poor girl's head off—

And then the man, in his glee and exultation, miscalculated.

He dove for Cobey without noticing that Cobey had started to turn over and inch away.

Just as the man dove, his hands reaching out for Cobey's throat, Cobey had a surprise for him.

A nice, white fist that he managed to throw, without very much leverage at all, directly into the man's face.

It was like watching a video game—face meets fist and then the explosion: in this case, the man's nose.

Cobey felt the man's nose disintegrate beneath his fist. And then blood exploded all over the man's face. And then the man cried out.

And Cobey, who'd never even played a scene like this on TV and therefore had no experience whatsoever with moments like this, jumped to his feet and kicked the man square in the side of the head.

At first, the blow seemed to have no effect.

Enraged because his nose had been broken, the beefy man in the white (and now bloodstained) T-shirt and white trousers started to grapple and grab at the air to reach his feet.

He started cursing and he started spitting blood and he started making huge, terrible fists.

"You sonofabitch, you sonofabitch," he said.

And then he fell over backwards. Almost like a comic pratfall.

Unconscious. Or maybe even dead.

He lay there in his white kitchen uniform, bloody and dirty and sweaty now, his eyelids closed and unmoving, his Popeye tattoo looking old and faded and sad.

"Shit," Cobey said. "*Shit.*"

All he'd planned to do was stop the guy from beating him and now look what had happened.

He started to bend down to make sure that the guy was still breathing when he heard, coming around the corner like the wail of a siren, a man shouting with great, theatrical urgency.

"There he is! There he is!"

Then the man followed his voice around the corner of the alley. He was dressed in the uniform of a Chicago policeman.

Cobey glanced miserably down at the unmoving form of the man in white.

And then, just as the cop started shouting again, Cobey started running once more. Harder than he'd ever run in his life.

3

Puckett called ahead for an appointment with Lilly Carlyle. She agreed to meet with him in a sandwich shop around the corner from her hotel.

When he arrived, two overworked waitresses were desperately trying to keep a crowd of impatient businessmen happy, Loop workers apparently putting in long hours, taking a dinner break between sessions in the skyscrapers.

Lilly Carlyle wasn't difficult to spot. She sat in the back, near a large window. She was the only person in the place, Puckett reckoned, who was wearing more than two thousand dollars on her back. Her beautifully tailored blue suit and high-necked white blouse and carefully combed blonde chignon gave her the look of an overweight but still attractive movie star who had peaked some years back. Puckett had seen many such melancholy creatures in Hollywood.

The first thing she said to him was, "You're late."

He checked his watch. "Three minutes."

"Five."

"Maybe your watch is wrong."

"Unlikely, given what I paid for it."

He sat down, looked at her, and smiled. "Are you usually this unpleasant?"

"I don't know about you, Puckett, but my time is valuable. Very valuable. So I naturally resent people who aren't prompt."

"In that case, I apologize."

"Apology accepted. Now, why don't you get to the fucking point?"

He saw a weary waitress drag by and he knew just how she felt. Five minutes ago, he'd been enjoying nighttime Chicago. Now he felt totally worn out. Lilly Carlyle was just as much a bitch as he'd always heard and it made his ass tired. Meeting people this unpleasant and despotic always made his ass tired. *Very* tired.

"Mind if I order a cup of coffee first?"

He signaled the waitress.

Lilly Carlyle picked up a package of gold Benson and Hedges 100's from the table, put one of the cigarettes in her mouth, and then picked up a very slender, elegant lighter and got her smoke going.

Ordinarily, Puckett was one of those nagging bastards who gave people a little speech when they lit up. He wasn't going to give Lilly Carlyle his save-your-lungs speech. In fact, he was probably going to start sending her a carton of cigarettes a day.

The waitress, a middle-aged lady with sad, nervous, brown eyes, took Puckett's order and then looked at Lilly Carlyle. "Anything for you, ma'am?"

"If there were, don't you think I'd say so?"

The waitress glanced at Puckett, sadder than ever, it seemed, and shuffled off.

"She's probably a nice, hard-working lady."

"Are you going to tell me that I should be nice to the little people?"

And then he said it—unprofessional as hell, but at the moment he didn't give much of a damn: "No, but what I am going to tell you is that you're a fucking, second-rate bitch agent with a second-rate stable of talent in a second-rate talent agency, so don't give me any more of your Beverly Hills bullshit or I'm going to say something we'll both be sorry for."

Even above the din of clanking dishes, even above the spit and hiss of background conversations, Puckett could be heard loud and clear.

Many eyes were on Puckett and Lilly Carlyle.

"Are you happy now? Is that what you fucking wanted?" he asked.

When she spoke, she whispered and blushed, obviously aware of all the attention he'd gotten them. "Why don't you try and calm down?"

"Why don't you try and shut the fuck up?"

So they sat there and glared at each other.

Once, she tried to get up and leave, but he grabbed her slender wrist and made her sit back down.

After a few minutes, people went back to their conversations—the stock market, the thieves running the government in Washington, D.C., the family member who was a) seriously ill; b) getting divorced; c) having trouble with his teenager.

Gradually, Puckett became embarrassed, as he always did when he lost his temper that way. Most of the time, he was a pretty cool and reasonable guy. But when he lost his temper . . .

"I'm sorry," he said. "I overreacted."

"I don't want any of your fucking apologies. I just want to get this over with."

The waitress brought Puckett's order. Lilly Carlyle glared at her. To her credit, the weary waitress was not intimidated. She glared right back.

Puckett sipped his coffee and nibbled at his french fries. He'd eat only a few and then congratulate himself for being such a wonderful guy.

"Did you know the Swallows girl, the one the police want to question Cobey about?"

"No," Lilly Carlyle said.

"Did you know that he was seeing her?"

"No."

"He never mentioned her to you?"

"No."

"You have no interest in Cobey's personal life?"

"None."

She was answering, but barely.

"Do you think there's any possibility Cobey might actually have killed her?"

"I don't know."

"If you aren't interested in his social life, why do you hate Veronica so much?"

"She's just some groupie he met in the bughouse."

"The bughouse?"

A smile of pure, malicious delight parted her soft and erotic lips. "The little darling didn't tell you that? That she was in the bughouse at the same time he was?"

Puckett shook his head.

"And guess why she was there? Because her very wealthy father arranged for her to be put in a mental hospital instead of being sent to prison."

"Prison? For what?"

"Sweet Veronica stabbed the family maid. Three times in the back. Said that the maid was hiding Martians in the closet."

"If they were both in the bughouse, that probably gives them something in common. A kinship."

"'A kinship.' How quaint you are, Puckett. Apparently you don't know much about groupies. When she was thirteen years old, Veronica managed to get into the dressing room of a rock star who was very much into youngsters. He didn't care which sex and he didn't care who knew. He deflowered her right there in his dressing room and then invited the other six members of the band to join in.

"When her father found out about it, he was outraged. Unfortunately, he couldn't get his pure little daughter to help the police arrest the rock star. So he went free and little Veronica was no longer a virgin. Does she sound like the happy homemaker Cobey is looking for?"

Her icy hatred of Veronica—and most others, for that matter—was impressive in a terrifying, implacable way. Through long and careful practice, she had turned herself into something that bore great resemblance to . . . but was not quite . . . human.

"Cobey disappeared several years ago."

"Ah, the famous disappearance. What would all those tabloids do without it? 'Child Star Runs Off To Have Sex Change Operation!' 'Child Star Dying In France Of AIDS!' 'Child Star Weds Dying Screen Beauty!' She smiled icily. "Personally, I thought he might have been abducted by a UFO."

"So you have no idea where he went for—how long was it?"

"Nine months."

"You have no idea where he went?"

"No. And I don't care where he went. All that matters is that the networks are interested in him again."

"How will the murder of this girl affect him?"

"If he didn't do it, he should be fine. The publicity may even help him in a perverse sort of way." She glanced at her very expensive, solid gold wristwatch. "Are you finished? Because even if you're not, I am, Mr. Puckett."

She stood up. For a woman of her formidable size, she was quite attractive. Until you looked closely at those dead, dead eyes. Then she scared the shit out of you.

"I remember how scared Cobey was when I brought him back from St. Louis," Puckett said. "I figure he's equally scared now. He could use a little help."

"Puckett, the Boy Scout. How noble."

And then she was gone.

Puckett sat and finished his coffee.

After a time, the weary waitress came over.

"Your wife left, huh?"

"Oh, she isn't my wife."

The waitress smiled. "Good."

"Good?"

She poked him on the shoulder. "You look like a nice, sweet guy. I was thinking you deserve somebody a lot nicer than she is."

Puckett laughed—and decided to double his tip. Not only was the waitress good at her job, she was also damned perceptive.

CHAPTER TWELVE

Cobey's Tapes
In re: Lilly Carlyle

You should have seen her face the day I came back from Dr. Silverman's and told her that he'd be calling her in a day or so. I was twelve years old at the time and had been living with Lilly in the big Tudor house just outside Bel Air for six years.

"Me? What for? What does he want?"

Even then, I think, she suspected what he was going to say. Dr. Silverman had been hypnotizing me, taking me a lot deeper than the previous shrinks had, and I was starting to remember things . . .

The day he called, I listened in on one of the extension phones. To be honest, I listened in on most of her calls, just the way she listened in on most of mine . . .

"Ms. Carlyle, I really think we need to set up an appointment."

"We? Meaning you and I?"

"You and I, yes. That's right, Ms. Carlyle."

"Dr. Silverman, I am paying you a great deal of money to find out why Cobey doesn't sleep well or eat well lately. I don't see what that has to do with me."

"It has a great deal to do with you."

Long pause. "Meaning what, exactly?"

Long sigh. "Meaning, Ms. Carlyle, that that's why I want you to make an appointment and come in and see me."

Long pause. "Exactly what are we talking about here, Dr. Silverman?"

"Well," said Dr. Silverman, and I could tell he was starting to lose some of his professional niceness, "to start with, we're talking about breaking the law."

"Breaking the law?"

"I know what's been going on out there, Ms. Carlyle."

"Out where?"

"In your home."

"Dr. Silverman, you seem to be forgetting the very first thing I told you about Cobey."

"And that was what, Ms. Carlyle?"

"That he lies. All the time. About everything."

"I see."

"That sounded awfully smug. 'I see.' I'll bet God sounds just the same way when He's being smug."

Long pause. "I don't think Cobey's lying about this, Ms. Carlyle, and, to be frank, it's foolish of you to pretend that he is."

"And just what is it that he's accusing me of?"

"He's not accusing you of anything. But under hypnosis—"

"Hypnosis!" And then she cackled that dismissive Lilly cackle of hers—the cackle known to studio heads, directors and actors throughout La-La Land. "Hypnosis! It's quackery, Dr. Silverman. In fact, I'm getting so pissed off that you'd even waste my money with it that I'm thinking about canceling Cobey's next appointment and taking him somewhere else. How do you like that, Dr. Silverman?"

"I could always go to the authorities, Ms. Carlyle."

"You just fucking try it, pal, and you'll have my lawyers all over you."

Long pause. "Cobey needs help . . . after everything that's happened."

"That's exactly why I sent him to you. For help."

"But I can't help him, Ms. Carlyle, until you and I have had a long conversation. And until . . . well, until I receive certain assurances that certain . . . practices . . . well, frankly, that certain practices will stop."

"That lying little fuck. Just wait till I—"

"No!" said the good Dr. Silverman. "I won't wait. Either you come and see me this afternoon . . . or I'll be calling a friend of mine over in Social Services. She's handled many cases like this one . . . and she'll know just what to do with you."

Long pause. "He's lying, Dr. Silverman. Whatever he's told you, he's lying."

"Perhaps he is."

"You mean that?"

"Well, I suppose there's always a possibility that Cobey—in his present state of mind—suffers from psychotic fantasies and sometimes talks about them as if they're real . . ."

They were both subdued and polite now.

"I'm sorry I yelled at you, Dr. Silverman."

"I wasn't trying to upset you, Ms. Carlyle. I was simply making the point that—"

"I understand, Dr. Silverman."

"Would four o'clock this afternoon be all right?"

"Four o'clock would be lovely."

"I'd appreciate it if you'd come alone."

"Of course, Dr. Silverman."

"Oh. One thing we *can* talk about on the phone."

"Yes?"

"Are you aware that Cobey has been sneaking whiskey from your liquor cabinet?"

"No."

"Well, he is. And I think that he's already got a drinking problem."

"He's only twelve years old!"

"It happens, Ms. Carlyle. I've seen active alcoholics his age before. You'd better lock up all your liquor. He's the kind of personality that becomes psychotic when he drinks . . . can't tell reality from his fears and dreams."

"I don't know what to say."

"I know all this is difficult for you. That's why I appreciate the opportunity to talk it through with you."

"Wait a minute," Lilly said.

"I beg your pardon?"

"Be quiet a minute."

"But—"

"Quiet!"

Long, long pause. "Cobey, are you on one of the extensions?" Pause. "Forgive me, Dr. Silverman, but I heard a noise and I know that Cobey's on this line. He does this all the time."

Long pause. "Cobey?"

I hung up. Quietly as I could.

It was shortly after this that I found the insurance policy in her desk. Lilly was always complimenting me on being "mature" for my age . . . and I suppose I was, in a certain, and very neurotic, way.

Smart enough, at any rate, to know the significance of the Prudential life insurance policy I found in her desk—we always snooped into each other's things; it was some weird part of our relationship.

$1,500,000.00

Looks lovely when you see it, doesn't it?

$1,500,000.00 of whole life taken out in the name of Cobey Robert Daniels.

With the beneficiary being . . .

But you're way ahead of me on that.

Lilly was the beneficiary of course.

If she ever got totally sick of me—of my alcoholism, of all my bad publicity, of always threatening to tell people about what really went on in that house of ours when I was a little kid—well, she could find some way of collecting on it.

But of course, Lilly wouldn't kill me. In her pathetic way, she still loved me. That's why she followed Beth and me around . . . and that's how she came to be in Beth's apartment that night . . . she sensed something wrong . . . and came up, part earth mother, part smothering bitch.

But would she have killed Beth and framed me? Could she collect if I died on death row?

Absolutely.

Oh, yes, Lilly, you vile bitch, I know just what you're capable of . . .

CHAPTER THIRTEEN

1

AFTER DRIVING BY RICHARD BOYLE'S MOTEL BUT FIND-ing him gone, Puckett stopped at a Denny's and ordered a cup of coffee and went right back to the pay phones and called the agency in Los Angeles. Right now, the daytime operations would just be closing down. He asked for the secretary and waited.

"You ready for Kevin?"

"Ready," Puckett said.

"He left a recorded message for you."

"Thanks."

Seconds later, Kevin McCoy said: "Hello, Mr. Puckett. I'm going to run down what I found out name by name, and I'll start with Veronica Hobbs.

"She's been put in mental hospitals twice, both times for having done something violent. She was in the hospital when Cobey was for stabbing somebody . . . and when she was thirteen, she was also put in a hospital. She'd stabbed a cousin of hers. Her father had to pay the girl's mother a lot of money to keep her from going to the police and the press. Veronica is not a very stable girl and, from everything I could find out, she's insanely jealous. She trashed half a restaurant once when she saw Cobey sitting there talking to a waitress. Very, very unstable, as I said."

Every few sentences, Kevin McCoy would pause and very consciously draw breath. He was not having an easy time talking. He sounded exhausted.

"Wade Preston hates Cobey. He's gone to his lawyer four times in the past fifteen years to dissolve his partnership with Lilly Carlyle because of Cobey. The word is that Preston is used to getting his way with women. He just can't believe that he can't get Lilly to marry him—but she never quite makes that commitment and Preston always blames Cobey.

"There's one other thing to consider. Lilly has a huge life insurance policy on Cobey—and maybe she'd decided it's time to cash in. Maybe she's just sick of him now and would rather have the money.

"Of course, their relationship—" Here he paused to cough and get his breath. "A psychiatrist I knew from the old days used to see Cobey and he shared some confidential information with me." He laughed softly. "The psychiatrist happens to be a pedophile and a junkie. Isn't it nice to know that shrinks are even crazier than we are?

"Anyway, Cobey saw this guy for two years, between the time he was fifteen and seventeen. This was just when he started getting into trouble. I think the first thing he did was steal a car. And right after that, he punched out a counter guy at a Baskin-Robbins, which gets you the same kind of publicity slapping a nun gets you. That's when the press really started turning on him.

"Anyway, the shrink: Seems that Cobey confided to him that, after Lilly took Cobey from his parents, would have been when he was about six, Lilly started sexually abusing him. He claimed that he was eight the first time Lilly actually seduced him. In case you're running for a medical encyclopedia to see if that's possible, yes, it is. Boys as young as four are capable of getting erections." A laugh again. "Hell, now *I* sound like a pedophile. Believe me, I'm not. It's just that I happen to remember another incident similar to this one.

"The point of all this being that Lilly Carlyle was seducing the little tyke almost all the time he lived with her." He broke into a racking cough again. "Cobey told this shrink that Lilly regularly searched his room for pictures of girls and screened all his calls. Very Oedipal. You know, the mother crushing all the life from the young boy. He also mentioned that the older he got, the kinkier Lilly got—they tried just about everything, including bondage, until he broke her shoulder one time—and then she got scared and stopped all the leather bullshit. Unfortunately, by then she had a serious hold on him. No matter how often he ran away, he couldn't help coming back. Just couldn't make it without her.

"Which takes us to his mysterious nine month disappearance. A friend of mine at the *Examiner* reminded me that one of our TV columnists had gotten a post card from Cobey during this time. The columnist was a big fan of Cobey's and was always defending him in print, even when Cobey was taking some pretty bad publicity shots. The card didn't say much, just that Cobey appreciated the guy's loyalty and all that, but the columnist remembered the postmark. Sparks, Nevada. Well, being the good gumshoe I am, I called Sparks last night and talked to this detective who told me a very curious story.

"Near the end of Cobey's disappearance, this cop gets—" The wracking cough again. "Don't let 'em kid you, Puckett. AIDS is a lot of fun. Ahem. Where were we? Oh, right, this cop. Well, in those days, he was a uniform guy. And he got this domestic violence call. But when he got there, he got a surprise. Most domestic violence calls involve a wife siccing the cops on her husband. This was the other way around—the wife had stabbed the husband in the shoulder. It was a pretty deep wound, but the guy didn't want to press charges and he didn't want to go to the hospital.

"The guy had a towel wrapped tight around his shoulder and the cop kept staring at him. The guy was pretty young, and he had dark hair and a long, dark beard, but then it hit the cop who this was—Cobey Daniels. He remembered about the kid disappearing from Hollywood—you know, that whole big search Lilly Carlyle staged, which amounted to a lot of great, free publicity—I mean, Cobey wasn't wanted by the law or anything, but a lot of people were sure looking for him.

"Anyway, the cop says to him, "Hey, you're Cobey Daniels, right?" And Cobey, who's probably pretty weak by then, doesn't put up any kind of defense. He admits he's Cobey and he says that he's trying to get his life straightened out and that, if the cop tells anybody about who he is or what happened tonight, Cobey will have to start running again.

"Cobey was pretty pissed that the neighbor in the apartment below his had called the cops anyway. Cobey says that he and this woman he lives with were both drinking and they got into this terrible argument and she picked up this butcher knife and—well, the way Cobey told it, she didn't really mean to stab him. She was just threatening him with the knife and then she tripped, and, well, that's how it happened, anyway.

"The cop says that the name Cobey gave him for the woman was Evelyn Day. D-A-Y. It's not a name familiar to me. But the story doesn't end there.

"Before the cop can say anything, Cobey goes over to this desk and pulls out two one-thousand-dollar bills and comes back and gives them to the cop. For being my friend, Cobey tells him.

"Well, the way this cop tells it now, he drove straight from Cobey's and gave the money to this sweet old Irish Catholic monsignor he knew, which I personally think is bullshit. I mean, for sure this cop went on a bender or something. Anyway, he let the whole thing slide.

He didn't report the accident and he didn't bring charges against the woman.

"In fact, he never saw the woman. She stayed in the bedroom all the time, with the door closed. The cop said he could hear her crying every so often. You know, like she was pretty screwed up.

"A week later, though, the cop gets kind of guilty about shirking his duty and he goes back there. Just to check things out. By this time, Cobey and the woman are gone. The landlord lets the cop in and the cop finds a bathroom all splattered and smeared with blood. Human blood. All the cop can liken it to is this place he saw one time where this cult sacrificed this old lady they'd kidnapped.

"The way the cop tells all this now, he was just trying to help out a lonely TV star. He wasn't personally interested in the two grand or anything. That went to that sweet old monsignor. That's the same price he demanded to tell the story this time, too. Two grand. I had to promise him that the agency would deliver a cashier's check in two hours.

"That's about it, anyway. I hope this helps, Puckett." The cough again, moist and deadly. "I'm going to take a small rest now. It's that time of day for me."

Still coughing, he clicked off.

2

On the way back to his hotel, Puckett tried Boyle's motel again.

Boyle was still gone.

3

"I like this."

"The dark?"

"Umm-hmm. No TV on. Just the dark and listening to the rain on the window."

"Any place special you want to go tomorrow?"

"You're not going to see Boyle?"

"After I see Boyle. You got any place in mind?"

"I wouldn't mind seeing the stained glass windows at the Second Presbyterian Church."

"You serious?"

"Real serious. I'm a sinner, Puckett. And so are you. It couldn't hurt."

"You're crazy."

"Yeah, but that's why you like me."

"C'mere a minute."

"Only a minute?"

CHAPTER FOURTEEN

1

BOYLE NEVER KNEW WHAT TO SAY TO THEM IN THE hard light of morning.

For one thing, none of them ever looked all that good, hair tousled, clothes wrinkled, makeup faded. They looked sad or scared or embarrassed or hurried if they had jobs to get to. Curiously, it was at this moment that Boyle felt his greatest tenderness for them—the way they looked young-old and so vulnerable there in the morning light streaming through the motel window as the day came alive . . . But he didn't ever express this tenderness, of course, because it just wasn't the sort of thing a guy said to a girl, especially not a girl who'd been nothing more than a one-night stand.

This morning's girl was named Monica and she claimed to be a runway model at Marshall Fields who was only "filling in" with a temporary gig as a clerk at Walmart. Right.

He lay in bed, lighting the day's first cigarette, watching her pull her panties up over the slope of her wide hips. She had ginger-colored pubic hair which, for some reason, fascinated him. She also had "blonde" hair badly in need of peroxide and a full body badly in need of a quick diet. Not to mention shaving the tops of her thighs to where the ginger-colored hair extended. It was a formidable bush, that.

He continued to watch as she drew her hands around her back and hooked the ends of her bra together. Watching her breasts rise a moment, the silver-dollar size nipples looking especially chewy, he felt heat stirring in his groin. But he was a night person, not a morning lover. He hated bad breath and sweat-tainted flesh and mussed hair. Hell, he was a romantic. Night was always better.

"You remember the pitcher?" she said, moving to the straight-backed chair where she'd draped her skirt and blouse.

He wanted to laugh. She'd said "pitcher" instead of "picture." This was funny because he'd decided to stay out near Evanston during the run of the play because he'd find a better grade of young women to pick up in the college bars and the discos that served the college crowd. The image playing in his mind was a very sexy Ph.D. who knew all sorts of kinky tricks that he could take back to Los Angeles with him.

And here he gets this kind of dumpy, puppy-dog-eyed girl who says "pitcher" instead of "picture." And who, for God's sake, works at effing Walmart. So much for his sexy Ph.D.

"Oh, yeah," he said. "Right."

He got out of bed in a single bound, a trick he'd learned as a boy from Superman. She modestly turned her eyes away when she saw his penis slapping against his leg. He was starting to come erect again, vaguely considering making an exception to his no-morning-loving rule.

The motel room was small and dingy because all he could afford was small and dingy.

The drawn curtains glowed at the edges with morning light. In the next room, a TV blared with Bryant Gumbel's smug laughter. Out in the parking lot, car doors opened and closed as an army of small-town tourists and low-rent salesmen made ready to descend on the Windy City.

Boyle's room smelled of disinfectant, hair spray (hers), cigarettes (his) and the vague scent of feces. She'd been in the bathroom a long time this morning, the water running the entire time, and when she'd emerged she looked apologetic.

Darling, he wanted to say, *it's all right with me that you have to take a big morning constitutional. I have to take them myself.*

The "pitcher" she referred to was on the desk that was bolted to the floor. (Who the hell would steal a desk?) It lay on a small stack of identical black and white glossy "pitchers," all of which showed Richard Boyle in all his TV sitcom glory . . . dark, curly hair, black Irish good looks (just narrowly missing pretty) and shining white capped teeth. Discreetly printed along the bottom of the glossy in two-point black type was the legend: "TV star and entertainer Richard Boyle."

He'd never been sure exactly what the hell "entertainer" meant. He couldn't sing, dance, juggle, play an instrument or do hand puppets. And hell, if most of the critics on the North American continent were to be believed, he couldn't act, either. About all he could do was stand there without his shirt and give the women of America one of his patented, blue-eyed, "smoldering" looks and wait for their thighs to get all wet and quivering with pure, unadulterated lust.

But he did look good in glossies. Correction: in glossies, he looked *grrrreaaaat!* (a little Tony the Tiger, if you please).

"Would you say 'love' on it?"

When she said this, he paused, sitting there bare-ass naked at the bolted-down desk in this shabby little room, and then he turned around and looked at her, really looked at her as a human being, and she goddamned near broke his heart.

He saw how scared and lonely and sad she was. She'd spend her life working at Walmart and then some stud from the stockroom would forget his Trojan one night and she'd give birth to the first of several little kids they couldn't afford at all and her body would mudslide early into middle-age and her husband would take a drunken punch at her every so often and there you'd go. And before you knew it her daughter would be working at Walmart and passing herself around to a whole new generation of stockroom studs and so the process would go on and on into eternal, black, meaningless, space and time, quick, sad, firefly lives on lonely planet Earth.

And to disprove all this—to prove that her life had meaning and order and dignity and point—she'd have this autographed picture of a fourth-rate TV "celebrity" and she'd show it to anybody who'd look. Hell, she'd probably rent a fucking sound truck and drive up and down the streets of suburban Chicago, pulling cars over, and waving housewives down to the curb from their porches.

And coyly, very coyly, she'd hint to them all that she'd gotten to "know" Mr. Boyle pretty well (if you know what I mean) and a nicer and more gentlemanly guy you couldn't ask for. You just couldn't ask for.

She would carry this photograph into the waiting oblivion of her future, clinging to it far more tenaciously than she'd ever clung to her virginity, because the picture would allow her to convince herself that her hours and months and years on this whirling, nowhere planet amounted to something after all.

He looked at her now and he fucking wanted to cry.

He stood up and he went over to her.

She watched him with a certain degree of apprehension, not certain of what he was going to do.

He took her hand and then he kissed her goodbye the way he always kissed his kid sister in North Hollywood goodbye, just a sweet little peck on the cheek.

"I'd be happy to put 'love' on it, Monica. You're a very nice young woman and I really enjoyed our night together."

And then she did it for him, standing there all mussed, standing there seeming to read his mind, she started crying and laughing, clearly not sure why she was doing either, squeezing his hand and then leaning over and putting a sweet little kiss of her own on his own sweet little cheek.

"So long, TV star," she said, snuffling her nose.

She was out of there in under ten seconds, the door opening, a blast of dirty sunlight angling into the room, the high, acrid stench of diesel fumes finding his nostrils, the roar and rumble of nearby truck traffic shifting the ground like a six pointer on the LA Richter scale.

Then, as always, he was alone.

2

But he was not alone for long.

Puckett knocked on his door.

"Morning," Puckett said. "You remember me?"

Boyle had to think a moment. "You were backstage with Cobey the other night."

Puckett showed him his ID.

"Gee, a Junior G-Man."

"Let's go have a cup of coffee."

"How about *please* let's go have a cup of coffee?"

"All right. *Please* let's go have a cup of coffee."

3

"So you didn't know Beth Swallows?"

"No."

"Never met her?"

"That's right."

"How about Cobey?"

"How about him?"

"I'm told there used to be bad blood between you."

"He chose me as director, didn't he?"

"You hear from him in the past day or so?"

"No."

"And you wouldn't have any idea where I could find him?"

"No."

"How'd you ever get to be this much of an asshole?"

"Practice."

"Figures."

CHAPTER FIFTEEN

Cobey's Tapes
In re: Boyle

Ah, the things friends won't do for each other.

Boyle, for instance. When it was apparent that I was going to be the star of *Family Life* and not him, Boyle called a gossip columnist and planted the item that, because his real love was directing, he'd "stepped aside to let me have the role."

Let me have it!

Boyle is so bad an actor that, even by sitcom standards, he's wooden. All he's got going is that Muscle-Beach tan and that pinup boy sulkiness.

And don't think I'm just being bitchy here. I don't like Boyle, but then, I've *earned* that right.

Item: 1983. Though I've never been able to prove this, I know it was Boyle, after he learned that I had just gotten the lead in a Movie of the Week he'd been after, who went to the LA County Morgue and bribed somebody there to cut the hand off a cadaver and sell it to him. And then he put the hand in the refrigerator in my dressing room along with a note that said: THE SOUND OF ONE HAND CLAPPING.

Item: 1984. He hires a young woman he knows I'll never be able to resist to, groupie-style, seduce me. Which she does. No problem there. But a few short weeks later, I find out that she's given me a very sweet little venereal disease—which she admits to doing on purpose, after Boyle paid her to do it. Bitch. Both of them.

Item: 1985. And this is the real pisser. While we were taping our last show, my trailer caught on fire. It so happened that everybody had taken a break and nobody was around. Except Boyle. He saved my life, hauling me out of there just before the smoke would have killed me. He even got an ambulance. They were afraid there might have been some residual brain damage because, apparently, I was in the smoke a long time.

So now I owe Boyle one! A big one! But yes, like you, I've also wondered from time to time if he might not have *set* the fire on purpose, just so he could save me and get himself a lot of publicity for his next series. And that's why I let him direct my show in Chicago. Because a) he'd actually become a very good director over the eight years we hadn't seen each other, and b) what am I gonna do? Say, "fuck you," to the guy who saved my life (even if he did start the fire—which I can't prove?).

The thing most curious about Boyle is his enthusiasm for hookers. Here's a very hetero guy with matinee-idol looks, a gym-perfect body and a very charming manner. He has dozens of girls to choose from, yet he spends a lot of his time with very young hookers. "Pure ones," he calls them, high school queens just out here from Nebraska or Colorado, working for "modeling" agencies to pay the rent. At a cast party one night, one of his chippies noted how many people were drinking Perrier instead of alcohol. She laughed. "That's a good thing. Customers come a lot faster that way."

But, and this is pure Boyle, rather than just pumping them and forgetting them, he pumps them and . . . tries to save their souls.

Tries to convince them to go back to Nebraska and give up the hills of Hollywood.

I guess I would be moved by all this—I mean, it is a nice thing to do to talk a girl out of being a prostitute—if I didn't know deep down that "saving their souls" was just part of a sexual game he likes to play with hookers.

Boyle is a tricky one.

You have to watch him.

Oh yeah.

CHAPTER SIXTEEN

1

THE GRAY LIMESTONE AND STAINED GLASS WINDOWS of the Second Presbyterian Church were even more beautiful than Puckett had expected.

They sat for a long time in the rear of the church, watching the way the sunlight played through the windows, vivid on one piece of glass for a time, then exploding elsewhere a few moments later.

Anne held his hand for a long time. "Do you feel holy, Puckett?"

"No. But I wish I did."

"I wish I did, too . . ."

After dinner at the Ristorante Italia, they went back to Puckett's room. As soon as they closed the door, the phone started ringing.

Puckett ran to it.

He recognized the voice immediately. "Where are you?"

Cobey told him.

He asked Puckett to meet him there in half an hour.

"I'll be there," Puckett said, and hung up.

"Is he all right?" Anne asked.

"He sounds exhausted and scared. About what you'd expect, I guess."

"Do you want me to go?"

"You mind if I take it alone? It'll probably be easier."

She smiled. "The code of the private eye?"

He smiled back and kissed her. "Yeah, something like that, anyway."

2

After hanging up, Cobey leaned his head back against the grimy glass of the phone booth and closed his eyes.

He stayed this way, taking deep, relaxing breaths, reciting again and again the mantra he'd gotten from his long-ago sessions on Sepulveda Boulevard in the true ways of the soul, and wishing he could clearly remember the night he'd awakened and found Beth's head in the refrigerator.

But Puckett would be here soon. Puckett would be able to help . . .

If he could recall the night exactly, maybe he could recall seeing the murder take place . . . or the murderer escape . . . Again, his mind returned to the fact that Lilly had just appeared at Beth's apartment that night. He couldn't remember calling her. How had she known to be there, known he needed help?

He opened his eyes.

Across the street, in the rain, a bulky man in an overcoat stood watching him. Only the man's eyes, which seemed the emerald color of a tiger's, were bright, the rest of the man's face was lost in shadow.

Suddenly, Cobey felt self-conscious, as if the booth were a display case.

Yes, it's me, Cobey Daniels, wanted for murder . . .

The phone booth reeked of piss and cheap wine. Cobey's nose was running. And his scalp had started to itch, apparently in some kind of reaction to the Lady Clairol he'd used yesterday morning.

The man dropped his cigarette in the gutter, then shoved both hands into his overcoat pockets.

He stood still, just watching Cobey.

And then he started across the street toward the booth.

The neighborhood was mostly warehouses and old shops. There was no traffic on the rain-slick street.

Just the man walking, walking, his footsteps echoing off the dark, empty warehouses.

Walking.

And then Cobey got scared.

He wasn't sure why. It was just some sense that this man was somebody Cobey didn't want to know, somebody who meant him harm.

Cobey opened the creaking door.

The night air was cold, his breath silver.

The man, head down in the mist, kept walking, walking, his footsteps louder now.

Cobey glanced up and down the dark street.

If the man had confederates anywhere, they were well hidden.

The man raised his head abruptly. His bright eyes stared right at Cobey. "That phone working?"

"Yes."

"Good. Have to call the wife."

The man nodded and brushed past Cobey, leaving the younger man to stand in the middle of the street. The street light waved in the wind, scattering blanched light across the pavement.

Cobey turned around and watched the man go in the booth.

When the light came on, the door closing, Cobey saw that the man was both older and heavier than he'd first appeared.

Even from there, Cobey could hear the metallic clank of the change dropping in the telephone.

And then he thought: *What if he's recognized me? What if he's calling the cops?*

Cobey felt sick and scared and cold again; and utterly, utterly baffled.

This was a nightmare, right? Some kind of horrible drug dream he was having?

The man opened the door abruptly and stared out of the phone booth, his eyes still seeming to glow.

"You got a match, son?" he said.

Cobey knew, then. This man was the enemy. The enemy.

He couldn't wait for Puckett now. By the time Puckett got here, this man would have arrested him.

Then he was running; running, the flapping of his soles on the wet pavement fading, fading as the man started talking on the phone.

Cobey was gone; gone . . .

CHAPTER SEVENTEEN

1

ALBERT KEMPER, THE MANAGER OF THE APARTMENT house in which Beth Swallows had been killed, was reading *Penthouse* when he thought he heard the noise upstairs. The time was 8:15 PM.

It was his habit, once he'd gotten every possible moment of pleasure from looking at the ladies, to go to the front of the hefty, glossy magazine and begin to read the articles. While his wife was alive, he hadn't dared bring the magazine home. His wife had been overly sensitive to any attention he paid to females, even ones in magazines. And a girlie magazine . . . But, as he thought this, he felt guilty. He loved his wife even now, and did not mean to dishonor her memory . . .

Overall, *Penthouse* was a pretty good magazine, journalistically speaking, one of the last refuges of liberalism. Kemper, though he was variously disenchanted with feminists, blacks, gays and foreigners, still called himself a liberal, even if, in his most secret heart, he was in fact something of a reactionary these days.

The noise caused him to set down his magazine—he was halfway through an article on which congressmen had mistresses on their payrolls. He looked up into the gloom of his ceiling.

Albert Kemper always read in the same armchair. With the same floor lamp spreading a bright coin of light in a small area encompassing the chair. The rest of the room was dark.

As he looked up now, he thought of two things: the torn, bloody head of Beth Swallows in the refrigerator and the fact that the police had sealed off Beth's apartment. Nobody was permitted in there, not even Albert Kemper, retired English teacher and apartment house super.

But he was sure the noise had come from Beth's apartment.

Sure of it.

He set the magazine down on the white doily that covered the surface of the stand. Following surgery years ago, his wife, Marjorie, had taught herself to crochet and it had been their joke that her enthusiasm would someday lead her to crochet such things as a refrigerator and a car. Kemper put his hands on his knotty knees and stood up.

His first impulse was to pick up the phone and call Detective Cozzens. Hadn't the detective told him to do just that?

The problem was, what if he was wrong?

On a windy night, in an apartment house usually noisy at this time of night anyway, how could he be sure that the sound had come from Beth's apartment? And who would be up there, anyway? The killer? Unlikely. For what reason?

He stood in the darkness surrounding the glowing chair, thinking.

Maybe it would be a waste of time to go up there at all. Maybe his hearing had just been playing tricks on him. Neither his vision nor his hearing were all that wonderful these days.

Then he sighed, drew tight his brown cardigan with the two buttons missing—he'd been not only a chauvinist but an obstinate one;

even with Marjorie gone all this time, he still hadn't learned how to sew, pricking himself every time he tried, and the button falling off right away the few times he'd succeeded—and went out into the hall.

VCRs competed with each other up and down the hallway. In the last five years, home videos had become the dominant form of entertainment, some people bringing home one or two at a time, others bringing home six or seven for a long weekend. A few apartments still watched regular television, though. As he neared the staircase, a human laugh came up over the inhuman laugh of the soundtrack, while in another apartment a popcorn maker simulated the sound of a Tommy Gun on the old *Untouchables* show.

The stairs were wearying. This was a big place, long out of fashion, of course, but the size guaranteeing each renter real privacy.

When he was halfway up, he saw Cosgrove, his newest tenant, coming down the stairs with a smiling, blonde woman walking in front of him single file. Cosgrove should have been the one smiling. As far as Albert Kemper was concerned, Cosgrove bore no resemblance whatsoever to Prince Charming, yet at least three times a week he sported a very nice looking woman. And a different one each time, too. He was this doughy Irish guy with a lot of greasy black hair and a somewhat sinister, film noir mustache. He always wore dark, double-breasted suits and bright silk ties. His success with women proved that the world was a mysterious and ultimately incomprehensible place.

The blonde smiled her empty blonde smile for Albert Kemper and kept on walking.

"Hey, Pops, how they hangin'?" Cosgrove said as he passed Kemper. He smiled his empty nightclub smile, obviously taking pleasure in the fact that calling Kemper "Pops" irritated and humiliated the guy. Then, "Hey, what's going on in that apartment where the chick got killed?"

Kemper froze on the stairway. "What?"

"Yeah, me 'n Denise here were just leavin' the apartment when we heard some kinda noise in there. Right, Denise?"

Denise nodded. Damn, she was good looking.

"What kind of noise?" Albert Kemper said.

"Who knows from noise? Just—noise."

"Like something falling maybe," Denise said.

Cosgrove shrugged. "Yeah, like somethin' fallin' maybe."

"I'll check it out," Albert Kemper said.

Cosgrove laughed. "Hey, maybe it's a ghost in there movin' around, right, Kemper?"

Denise shuddered. Cosgrove winked at Albert Kemper. They were both, or so thought Cosgrove, in the same club, with ladies far too frail to ever join.

"Stuff like that really scares me!" Denise said on the way down the stairs.

Albert Kemper walked in the opposite direction. When he reached the second floor, he started thinking about strange noises and how they affected him. They scared him, too.

Maybe he should go back downstairs and call Detective Cozzens and let him go see for himself what was going on in the apartment.

Albert Kemper paused, though, then shook his head and continued down the hall, past doors that smelled of roast beef and chili and baking bread. Albert Kemper might be losing his vision and his hearing, but he had a fine, keen nose.

When he got to Beth's door, he stopped, gaped.

All the yellow tape designating the apartment as a CRIME SCENE: DO NOT ENTER was still in place. The door looked like a gift, tied up in yellow ribbon.

If somebody was inside, how in the world had he gotten in there?

For a long moment Albert Kemper considered, with a certain relish, the notion of ghosts. As a boy, he'd always loved campfire tales that made him shiver. A certain kind of fear was even enjoyable, lights out, lying next to the other Scout in the pup tent, trying to see who could do the best job of scaring the other guy.

But this was different.

A young woman had had her head severed from her body. Then somebody had placed the head, ragged and dripping blood, into the refrigerator.

No, this was very different from campfire tales. Very different.

He approached the door, taking notice of the fact that his heart rate had increased, and that a fine, invisible sweat had broken out chill along his arms and shoulders and back.

Imagining how Beth's head must have looked in the refrigerator, he decided to make sure that the door was actually sealed, that some-body hadn't broken the seal, in fact, and then head back downstairs.

From what he could see, peering closely, the yellow plastic tape was just as the police had left it. The apartment was sealed off.

He leaned his head closer to the door, listened.

The apartment house was a cacophony; an electric blender erupted somewhere, accompanied by the din of MTV, which was in turn drowned out by the Colemans' baby. Marsha and Dave Coleman were the only parents in the entire apartment building.

His ears strained to hear something within Beth's apartment.

But—nothing.

He waited a moment longer, shrugged, then turned around and headed back downstairs.

Once in his own apartment, he went into the bathroom, took a nice, long pee, washed his hands and then went out to resume reading his magazine.

But twenty minutes later, he found himself unable to concentrate on his reading.

Hadn't Detective Cozzens said to call him if anything untoward happened?

And wasn't it even stranger that Cosgrove and Denise had also heard something in there?

Albert Kemper stood up, walked out of the circle of light, and went over to the dark corner where his desk lay, the aged, black, dial phone atop it.

He didn't even say hello; he didn't even identify himself.

He said, first thing, in a bluster, "I'm sorry, Detective Cozzens, for phoning you like this. I really am."

So Cozzens had to back him up a little and find out a) who was calling, and b) why he was calling.

After that, the two men got along just fine.

2

The cab pulled up to the phone booth where, twenty minutes earlier, Cobey Daniels had stood.

Now the booth was empty, the dark street shiny with the recent rain.

Puckett told the cabbie to wait while he walked up and down the block of warehouses trying to find Cobey.

But Cobey was gone; gone . . .

3

"Yes?"

"I was wondering if I could get into Cobey Daniels' apartment."

"You a cop?"

"Private cop."

"Private eye, you mean?"

"Something like that."

"What's your name?"

"Puckett."

"Cops told me I was supposed to tell them if anybody tried to get into Cobey's apartment."

"It's all right with me if you tell them after I leave. I'll need a while up there, though."

"How long?"

"Hour-and-a-half. Maybe two."

"Now why would I go and let you do a thing like that?"

"Because I'm going to give you this."

"Say, you must make a lot of money in the private eye business."

"I do all right."

"Hour-and-a-half you say?"

"Or two."

"Or two. And you don't tell the cops I let you go up there?"

"I don't tell the cops anything."

"Good enough."

He spent two hours and twenty-three minutes going through virtually everything that was in the tiny efficiency apartment Cobey had rented for the run of the play.

He found nothing; nothing.

4

Being a smart-ass cop, Cozzens decided to play it like a smart-ass cop. He parked in the rear of Albert Kemper's apartment building and walked through the wind and the cold, spattering rain to the fire escape. He would not announce his presence. He would see Kemper later.

Kemper did a good job of keeping the place neat and orderly. Two dumpsters and six large galvanized steel garbage cans lined the rear wall. A newly painted door led to the basement and the two clothes-line poles had been painted silver recently. The rear steps, steel and doubling as a fire escape, were also in good repair.

Cozzens stood a moment in the shadowy light, looking up at Beth Swallows' apartment window. The glass was dark. In other apartment windows, light was warm and cozy. He thought of his old days as a family man. Damn! Now wasn't the time for melancholy.

He went over to the steps and started climbing. The metal rail was cold to his touch.

He went up past the noise of a TV set playing rap music, past the noise of four people playing bridge, past the noise of a couple laughing. For a moment, he knew how a killer would feel out here in the vast, dark, night—knowing, superior, dangerous, one with the shadows, the bringer of violent and unexpected fate.

At this, he smiled. He was reading too many paperback serial killer novels. Maybe it was time to switch back to the science fiction of his youth.

When he reached Beth Swallows' floor, he took out his burglar tools and went to work. The lock yielded entrance in less than a minute-and-a-half and he went inside and stood for a moment in the hallway.

He smelled warmth and the lingering aromas of several dinners. He heard competing TVs; competing conversations; a phone ringing.

Beth Swallows' door was right in front of him.

From his trench coat pocket, he took a black leather glove and tugged it onto his right hand.

He wrapped his fingers around the doorknob, turned it. Locked.

He examined the yellow tape. The door was completely sealed off, just as the officers had left it.

If somebody was in there, he hadn't gone in through the door.

Cozzens stuffed the glove back in his pocket and then went outside on the rear stairs again. The contrast between the heat of the apartment house and the cold of the rear steps was like a bracing slap in the face.

He walked over to the rear window of the Swallows apartment and peered in. He could see nothing more than the shape of bedroom furnishings, a double bed, bureau, a closet door left ajar. Nothing stirred. Nothing looked unusual or wrong.

He took out the glove again, jerked it on, and tried to push up the window frame.

The window eased open.

He stood there in the rushing, dark, night, letting his cop judgment dry the sudden hot sweat on his face.

He did not want to race to any conclusion. Any number of explanations could be given for the window being unlocked, namely that one of the officers had failed to do his or her duty in securing the crime scene.

As for the noise that Albert Kemper and at least one of his tenants had heard, people living in a house where a murder had taken place were often spooked for months following. The slightest noise convinced them that something sinister was afoot, and they frequently made calls to the precinct with hysteria riding high in their voices.

Cozzens took out his weapon. It was an old-fashioned Smith and Wesson .38, his first official police gun, and the only weapon he'd ever been sentimental about—he hated to think of the phallic implications of that—and the weapon that had seen him through three shoot-outs and any number of robbery scenes. The contours of the gun felt welcome and familiar in his hand.

Cozzens was betting on his cop hunch, betting that despite all good reason, despite all the long odds, somebody was in there.

He had no idea who, he had no idea why, but he was just about to find out.

Sliding the window up all the way, he pushed a leg over the window ledge and proceeded to climb in. Not so easy when you were wearing your official Mike Hammer trench coat.

As soon as he was inside, standing in the darkness, the .38 filling his gloved hand, his blue, Irish eyes scanning the shadows, he smelled the blood and entrails.

No disinfectant ever created could rid a close quarters crime scene such as this one of its stench. Only time could do that—long periods of time. The way that poor young woman had been cut up, head severed from torso, torso worked on with unyielding savagery . . .

The stench would be in this apartment for a long time, despite all the best efforts of poor little Albert Kemper.

Cozzens started his search.

He kept thinking about calling for backup but decided against it. He wasn't the macho sort. He was, in fact, the sort who found a great deal of police work pretty frightening, but he had to admit that he had found the past half hour to be exhilarating.

Ever since splitting up with his wife, Cozzens had existed in a kind of funk. He couldn't quite bring himself to focus on anything. But ever since Albert Kemper's phone call—

Talk about focus. Talk about attention to duty.

Cozzens' heart was pounding. His eyes were keen as an animal's. And there was the undeniable wish in his heart for violence, for some kind of purgation of all his emotional pain, some blinding, blood-filled moment of pure exorcism, his demons on the run at last.

His grip tightened on the handle of his weapon.

He started his search of the bedroom, taking the closet on the right first and finding it empty, and then checking the other closet. Nothing.

He went out into the living room. Chalk marks still indicated where Beth Swallows had been killed originally. Only after that had she been beheaded, her body dragged to the kitchen closet.

He found nothing in the living room, nothing in the front closets.

He paused by the front window, looking down at the street that appeared clean and shiny and new after the rain. He felt as if he were hiding in some dark perch, a tree house made exclusively for grown-ups. A silver XKE went past below and he thought of how enviable the owner's life probably was. Lots of fun, lots of women. Or maybe not. As a cop, Cozzens had learned that few lives were all that enviable under close scrutiny.

When he heard the noise, he whipped around in a crouch, ready to fire like a gunfighter of old.

Heart slamming against his chest, body trembling beneath cold sweat, gun hand twitching violently, he peered into the gloom.

He hadn't imagined the noise. That he knew for sure.

But where had it come from? And exactly what had it been?

He started having doubts about his decision to face this down alone. Maybe he was being macho, after all. Maybe he should walk over to that phone and call in and . . .

And then the noise came again.

Right below his feet.

He grinned. He couldn't help it. This big-ass grin of relief.

Somebody in the apartment below had dropped something on the floor, and had just now dropped it again.

He looked down at his hand.

Still shaking. God, inside his thick, Irish body beat the heart of Barney Fife.

He grinned again, at the image of Andy Griffith and Mayberry. He hoped heaven was just like Mayberry.

Then, good, reasonable and competent cop that he was, he set about finishing his search, moving down the narrow hallway to the kitchen.

The stench here was much worse. Images of the headless torso flashed in his mind. He felt sick.

He found more chalk marks on the tiled kitchen floor. The white appliances looked dim and dirty in the gloom. His eyes fixed on the refrigerator. He could still see Beth Swallows' head inside there, staring out at him, as if she were waiting for human company. Next to the refrigerator was the tall, narrow pantry where he'd found the headless corpse. The door was closed. He tried not to remember how obscene she'd looked with her head gone.

Inexorably, he walked slowly toward the refrigerator.

He pictured himself the night the body was discovered . . . moving at about the same pace . . . walking closer, closer to the refrigerator.

Putting forth his right hand, as now.

Taking the silver refrigerator handle, next to the built-in juicer, and pulling it back with his gloved hand.

Watching the door come open, the bright burning light from the refrigerator interior painting him a wan silver color.

And then the door opening all the way—

And the light growing brighter, brighter—

And sitting right there, staring right up at him, the most horrible sight he'd ever—

But there was no bloody and begrimed head waiting for him tonight. Somebody, Albert Kemper probably, had scoured the refrigerator until it shone white and clean.

Cozzens shook his head, the image of Beth Swallows' head vivid again, and—

He didn't see it in time. Or hear it in time.

The other closet door opening.

The woman stepping out, the butcher knife in her hand.

Only too late did his eyes move to his left.

Only too late was he aware of the knife coming down in a flashing arc, directly into his right eye.

He screamed and tried to fire but she was stronger than she'd appeared in his momentary glimpse of her.

She tore the knife from his eye and pushed him into the refrigerator door, the gun falling, unfired, to the floor.

So much hot blood. So much screaming pain. He was blind; he was frenzied.

And then, distantly, as if it was happening to someone else but somehow his own body was registering the pain, he felt the butcher knife begin to move in and out of his chest in a rhythm that was almost sexual.

He tried to scream for help but somehow no sounds came.

He tried to push away from her but somehow there was no place to go.

He was seven years old and swimming in a municipal pool with his cousin Harry; he was eleven years old and hitting the winning home run in a softball game; he was twenty-two and making love to his wife on their wedding night. He was—

He was dying, and reviewing his life in the process.

He was beyond pain now as he slid down the refrigerator, coming to sit almost comically on the floor, legs spraddled, palms turned outward.

This time, she put the butcher knife right in the center of his forehead and left it there.

He didn't mind. There were only moments left before all history came crashing down, all life, all human utterance and aspiration, gone forever, his life gone forever. He was about to learn the answer to the question most fervently asked by each generation: *Is There Life After Death?*

No, he didn't mind at all.

He just sat there, bleeding, dying.

Waiting, but for what he was not sure . . .

5

When she was done vomiting, she went back down the hall to the kitchen and took another look at him. Even with the stench, even with the steaming blood, there was something dreamy and unreal about it, just as there had been something dreamy and unreal about killing Beth, and she had to be sure, as if she'd just awakened from a terrible sleep, had to make sure that it really had happened.

Detective Cozzens had fallen over on his side. He looked like a drunk in a high school sketch. Even the butcher knife handle protruding from his forehead had a certain loony quality to it.

She touched trembling fingers to her face. She was afraid she was going to be sick again. But she was glad she'd come back here. The night she'd killed Beth Swallows here, she'd dropped an earring and had to flee just as Cobey was starting to wake up, the earring falling down a floor grate. Tonight, she'd opened the grate and found the earring lodged down there where the police hadn't searched . . .

She began to back slowly out of the kitchen, the image of the dead detective receding, receding.

She was afraid now, and confused, and the taint of blood was high and hot in her nostrils.

She moved through the shadows of the apartment until she found the same window she'd come in.

Then she was gone; gone . . .

CHAPTER EIGHTEEN

1

CLOUDS OF STEAM ROLLED AND TUMBLED WITHIN the narrow glass shower stall. The pink and appealing flesh of Anne Addison was lost somewhere inside.

As always, hot soapy water gave her the feeling she sought, one of cleansing not only her body but her soul as well.

She parted her legs, working the bar of Dove high up the sleek inside of her thigh. She was careful not to touch herself sexually, because the notion of sex would again ignite memories she was constantly trying to forget.

She hummed to herself, an old show tune. In both high school and college she'd been in many plays, always minor roles, limited by the fact that her voice was terrible. But in the shower . . .

She smiled to herself and soaped her face once again, long fingers tapering down the luxurious angles of her cheekbones.

She enjoyed holding her face up close to the shower nozzle, the pain almost pleasure. She closed her eyes, letting the steady blast of the shower numb her face, push her off into some other world where there were no memories, no regrets, no guilt . . .

Five minutes later, her right hand groping out of the shower door and snatching a big, nubby, pink towel from the rack, she heard the phone ring out there in the darkness of the hotel room.

She had to rush through the shadows to the phone.

Now, towel-wrapped in the shadows, Anne shivered, goose bumps hard as BBs covering her body.

"Hello?"

Long silence.

"Hello?" Anne's irritation clear in her tone.

Long silence.

"Hello."

Then, "Anne?"

"Yes."

"It's me. Cobey."

"Cobey! God." Her gaze fixed on the neon green and yellow raindrops sliding down the window. "Where are you?"

"I need to talk to Puckett, Anne."

"Puckett? God, Cobey, it's me, Anne."

"Anne, please, listen. Don't get your feelings hurt as usual."

Anne's anger was swift and certain. It lent her body a genuine warmth, dispelling the trembling effects of the goose bumps. "Are you going to start calling me overly sensitive again, Cobey, the way you used to before—"

Then she fell silent. As did Cobey.

She'd almost said it, almost given voice to the terrible incident that had ended their nine-month romance the time Cobey disappeared.

She said, "I'm sorry, Cobey."

"I know. It's just the way you are, Annie."

Annie. God, every time he'd called her that during their time together she'd gotten positively girly and weak. There had been a time when the most romantic word ever uttered was her own name coming from the sensual lips of Cobey Daniels.

"Annie."

"Yes?"

"I need to talk to Puckett. I really do."

"Where are you?"

"I'd rather not say."

"You don't trust me?" The hurt tone was back in her voice again.

"It's not that, it's . . ." He sighed. "Of course I trust you, Annie."

"Good. Because I trust you."

"Then you don't think I killed Beth?"

"No, I don't."

"It's great to hear you say that, Annie. It really is." A pause again. "I'm over near the Daley Center. You know where that is?"

"Yes. Of course."

"I'm in a phone booth." The pause again. "I don't know what to do, Annie. I was hoping that Puckett could help me."

"I could help you."

"Oh, no, Annie, I don't want to get you involved in this. You're—" He stopped himself.

"I'm what?"

"Oh, Annie, I wasn't going to say anything terrible."

"No?"

"No."

"Just what were you going to say?"

"Annie, let's not argue. I—"

"Just tell me what you were going to say."

"Jeez, Annie, this is how you always get."

"Then let me say it for you. You don't want me to help you because I'd just get overly emotional and end up going into one of my depressions. And maybe I'd even start drinking again."

"I wasn't going to say that, Annie. I mean, you do get upset about things very easily, but I'd never say you were going to start drinking again. I know you've kicked it and you'd never—"

"I'll be there in half an hour."

"What?"

"Half an hour. In a cab. Now, tell me exactly where you are."

"But, Annie, I—"

"I want to know exactly where you are. I want to help you. Aren't we still friends?"

He didn't say anything for a time. Then, in little more than a whisper, "You really still think of us as friends? After what happened and all?"

"Still friends, Cobey. Still friends."

"You know," he said, "at least once a day I think about that. Sometimes, I even have nightmares about it. I wake up covered in icy sweat and I'm screaming and I—"

"I've forgotten about it."

"You have? Really?"

"It's in the past, Cobey. I just look to the future."

"But you were so angry. I thought—"

She was in control of herself again. For a long moment, thinking about what had happened there at the end of her nine month time with Cobey . . . Well, thinking about it all again, she'd started to lose it. Felt the old rage once more.

But now . . .

She stood in the shadows, slender and lovely inside the nubby towel, watching the neon-tinted raindrops, and said, "Tell me where you are, Cobey. The longer you're out on the street, the better your chances of getting caught."

"You're sure you want to get involved?"

"Oh, yes," Anne said. "Yes, Cobey, I want to get involved."

So Cobey, sounding relieved at the prospect of a friend helping him out, told Anne again where he was.

Exactly where he was.

Ten minutes later, her hair still wet beneath the suede, turquoise beret she wore, she reached the elevator.

Two-and-a-half minutes after that, she was stepping into a Yellow cab that smelled of defroster heat and cigar smoke.

I'm coming to you, Cobey, she thought.

After all this time, I'm finally coming to you.

The cab pulled away.

Anne leaned her head back and closed her eyes as if she were praying.

The time was finally here. At last; at last.

2

She was gone.

Puckett stood just inside his hotel room looking at the dark, empty room, the only light coming from the rain-dappled window. No place is lonelier than an empty hotel room, especially on a rainy night.

She was gone and something was wrong. That, Puckett was certain of.

He should have come back to the room earlier but instead he'd made the rounds of the discos where Cobey was known to hang out. He hadn't turned up anything.

He closed the door behind him and started to walk toward the window. Halfway there, he noticed the curled, wet leaves on the rug.

He bent down, knees cracking, and picked up one of the birch leaves. The dampness gave it the slick feeling of a fish.

So she had gone out tonight and then come back.

And had now gone out again.

All he could think of was that Cobey had called while he was out and that Anne had taken the call and had gone off somewhere to help Cobey.

Nothing else made sense. Not at this hour.

He stood up, looking at the antiseptic, lonely room. He wanted to hear her laugh, feel her hug him in that urgent, girlish way of hers, as if she were clinging desperately to him for support. He enjoyed being needed. It made him feel that he belonged to somebody.

He went over to the bed, sat down on the edge and started to pick up the phone when he noticed the stack of magazines with Anne's pen name material in them.

He flipped on the goose neck lamp on the ledge between the two beds and picked up the phone.

He dialed the desk, giving his name and room number when a male voice answered. He asked the clerk if he'd happened to see Anne recently.

"I've just come on duty, sir, but Michael is still here. He was on since three this afternoon. Let me go ask him."

"Thank you."

As he waited for the clerk to return, Puckett thumbed through the magazines. Each of Anne's pen name articles was flagged with a yellow sticky on the title page. He was struck, first, by the fleeting nature of fame as represented by these glossy pages. More than half of the "hot" stars that Anne had written about a few years ago were not working much these days.

He smiled at some of the pen names: Amy Conners, Rachel Forrest, Evelyn Day, Dorothy Todd. If all else went bad for Anne, she always had a future as a bad check artist. She was good at inventing names.

The clerk came back on. "Sorry I took so long."

"I appreciate your trouble."

"Michael did see her leaving. About an hour ago, he said. He also saw her leave earlier in the evening."

"The last time he saw her—did he see her get into a cab or anything?"

"Yes. A Yellow cab. He thinks it was Marty's."

"Marty's?"

"Marty Gresham. He usually parks out front. His brother is a bellman here and so they kibitz a lot."

"Is Marty out there now?"

"Just a second. I'll check."

The desk clerk went away, came back. "Not yet. I can call you as soon as I see him, though."

"I'd appreciate it."

And then, sitting there on the edge of the bed, the name came back to him, one of the pen names she'd used on her articles. Evelyn Day. Something familiar about that . . .

The name teased at his mind but bore no meaning. Evelyn Day. Why did that seem familiar?

He went in the bathroom and cleaned up. Hot water and soap felt good on his beard-stubbled face. He splashed on Brut and then did his pits and rolled on some new deodorant.

All the time he kept waiting for the phone to ring.

All the time he kept thinking about the name Evelyn Day. Why did that sound familiar?

He went out to the room and started looking for notes. Maybe she'd left him one and he just hadn't stumbled across it yet. This was unlike her, taking off this way with no kind of note.

He was on the third dresser drawer when he remembered why the name Evelyn Day sounded so familiar to him. A burning sensation started in his stomach and began working up his chest. Icy sweat dappled his long arms and his sloping, muscular back.

He turned his head to look at the phone, praying for it to ring.

3

At this time of night, the only people moving inside the Daley Center were the security guards. Otherwise, the windows in the vaulting white building sitting in the middle of the large plaza were dark.

Outside, hiding behind the enigmatic Picasso sculpture that Chicagoans had been arguing about for long years, Cobey Daniels searched the street for any sign of a taxi.

He still wished he'd been able to get hold of Puckett instead of Anne. After everything that happened . . .

Several years ago, one of the big, slick, entertainment magazines had assigned Anne to write an article about Cobey. He'd been out of the asylum for less than a year and was doing bit parts at the time. Lilly had taken an instinctive dislike to the woman. Apparently, she'd sensed intuitively that there was a strong attraction between Anne and Cobey.

On the night of Anne's last interview with Cobey, after two weeks of her following him around like a valet, she invited him out to dinner and he accepted. They drove out to Malibu on one of those Technicolor evenings that recalled a fifties musical, impossibly gorgeous, impossibly romantic . . .

Not much later that evening, Cobey called Lilly and told her that he wouldn't be able to keep his weekend mall gig. He said he'd just come down with the flu and would be staying in his apartment.

Lilly, of course, didn't trust him. She drove over to his apartment at once and found him gone. She spent the entire weekend frantically phoning his place and driving over there on the off-chance that he'd returned and simply wasn't answering his phone.

Meanwhile, Cobey and Anne flew to Las Vegas for the weekend, following a chance remark by Cobey that he'd always wanted to see if the place was just as tacky as everybody said. It was—but it was also exciting as hell.

It was, perhaps, the finest weekend of Cobey's life and, by the end of it, he was in love with Anne Addison. True, she was a few years older than he and true, the loss of her son frequently sent her into deep depressions. But she was funny and tender and gentle, and she gave him the best silken sex he'd ever had. They quickly developed a mutual need that bordered on a sick kind of dependency, but if either noticed it at this juncture, they said nothing. They just accepted the dependency as part of their relationship—quick jealousies, constant phone calls if they were apart for even an afternoon, and incessant reassurances that she really truly loved him and that he really truly loved her.

Cobey lost all interest in his career. He started canceling publicity dates, on the set he was forlorn because Anne wasn't around, and he was constantly battling both Lilly and Wade, who saw his career start-ing into a serious decline. He even did the most unexpected thing, quit drinking.

Lilly set private detectives on them, but the detectives were unable to learn Anne's identity. Cobey and Anne took child-like delight in eluding the detectives, in setting traps for them, in planting false clues.

And then one day Cobey was gone.

Lilly called the police and a nationwide search was set in motion for the TV star.

Cobey and Anne, hair dyed, had rented a farm in Pennsylvania under a false married name. Cobey loved Pennsylvania, especially the steep, wooded hills and mountains. If anything, the relationship between the pair was stronger and more fulfilling than ever. Anne and Cobey would spend their lives together. That went without saying.

And then the spells came.

At least, that's what Cobey called them. Anne had started having nightmares about her little boy running out into the street and being struck and killed by the car. She'd started seeing his death as somehow her fault, even though, in reality, there had been nothing she could do to prevent it.

Cobey got her to a shrink, an irony not lost on him—crazed Cobey taking someone else to a psychiatrist. For a time, Anne was better.

And then one morning, dawn still muzzy in the dusty farmhouse window, the boards of the floor cold on the white pads of her soles, she stood looking out at the ground fog that was now touched with gold as the sun rose to take the sky, and said, "I'm pregnant."

He watched as she turned to him, startled by the look on her face. No surprise, no joy; only a somber, even anxious look.

"Don't you see what this means?" she said. "It means God is giving me another chance. I didn't take care of my first son, but he's giving me another chance to take care of this one. Don't you see that, Cobey?"

She came over to the bed and fell into his arms, where they stayed the rest of the morning. He was going to be a father. Cobey Daniels. Punk of punks, assbandit of assbandits, a father if-ya-could-fer-God's-sake-believe-it.

The next two months were out of a sentimental forties romance movie—maybe one with June Allyson. Cobey was a big fan of old movies, always wondering what it would have been like to screw those older actresses. Cobey played the attentive expectant father, Anne the lovely, serene expectant mother. And then one afternoon, a late rainy afternoon when he'd gone off to do the grocery shopping, he stopped in a bar and—just some wild, irresistible hair up his ass—had a couple of drinks and came home in the only mean mood he'd ever shown Anne . . .

Terrified that something had happened to him, she was hurt and angry when she saw why he was late. She slapped him hard across the face and then he just reacted. Didn't plan to. Didn't want to. Immediately wished he hadn't.

He raised his hand and brought it down in a chopping motion against the side of her face, brought it down with an obscene grace and power, brought it down hard enough to send her slamming backwards into the spindly coffee table, and falling over it, her thin arms windmilling, her face sweet and vulnerable and terrified. And he tried to grab her, oh, God, he tried so hard, but it was too late, her head banging against the hard corner of the couch arm, her torso folding in half as her bottom slid between the coffee table and the couch.

He was next to her in seconds, helping her up, crying out crazily *I'msorryI'msorryI'msorryI'msorry* and kissing her face and wailing some insane animal wail and seeing in nightmare truth what booze did to him every time he touched a single flicking drop. And then she ran to the bathroom and started throwing up and he came in and got down on his knees next to her at the bowl and said, "Is the baby all right? Is the baby all right?" with that same loony repetition panic always induced in him.

She looked at him and said, "I don't know. I don't feel very well and I'm scared. You hurt our baby! You hurt our baby!"

And then he got her on the bed and she began sobbing so hard the mattress squeaked with the rhythms of lovemaking. He went in and sat down next to her and gently touched a hand to her tear-soft, tear-warm cheek.

By now the rain was coming down hard outside. He lay down next to her in the dark bedroom, the small lamp out in the living room the only light in the entire farmhouse and she cried softly for an entire hour. He said nothing. He just smelled the damp, cold rain and smelled the dark consuming night and smelled the tart whiskey on his breath. Then he went to sleep.

He heard her, several hours later, screaming in the shadowy bedroom, standing over him and looking down at him. At first, coming up from the depths of sleep, he was disoriented and unable to tell what she was pointing at and screaming about. But then he rolled over and felt the sticky, bloody mess beneath him on the bed and knew instantly that she'd had a miscarriage.

She kept screaming and pointing and screaming and pointing until all he could think of to do was get her in the shower and run the water so cold that it brought her back to at least a semblance of sanity . . .

Four nights after this, she packed her bags and left in the middle of the night. He didn't hear from her for a week and he started drinking again. He managed to get his hands on twenty Halcyon pills and considered downing them along with a pint of Old Crow. Good-fucking-bye and good-fucking-riddance. But the night he considered this, his phone rang near midnight and she said, "Sparks, Nevada, if you're interested," and then hung up.

Late the next dusty afternoon, Cobey stood on the runway in Sparks. By nightfall, at his paternal and adamant insistence, they were living in a nice, middle-class apartment where hubbies ran to accountants and ad men and wifies ran to school teachers and travel agents.

For fifteen days and nights Cobey told her how sorry he was, how devoutly he begged for her forgiveness.

For fifteen days and nights Anne told him that she knew he was sorry and that she had indeed forgiven him and that there was no point in talking about it further.

Her eyes and some inexplicable turmoil in the cool Nevada air said otherwise. But, finally, he began to believe her. For six days and nights he believed her completely. She had forgiven him and everything was fine and they would try again to have a child and things would be even better than they had been before.

On the seventh night, Cobey was watching some old Road Runner cartoons when she came up behind him and stabbed him deep in the shoulder and he cried out in fear and pain so loud that one of the hubby accountants or one of the wifey school teachers called the law and when they came they insisted that Cobey press charges but he insisted otherwise.

By one AM, he was on a plane to LA.

By then, and for the first time, he understood the full consequences of his actions.

He had killed their baby.

Not until she'd walked into his dressing room several days ago had he seen or heard from her again.

Now she was picking him up in a cab.

Now she was going to save him, at least temporarily, from the night and the police cars that seemed to be prowling every other block. The thought of being alone with her made him uncomfortable. What if she started shrieking at him? But he was exhausted and completely empty of ideas. He felt as young as a child, and long, long deserted . . .

A Yellow cab, made spectral by the misty rain, pulled up to the corner and stopped. At first, Cobey wasn't sure if the cab was waiting for him or if the cabbie was just taking a break and parking. The cab seemed to glow eerily in the gloom.

He moved out from behind the Picasso statue, turning his collar up and hunkering inside his jacket in case a cop suddenly appeared.

He was a lone, dark figure moving across the plaza at an angle to the taxi. His body language told you that he was ready at any moment to start running. When he walked through puddles, his shoes made a *whapping* noise.

The back door of the taxi opened.

Country and western music whined from the dark opening.

From here, Cobey couldn't see anybody inside. He had a Twilight Zone kind of thought, born of paranoia and exhaustion. What if he reached the cab and found it empty? That would sure scare the shit out of him, wouldn't it?

He kept walking. He didn't know what else to do. The music got louder. Faintly, he made out the shape of somebody in the back seat.

Cars splashed by in the street. He wanted to hail one and say *Please take me. There's trouble for me in that taxi. I can feel it. Man, I really can.*

Anne leaned out of the back seat darkness and smiled. "C'mon, you can walk faster than that. We don't want to make the cab driver rich, do we?"

The impulse to turn and run was now almost overwhelming. He was filled with this dread, the same kind of oxygen-robbing panic he used to feel on the sitcom set when he had an anxiety attack.

He wanted to *puke*.

Anne leaned out even further into the light of the plaza. Her looks never let him down. The vulnerability, maybe even the craziness, was as erotic to him as anything he'd ever known.

He smelled her now, her perfume, and the scent of her flesh, and it steadied him.

A long, slender hand came out of the shadowy back seat. He reached out and took it, soft and warm to the touch, reassuring.

Cobey got inside the cab and closed the door.

He glanced in the rearview mirror where he met the hungry brown eyes of the driver. No doubt what this man was thinking: some shambling piece of shit like this kid gets this kind of pussy, and what do I get? I get to drive around fucking Chicago all night long and risk my ass on niggers for a couple bucks an hour.

The cabbie ground the gears as he pulled away.

Cobey was jerked back in his seat.

Then Anne moved over.

She gave the cabbie plenty more reason to be envious.

Her mouth found Cobey's, and her hand found his cock.

4

It seemed like hours before the phone rang.

"Mr. Puckett?"

"Yes."

"This is Richard at the desk. Marty just pulled in."

"Thank you."

"I hope everything turns out all right, Mr. Puckett."

"So do I, Richard. Thanks again."

"You're most welcome, Mr. Puckett. Enjoy your stay."

He knew he had to hurry. Had to.

He took the lobby in long strides, Richard the desk clerk waving at him just as Puckett reached the glass front doors. To the right of the impressive, impassive doorman, all gussied up to be in a Sigmund Romberg musical about merry old Vienna, were three Yellow cabs. Drivers sat behind the wheels reading newspapers. Given the shadowy interior of the cabs, the drivers must have been reading by some kind of radar.

"Marty?"

The driver glanced up. Puckett's voice had a frantic edge to it now. "'fraid not, pal. Marty's back two cabs."

"Thanks."

Out here, the night smelled of rain and cold and exhaust fumes.

Puckett half-jogged to the last cab in line, then knocked quickly on the rolled-up driver's window.

"Hop in," Marty said, putting down his paper in a quick rustle.

"You're Marty?"

"Yeah." Suspicion colored his tone. "Anything wrong with that?"

"I need to know where you took a red-haired woman about an hour ago."

Now the suspicion was in Marty's gaze. He was a squat, thirtyish man in a red-gold cap and a vinyl bombardier jacket. His taxi smelled of cigar smoke.

"She your wife?"

"My lady friend."

Marty sighed and stared straight out his windshield. "I hate gettin' involved in stuff like this."

"It's very important, Marty."

Marty sighed. His eyes, turned toward Puckett again, looked sad.

"She picked up some guy."

"Some guy?"

"Some young guy over to the Daley Plaza."

"Then where did you take them?"

"The harbor."

Wade Preston's yacht. Of course, he remembered Anne telling him that Preston had been pursuing her so desperately that he'd even given her the key to his yacht.

"That's where I need to go," Puckett said, and opened the back door.

When he was seated inside, and closing the door, Marty looked at him in the rearview and said, "I hope you don't do nothin' crazy, pal. I sure wouldn't want to be involved in anything like that."

Marty here was under the impression that they were dealing with adultery.

If only it were that simple, Puckett thought.

Marty ground the cab into gear and pulled out from the towering, luxury hotel, a battered yellow vehicle among fine, shiny Rolls-Royces and Jaguars.

CHAPTER NINETEEN

1

HE JUST HAD A SENSE OF SOMETHING BEING WRONG. There was no other way to explain it.

As he moved a few steps behind her onto the yacht, the pitch and sway of the craft making him vaguely nauseous already, Cobey once again felt the impulse to simply flee.

But where would he go? He had no energy left for running. He needed time to gather himself, and then time to talk to Puckett, before turning himself in.

The mist and shadow of the night reminded Cobey of the Conan books he enjoyed so much, ancient sailing craft leaving strange ports in the middle of stormy nights. The entire harbor was dark, the burglar lights of boats shining like the red, malevolent eyes of hungry beasts. He shuddered from the cold, and the fine, chilly spray of water as waves continued to hurl themselves against the boat. In the distance, the skyline of Chicago glowed with a radioactive glee behind a veil of fog. Tug boats hooted like hoarse dinosaurs, plying the wintry black waters.

"Hurry up, Cobey. You must be freezing."

Anne's voice was disembodied again, the way it had been earlier in the cab.

For some reason he could not quite explain, an image of the night she miscarried flashed across his mind. *He raised his hand and half-clubbed her with it, sending her sprawling back across the coffee table—*

"Hurry up, Cobey."

Voice only from the dark pit of cabin below; fine, cold spittle of spray across his face; needing to piss and piss badly; and weariness, so much fucking, pure, overwhelming *weariness.*

Now he no longer thought of running.

He was too tired.

He'd go below to the cabin, maybe even get a little sleep. Just stay there in the darkness, listening to the waves slap the yacht, feeling the pitch and pull of the dark, eternal waters.

"Cobey."

He started across the yacht, toward the waiting cabin door.

Hell, maybe he'd even score with her. He knew it was wrong to think this way—Veronica was such a true-blue girl, and here he was licking everybody who gave him half a chance; and for sure it would not be fair to Puckett—but who would know if, in the shadows of the cabin below, they just kind of snuggled up against the cold wet night and, just naturally, he slipped himself into her and—

From the darkness, he saw the faint shape of her hand.

She slid her fingers over his and he was startled by the frozen quality of her flesh. All he could think of was one of the reissues of the old DC Comics where the Cryptkeeper held out his hand to the little girl and the little girl screamed because the hand was so cold . . .

She led him down the four stairs to the cabin, never letting go of his hand.

Faintly, he could make out the contours of furniture and a bar. Nice place. Of course, you wouldn't expect less from Wade Preston. He was such a status-conscious sonofabitch.

And then he was in her arms. Without a word. And then her tongue, was in his mouth and he felt her crotch pressing urgently against his crotch.

And then she was easing off his jacket. And pushing him slowly back toward the couch.

By this time, he had slid his hand inside her blouse. She wasn't wearing a bra and he'd always loved her breasts.

Her mouth tasted sweet, of gum.

She had a sweet-tasting pussy, too. He remembered that going down on her had always been one of the abiding pleasures of their sex life.

It all started fading away then. Beth Swallows being dead. Being wanted by the police. Running; running. Veronica's soft green gaze. Puckett's friendship.

None of it mattered now.

There was just the two of them here on this yacht, the pitch and pull of the waters, the faint scent of scotch whiskey from the bar—

Ohshit ohsweetChrist ohgogogogo—

She'd unzipped his pants and gotten his cock out.

He looked down, watched as she got the big, urgent rod in her mouth and started working on it with her moist, masterful tongue.

Ohshit. He was going to go blind from pure pleasure.

He'd forgotten just how good she really was.

He was so far gone, in fact, that at first he didn't recognize the instrument that she'd brought up from the floor.

By the time it registered on his brain, it was far too late.

She pulled her head up and brought down the long, shining blade of the butcher knife.

And lobbed his cock off right at the root, the hole that was left splashing blood over both of them.

He screamed; he was aware of the sound he made.

But by then she was already stabbing the knife again and again and again into his chest . . .

2

The parking lot adjacent to the harbor was empty as the Yellow cab emerged from the fog and mist and stopped just below the high, wooden stairs leading to the water. The mercury vapor lights, enshrouded in swirling silver clouds, resembled the glowing heads of aliens.

The rear door opened and Puckett emerged, throwing a fifty dollar bill at the driver, slamming the door shut behind him.

As the cab backed away, its reverse gear whined as if under a terrible strain.

Puckett ran through the fog, his footsteps making flat, slapping sounds against the wet asphalt.

When he reached the hill, he paused to glance down along the harbor. He smelled the polluted lake and his own heat and sweat. He was trembling.

No lights shone on Wade Preston's yacht.

Puckett drew his service revolver and began running for the pier, slipping once and nearly pitching forward.

He ran along the slippery pier, the ghost boats lining it little more than vague shapes in the fog, the hoot of tugs faint.

He jumped from the pier to the Preston yacht without slowing down.

Only then did he stop, his breath coming in hot, lung-aching gasps. He listened for any human sounds below deck, but all he could hear was his own heartbeat pounding in his ears.

He approached the cabin, revolver ready, and stopped.

He put his ear to the door. Heard nothing below.

He put the weapon in his left hand and tried the door handle with his right. Unlocked.

He opened the door, pushed his head in a few inches. With the curtains drawn, the cabin was pitch dark.

He went down the four steps and stood in the open room, his feet spread wide to absorb the pitch of the yacht.

Gradually, his eyes began to define certain shapes: couch, bar, small refrigerator. Gradually, his nose began to define the terrible odor filling it.

A terrible thought came to him, then, just standing there, just trying to give his body time to calm down, just trying to understand the revelations of the past hour-and-a-half.

He tried to dismiss the thought, tried to persuade himself that he was only being ghoulish or silly, tried to fix his mind on something else.

But the thought would not go away. He knew that there was only one way to dispel it. He had to prove to himself that the thought was nonsense.

Feet crossing the dark carpeting, knees giving a little to accommodate the sway of the craft, he went directly to the small, kitchenette-style refrigerator and opened the door.

The interior light was very, very bright.

Staring up at him were the blue, blue eyes of Cobey Daniels . . .

Somebody had sawn Cobey's head from his shoulders and then placed the head in the refrigerator, just as Beth Swallows' head had been placed in a refrigerator.

That had been the stench, of course, the way Cobey had been butchered so as to fit his head into the refrigerator. The white bottom of the refrigerator was a mess of blood. The white walls were badly splattered, too. A bottle of 7-Up was painted a dark red with the stuff.

There was no mistaking the sensation he next felt. Even bending over, even unable to see the instrument, he knew what it was and he knew who wielded it.

"Put the gun on the refrigerator, Puckett," Anne said behind him.

She had pushed the butcher knife so hard into his back that it had cut through his London Fog and his sport coat and his shirt.

He put the gun on the refrigerator.

"Did you know he killed our child?" she said.

He didn't know what she was talking about. In fact, there was only one thing at this moment that he knew at all. He knew that Anne was insane.

"Those nine months he was missing?" she said. "He was with me."

"I want to help you, Anne," he said quietly. "I want to help you."

She laughed. "Oh, Puckett, I wish you were a shit like all the other men I've known. Why do you have to be so decent?"

"I'm afraid for you, Anne. I'm afraid of what might happen to you."

Slap of waves; pitch of ship; high, wet stink of human meat.

"Stand up and turn around," she said. "Slowly."

He complied.

When he got turned around and saw her standing there, the butcher knife huge and terrible in her fine, small hand, he was shocked at the amount of blood splattered across her face and white blouse. It even tainted her coppery hair. She looked as if she'd worked a hard, pitiless shift on a killing floor.

She held the knife out straight at his chest so that he would not be inclined to lunge at her. Then she stooped slightly and reached around him and picked up the gun from the top of the refrigerator.

In her hand, the weapon looked outsize, even comic, like an ugly German handgun in the tiny hand of a little girl.

"I wish it could have worked for us, Puckett," she said. "I really do. But it was too late. Everything was already set in motion. Inside my head, I mean. A lot more than I knew."

She looked right at him, pretty, delicate, mad. "I want you to help me, Puckett."

"I want to help you, Anne."

"I want you to hold me."

There was no evidence of fear, no evidence of sadness. He had never seen her more controlled.

"All right," he said.

"Don't try to take the gun from me."

"All right."

"You promise?"

"I promise."

He took a step forward, letting more of the backglow into the room.

The refrigerator light was unkind to her face, gave her hollows and angles where they were not becoming. And all the while, he could feel Cobey's blue eyes on them, staring, staring.

"I really was starting to love you again, Puckett. I really was."

She walked toward him one, two steps, and he slid his arms around her and gently took her to him, lover, brother, father, priest.

He heard the knife hit the floor.

He held her even tighter.

"I love you, Anne."

"Even after all I've done?"

"Yes. I think I loved you the first time I ever saw you. It was just—that way. Nothing I could do about it."

"I'm sorry, Puckett."

"It's all right."

"You know what I'm going to do?"

"Yes."

"Will you help me?"

"No. No, I couldn't do that, Anne."

"But you said you loved me. You'd help me if you loved me."

"I'm sorry, Anne. You'll have to do it yourself."

"I'm afraid . . ."

"I know."

"Hold me tighter, Puckett. Hold me tighter than you've ever held me before."

And so he did, there on the pitching yacht in the rolling, foggy, isolated darkness. He held her until he felt her get the gun set in the proper direction, and slip her finger against the trigger, and jerk backward as the bullet ripped through her ribs.

"Oh, Puckett," she said. "Oh, Puckett . . ."

And then he thought she might cry, but of course, it was too late for that.

She was dead.

3

"I suppose she loved him," Veronica said at O'Hare the next day as Puckett was headed west and she east. "Even though she killed him. I mean, just because you kill somebody doesn't necessarily mean that you don't love them."

And what, exactly, was one to say to that?

4

There were a lot of nasty jokes in Hollywood that next week about how Cobey Daniels had lost his head over the woman who'd killed him.

There were three hundred people at Cobey's funeral, six hundred if you counted press, and Puckett and Veronica stood in the front line graveside, right next to Lilly Carlyle and Wade Preston, both of whom were dressed in dramatic black outfits straight out of *Sunset Boulevard*. Lilly kept shooting angry glances at Preston.

The grass was very green and the sky very blue and there was a sweet, soft, April breeze.

By now, Puckett knew everything that had happened. Anne had left a letter for him and the police gave him copies of the tapes Cobey had made.

Veronica had admitted, just as they'd entered the church in Beverly Hills, that she'd "stoked up on franks." She seemed almost oblivious to everything that was going on. He envied her.

After the ceremony, Puckett gave her a ride to LAX, where she gave him a chaste kiss good-bye.

In the afternoon, Puckett went to a pet store and bought the tiniest, most heartbreaking little kitten he'd ever seen and he wasn't even sure why.

He took her back home and set up her food bowl and her water bowl and her litter box.

And then he spent the rest of the day following her around like some moonstruck adolescent.

He did not consider it sentimental to call her by the name of Anne . . .

From the December 2, 1994 edition of *The National Tattler*

"Starmaker" Finds New Youngster

Discoverer of Cobey Daniels says new boy "even more appealing and handsome"

———

Lilly Carlyle, the Hollywood talent agent who discovered and built the late Cobey Daniels into a teenage mega-star, says that five-year-old Brad Cudahy will soon be the "biggest child star to ever hit TV."

As she did with the late Cobey Daniels, Carlyle sought permission to take the boy from his parents on an Illinois farm. After getting their agreement, Carlyle, who first saw Brad on a Chicago talent show, flew the boy to Los Angeles where he will live with her and receive the same kind of "special treatment" that Cobey Daniels enjoyed.

Of Daniels, all Carlyle would say was, "The pressures of fame were just too much for him."

Cobey Daniels was killed last year in a grisly Chicago murder.

"I'm really looking forward to living with Brad," Lilly Carlyle told our reporter enthusiastically. "There's so much he can learn from me."

OTHER SINISTER STORIES OF SHOW BUSINESS

SCREAM QUEEN

ALLOW ME TO INTRODUCE MYSELF. MY NAME'S JASON Fanning. Not that I probably need an introduction. Not to be immodest but I did, after all, win last year's Academy Award for Best Screenplay.

Same with my two friends, Bill Leigh the Academy Award-winning actor. And Spence Spencer, who won the Academy Award two years ago for Best Director. People with our credentials don't *need* any introductions, right?

Well . . .

That's the kind of thing we talked about nights, after Vic's Video closed down for the night and we sat around Bill's grubby apartment drinking the cheapest beer we could find and watching schlock DVDs on his old clunker of a TV set. Someday we were going to win the Academy Award for our respective talents and everybody who laughed at us and called us geeks and joked that we were probably gay . . . well, when we were standing on the stage with Cameron Diaz hanging all over us . . .

We had special tastes in videos, the sort of action films and horror films that were the staples of a place like Vic's Video.

If it's straight-to-video, we probably saw it. And liked it. All three of us were on Internet blogs devoted to what the unknowledgeable (read: unhip) thought of as shitty movies. But we knew better. Didn't Nicholson, Scorsese, De Niro and so forth all get their start doing low-ball movies for Roger Corman?

That's how we were going to win our Academy Awards when we finally got off our asses and piled into Spence's eight-year-old Dodge Dart and headed for the land of gold and silicone. We knew it would be a little while before the money and the fame started rolling in. First we'd have to pay our dues doing direct-to-video. We were going to pitch ourselves as a team. My script, Bill's acting, Spence's name-above-the-title directing.

In the meantime, we had to put up with working minimum wage jobs. Mine was at Vic's Video, a grimy little store resting on the river's edge of a grimy little Midwestern city that hadn't been the same since the glory days of the steamboats Mark Twain wrote so much about.

Even though we worked different gigs, we all managed to go hang at Bill's, even though from time to time Bill and I almost got into fist-fights. He never let us forget that he was the normal one, what with his good looks and his Yamaha motorcycle and all his ladies. We were three years out of high school. We'd all tried the community college route but since they didn't offer any courses in the films of Mario Bava or Brian De Palma, none of us made it past the first year.

I guess—from the outside, anyway—we were pretty geeky. I had the complexion problem and Spence was always trying to make pharmaceutical peace with his bi-polarity and Bill—well, Bill wasn't exactly a geek. Not so obviously, anyway. He was good-looking, smooth with girls and he got laid a lot. But he was only good-looking on the outside . . . inside he was just as much an outcast as the seldom-laid Spence and I . . .

Do I have to tell you that people we went to high school with smirked whenever they saw us together? Do I have to tell you that a lot of people considered us immature and worthless? Do I have to tell you that a big night out was at GameLand where we competed with ten and twelve-year-olds on the video games? If Spence was off his medication and he lost to some smart-ass little kid, he'd get pretty angry and bitter. A lot of the little kids were scared of us. And you know what? That felt kinda good, having somebody scared of us. It was the only time we felt important in any way.

And then Michele Danforth came into our lives and changed everything. Everything.

Spence was the first one to recognize her. Not that we believed him at first. He kept saying, That little blonde chick that comes in here every other night or so—that's Michele Danforth. But we didn't believe it, not even when he set three of her video boxes up on the counter and said, You really don't recognize her?

Michele Danforth, in case you don't happen to be into cult videos, was the most popular scream queen of all a couple of years ago. A scream queen? That's the sexy young lady who gets dragged off by the monster/ax-murderer in direct-to-video horror movies. She screams a lot and she almost always gets her blouse and bra ripped off so you can see her breasts. Acting ability doesn't matter so much. But scream ability is vital. And breast ability is absolutely mandatory.

The funny thing is with most scream queens, you never see them completely naked. Not even their bottoms. It's as if all the seventeen-year-old masturbation champions who rent their videos want their scream queens to be pretty virginal. Showing breasts doesn't violate the moral code here. But anything else—well, part of the equation is that you want your scream queen to be the kind of girl you'd marry. The marrying kind never expose their beavers except in doctors' offices.

Couple quick things here about Michele Danforth. She was very pretty. Not cute, not beautiful, not glamorous. Pretty. Soft. A bit on the melancholy side. The kind you fall in love with so uselessly. Uselessly, anyway, if your life's work is watching direct-to-video movies. And those sweet breasts of hers. Not those big plastic monsters. Perfectly shaped medium sized good-girl breasts. And she could actually act. All the blog boys predicted she'd move into mainstream. And who could disagree?

Then she vanished. Became a big media story for a couple weeks and then some other H-wood story came along and everybody forgot her. Vanished. The assumption became that some stalker had grabbed her and killed her. Even though she always said she couldn't afford it—scream queens don't usually make much more than executive secretaries—she had to hire a personal bodyguard because of all the strange and disturbing mail she got.

Vanished.

And now, according to Spence, she resurfaced 1500 miles and three years later. Except that instead of dark-haired, brown-eyed and slender, she was now blonde, blue-eyed and maybe twenty-five pounds heavier. With very earnest brown-rimmed glasses sliding down her nose.

We had to admit that there was a similarity. But it was vague. And it was a similarity that probably belonged to a couple of million young women.

The night the question of her identity got resolved, I was starting the check-out process when the door opened up and she came in.

She went right to the Drama section. I'd never seen her go to any of the other sections. Her choices were always serious flicks with serious actors in them. Bill and Spence had taken off to get some beer at the supermarket, the cost of it being way too much at convenience stores.

I'd agreed to the little game they'd come up with. I thought it was kind of stupid but who knew, maybe it would resolve the whole thing.

It was a windy, chill March night. She wore a white turtleneck beneath a cheap, shapeless thigh-length brown velour jacket. She was just one more Midwestern working girl. Nothing remarkable about her at all. She always paid cash from a worn pea-green imitation-leather wallet. Tonight was no different. She never said much, though tonight, as I took her money, she said, Windy. She went under the name Heather Simpson.

Yeah. Where's that warm weather they promised?

She nodded and smiled.

I rang up the transaction and then as I handed her the slip to sign, I nudged the video box sitting next to the cash register out in front of me. *Night of the Depraved* was the title. It showed a huge, blood-dripping butcher knife about to stab into the white-bloused form of a very pretty girl. Who was screaming. The girl was Michele Danforth. The quote along the top of the box read: *Depraved* to the Max . . . and scream queen Danforth is good enuf to eat . . . if you know what I mean!—Dr. Autopsy.com

Oops, I said, hoping she'd think this was all accidental. You don't want that one. I picked up the box and looked at it. I wonder what ever happened to her.

She just shrugged. I wouldn't know. I never watch those kind of movies. She took her change and said, I'm in kind of a hurry.

I handed her the right movie and just as I did so she turned toward me, showing me an angle of her face I'd never seen before. And I said, It's you! Spence was right! You're Michele Danforth!

And just then the door opened up, the bell above it announcing customers, and in came Bill and Spence. They'd left the beer in the car. Video Vic would've kicked my ass all the way over into Missouri if he ever caught us with brew on the premises.

She turned and started away in a hurry, so fast that she brushed up against Spence. The video she carried fell to the floor.

Bill picked it up. He must have assumed that I had played the little game with her—bringing up Michele Danforth and all—because after he bent to pick up the video and handed it to her with a mock-flourish, he said, I'm pleased to present my favorite scream queen with this award from your three biggest fans.

She made a sound that could have been a sob or a curse and then she stalked to the door, throwing it open wide and disappearing into the night. My mind was filled with the image of her face—the fear, the sorrow.

She'll never be back, I said.

I told you it was her, Spence said. She wouldn't have acted that way if it wasn't.

I wanna fuck her, Bill said, and I'm going to.

Spence said, Man, she's nobody now. She's even sort of fat.

Yeah, but how many dudes can say they bopped Michele Danforth?

Wait'll we get to La-La Land, Spence said, we'll be boppin' movie stars every night. And they won't be overweight.

Our collective fantasy had never sounded more juvenile and impossible than it did right then. In that instant I saw what a sad sham my life was. Shoulda gone to college; shoulda done somethin' with my life. Instead I was just as creepy and just as pathetic as all the other direct-to-video freaks who came in here and who we all laughed at when they left. Video Vic's. Pathetic.

Hey, man, hurry up, Bill said to me. I'll get the lights. You bag up the money and the receipts. We'll drop it off at the bank and then tap the beer.

But I was still back there a few scenes. The terror and grief of her face. And the humiliating moment when Spence had spoken our collective fantasy out loud. Something had changed in me in those moments. Good or bad, I couldn't tell yet. I got this sore throat.

Yeah, Bill said, it's such a bad sore throat you can't even swallow beer, huh?

Spence laughed. Yeah, that sounds like a bad one, all right. Can't even swallow beer.

I could tell Bill was looking at me. He was the only one of us who could really intimidate people. So what the hell's really goin' on here, Jason?

I sounded whiny, resentful. I got a sore throat, Lord and Master. If that's all right with you.

It's when I said I'm gonna fuck her, wasn't it? He laughed. In your mind she's still this scream queen, isn't she? Some fucking virgin. She's nobody now.

Then why you want to screw her so bad? I said.

Because then I can say it, asshole. I can say I bopped Michele Danforth. He looked at both me and Spence. I'll have actually accomplished something. Something real. Not just all these fantasies we have about going to Hollywood.

I shouldn't have done it to her, I said. We shouldn't have said anything to her at all. She had her own reasons for vanishing like that.

Yeah, because she was getting fat between movies and they probably didn't want her any more. He laughed.

Hard to tell which rang in his voice the clearest—his cruelty or his craziness. Bill was climbing out on the ledge again. Sometimes he lived there for days. Times like these, we'd get into shoving matches and near-fights.

Spence's attitude had changed. You could see it in his dark eyes. He'd thought it was pretty funny and pretty cool, Bill screwing a scream queen like this. But now I could tell that he thought it was just as twisted as I did. Bill always got intense when he went after something. But this went beyond intensity. He actually looked sort of crazy when he talked about it.

Maybe Jason's right, Bill, Spence said gently. Maybe we should just leave her alone.

The look of contempt was so perfectly conjured up, it was almost like a mask. So was the smirk that came a few seconds later. The Wuss brothers. All these fantasies about what great talents you are. And all the big times you're gonna have in Hollywood. And then when you get a chance to have a little fun, you chicken out and run away. We could all screw her, you know. All three of us. A gang-bang.

Yeah, I said, now there's a great idea, Bill. We could kill her, too. You ever thought of that?

Now who's crazy? All I was talking about was the three of us—

I was as sick of myself just then as I was of Bill. I was already making plans to go call the community college again. See when I needed to enroll for the next semester. I knew that maybe I wouldn't go through with it. But right then with Bill's mind lurching from a one-man seduction to a three-man rape . . . Prisons were filled with guys who'd had ideas like that. And then carried them out.

I got to finish up here, I said, working on the cash register again.

Yeah, c'mon, Spence, let's leave the Reverend here to pray for our souls. We'll go get drunk.

Spence and I had never been very good about standing up to Bill. So I knew what courage it took for Spence to say, I guess not, Bill. I'm not feeling all that well myself.

He called us all the usual names that denote a male who is less than masculine. Then he went over to a stand-up display of the new direct-to-video Julia Roberts movie and started picking up one at a time and firing them around the store. They made a lot of noise and every time one of them smashed into something—a wall, a line of tapes, even a window—both Spence and I felt a nervous spasm going through us. It was like when you're little and you hear your folks having a violent argument and you're afraid your dad's going to kill your mom and you hide upstairs under the covers. That kind of tension and terror.

I came fast around the counter and shouted at him. Then I started running at him. But he beat me to the door.

Good night, ladies. He stood there. Every time I see you from now on, I'm gonna punch your ugly faces in. You two pussies've got an enemy now. And a bad one. He'd never sounded scarier or crazier.

And with that, he was gone.

◆ ◆ ◆

It was misting by the time I got back to my room-and-a-bathroom above a vacuum cleaner repair store. I had enjoyed the walk home.

The mist was dirty gold and swirling in the chilly night. And behind it in doorways and alleyways and dirty windows the eyes of old people and scared people and drug people and queer people and insane people stared out at me, eyes bright in dirty faces. This was an old part of town, the buildings small and fading, glimpses of ancient Pepsi-Cola and Camel cigarette and Black Jack gum signs on their sides every other block or so, TV repair shops that still had tiny screens inside of big consoles in the windows for nostalgia's sake, and railroad tracks no longer used and stretching into some kind of Twilight Zone miles and miles of gleaming metal down the endless road. There was even a dusty used bookstore that had a few copies of pulps like *The Shadow* and *Doc Savage* and *Dime Detective* in the cracked window and you could stand here sometimes and pretend it was 1938 and the world wasn't so hostile and lonely even though there was a terrible war on the way. It was a form of being stoned, traveling back in time this way, and a perfect head trip to push away loneliness.

To get to my room you took this rotting wooden staircase up the side of the two-story stucco-peeling shop. I was halfway up them before I looked up and saw her sitting there. The scream queen. If the misting bothered her, she didn't seem to mind it.

She smoked a cigarette and watched me. She looked pretty sitting there, not as pretty as when she'd been in the movies, but pretty nonetheless.

How'd you find me?

Asked the guy at the 7-11 if he knew where you lived.

Oh, yeah. Dev. He lives about three down. I smiled. In our gated community.

Sorry I got so hysterical.

I shrugged. We're video store geeks. We can get pretty hysterical ourselves. You should've seen us at our first Trekkie convention in Spock ears and shit. If you had any pictures of us from back then, you could blackmail us.

She smiled. That's assuming you had any money to make it worthwhile.

I laughed. I take it you know how much video store geeks make.

I must've done three hundred signings in video stores. The smile again. It was a good clean one. It erased a lot of years. Most of you are harmless.

We could always go inside, I said.

◆ ◆ ◆

After I handed her a cheap beer, she said, I didn't come up here for sex.

I didn't figure you did.

She glanced around. You could fix this up a little and it wouldn't be so bad. And those *Terminator* posters are a little out of date.

Yeah. But they're signed.

Arnold signed them?

I grinned. Nah, some dude at a comic book convention I went to. He had some real small part in it.

She had a sweet laugh. Played a tree or a car or something like that?

Yeah, you know, along those lines.

She'd taken off her brown velour jacket. Her white sweater showed off those scream queen breasts real real good. It was unsettling, sitting so near a girl whose videos had driven me to rapturous self-abuse so many times. And I had the hairy palms to prove it. Even with the added weight, she looked good in jeans. I'll make you a deal, Jason.

Yeah? What kind of deal. I mean, since we ruled out sex. Much to my dismay.

Oh, c'mon, Jason. You don't really think I just go around sleeping with people do you? That's in the movies. This is straight business, what I'm proposing. I'll clean your apartment here and fix it up if you'll convince your two friends not to let anybody know who I am or where I am.

Spence won't be any trouble.

Is he the good-looking one?

That's Bill.

He looks like trouble.

He is.

She sank back on the couch—one night Spence and I managed to get a couple of girls up here and we all played a game of Guess the

Stain with the couch—and covered her face with her hands. I thought she was going to cry. But no sounds came. The only thing you could hear was Churchill, my cat, yowling at cars passing in what was now a downpour.

You OK?

She shrugged. Said nothing. Hands still covering her face. When she took them down, she said, I left LA for my own reasons. And I want to keep them my reasons. And that means making a life for myself somewhere out here. I'm from Chicago. I like the Midwest. But I don't want some tabloid to find out about me.

Well, like I say, Spence won't be any trouble. But Bill—

Where's he live?

I was thinking about what Bill had said about screwing a scream queen. Even if she wasn't a scream queen anymore. It didn't make much sense to me but it sure seemed to make a lot of sense to him.

Why don't I talk to him first?

She looked relieved. Good. I'd appreciate that. I'm supposed to start this job next week. A good job. Decent bennies and from what everybody says, some real opportunities there. I want to start my life all over.

I'll talk to him.

She was all business. Grabbing her coat. Sliding into it. Standing up. Looking around at the stained and peeling wallpaper and all the posters, including the latest scream queen Linda Sanders. She's a nice kid. Had a real shitty childhood. I hope she can beat the rap—you know, go on and do some real acting. I saw her at a small playhouse right before I left LA. She was really good.

I liked that. How charitable she was about her successor. A decent woman.

Churchill came out and rubbed his head against her ankle. She held him up and gave him that smile of hers. We both need to go to Weight Watchers, my friend.

He stays up late at night and watches TV and orders from Domino's when I'm asleep.

She gave him a kiss. I believe it.

She set him down, put out her hand and shook, that formal forced way people do in banking commercials right after the married couple agrees to pay the exorbitant interest rates. I really appreciate this, Jason. I'll start figuring out how I'm going to fix up your apartment. I live in this tiny trailer. I've got it fixed up very nicely.

You didn't screw her, did you? Bill said when he came into the store.

He'd been hustling around the place, getting the displays just so, setting up the 50% OFF bin of VHS and DVD films we hadn't been able to move, snapping Mr. Coffee to burbling attention. When I told him she'd come over to my place last night, he stopped, frozen in place and asked if I'd screwed her.

Yeah. Right on the front lawn. In the rain. Just humping our brains out.

You'd better not have, you bastard. I'm the one who gets to nail her.

At any given time Bill is always about seven minutes away from the violent ward but I couldn't ever recall seeing him this agitated about something.

She isn't going to screw anybody, Bill. Now shut up and listen.

Oh, sure, he said, now you're her press agent? All the official word comes from you?

She's scared, asshole.

Listen, Jason. Spare me the heartbreak, all right? She's been around. She doesn't need some video geek hovering over her. Then: That's how you're gonna get in her panties, isn't it? Be her best friend. One of those wussy deals. Well, it's not gonna work because she'll never screw a pus-face like you. You checked out your blackheads lately, Jason?

I swung on him, then. When my fist collided with his cheek, he gaped at me in disbelief, then sort of disintegrated, started scream-ing at me real high-pitched and all, as he stumbled backwards into a display of a new Disney family movie. Most surprisingly of all, he didn't come after me. Maybe I'd just stunned him. He'd always seen Spence and I as his inferiors—we were the geeks, according to him; he wasn't a geek; he was a cool dude who pitied us enough to hang out with us—and so maybe he was just in shock. His slave had revolted and he hadn't had time to deal with it mentally yet.

She's afraid you'll tell somebody who she is, I said. And if you do, you're going to be damned sorry.

And then I couldn't believe what I did. I hit him again. This time he might have responded but just then the front door opened, the bell tinkled, the first customer of the day, a soccer-mom with a curly-haired little girl in tow, walked in with an armload of overdue DVDs. Mrs. Preston. Her stuff was always overdue.

I had just enough time to see that a pimple of blood hung from Bill's right nostril. I took an unholy amount of satisfaction in that.

Michele didn't want to see me. She was nice about it. She said she really appreciated me talking to Bill about her and that she really appreciated me stopping by like this but she was just in a place where she wanted to be alone, sort of actually needed to be alone and she was sure I understood. Because that was obviously the kind of guy I was, the understanding kind.

In other words, it was the sort of thing I'd been hearing from girls all my life. How nice I was and how understanding I was and how they were sure, me being so understanding and all, that it was cool if we just kind of left things as they were, you know being just friends and all. Which is what she ended up saying.

As usual, I'd gotten ahead of myself. By this time, I had this crush on her and whenever I get a crush of this particular magnitude I start dreaming the big dream. You know, not only having sex but maybe her really falling in love with me and maybe moving in together and maybe me getting a better job and maybe us—it could happen—getting married and settling down just as the couples always do in the screwball comedies of the Thirties and Forties Bill and Spence always rag on me for liking so much.

Over a three-day period I must have called Spence eight or nine times, always leaving a message on his machine. He never called back. I finally went over there after work one night. He had a two-room apartment on a block where half the houses had been torn down. I was just walking up to the front door when Spence and Bill came out.

They were laughing until they saw me. Beery laughter. They'd both been gunning brew.

Bill was the one I watched. His hands formed fists instantly and he dropped back a foot and went into a kind of boxer's crouch. You got lucky the other day, Jason.

I don't think so, Bill. I think you got lucky because Mrs. Preston came in.

Spence's face reflected the disbelief all three of us were probably feeling. I couldn't believe it, either. I'd stood up to Bill the other day but I think both of us thought it was kind of a fluke. But it wasn't. I was ready to hit him again.

The only difference between the other morning and now was that he was half-drunk. Brew makes most of us feel tougher and handsomer and smarter and wittier than we really are. Prisons are packed with guys who let brew addle their perception of themselves. Or dope. Doesn't matter.

He came at me throwing a roundhouse so vast in scope it couldn't possibly have landed on me. All I had to do was take a single step backward.

I don't want to fight you, Bill. Spence, pull him back.

Whatever Bill said was lost in his second lunge. This punch connected. He got me on my right cheek and pain exploded across my entire face. He followed up with a punch to my stomach that doubled me over. Kick his ass, Bill, Spence said.

Even though I was in pain, even though I should have been focused on the fight I was in, his words, the betrayal of them, him choosing Bill over me when it should have been Spence and I against Bill—that hurt a lot more than the punches. He'd been my friend since third grade. He was my friend no longer.

Bill hit me with enough force to knock me flat on the sidewalk, butt first. If this had been the other night, I would've jumped to my feet and started swinging. But I was still hearing Spence say to kick my ass and I guess I didn't have enough pride or anger left to stand up and hit back. I just felt drained.

You all right? Spence said to me. I could hear his confusion. Better to stick with Bill. But still, we'd been friends a long time and to see me knocked down—

He's just a pussy, Bill said. C'mon.

I didn't stand up till they were gone. Then I walked home slowly. I took the long way so that I'd go past Michele's place. The light was on. I turned off the sidewalk and started moving toward the house but then I stopped. I wasn't up for another disappointment tonight.

Video Vic's real name wasn't Vic it was Reed, Reed Patrick, and when I called him next morning and gave him my week's notice, he said, You don't sound so good, kiddo. You all right?

I just need to be movin' on, Reed. I enjoyed working for you, though.

You ever want to use me for a reference, that'll be fine with me.

Thanks, Reed.

That night, I surprised my folks by showing up for dinner. Mom had made meat loaf and mashed potatoes and peas. I figured that was about the best meal I'd ever had. They were surprised that I'd quit my job but my dad said, Now you can start looking for something with a future, Jason. You could start taking classes again out to the college. Get trained for some kind of computer job or something.

Computers, honey, my mom said, patting my hand. Jobs like that pay good money.

And they've got a future.

That's right, Mom said, computers aren't going anywhere. They're here for good.

You should call out there tomorrow, Dad said. And my buddy Mike can get you on at the supermarket he runs.

I pretended to be interested in what he was saying. I'd never seemed interested before. He looked happy about me, the way he had when I was a little kid. I hadn't seen him look this happy in a long time. He also looked old. I guess I hadn't really, you know, just looked at him for a real long time. The same with Mom. The lines in their faces. The bags under their eyes. The way both my folks seemed kind of worn out through the whole meal. When I left I hugged them harder than I had in years. And all the way back to my little room, I felt this sadness I just couldn't shake.

Over the next week, the sadness stayed with me. I'd realized by then that it wasn't just about Mom and Dad, it was about me and everything that had happened in the past couple of weeks. I tried Michelle a couple more times. The second time she was real cold. You know how girls are when they aren't happy to hear from you and just want to get you off the phone. After I hung up, I sat there in the silence with Churchill weighing a ton on my lap. I felt my cheeks burn. It was pretty embarrassing, the way she'd maneuvered me off the phone so fast.

The next night, no longer gainfully employed, I walked over town to the library. I was reading the whole run of George R.R. Martin fantasy novels. He was one of the best writers around.

Even though they'd bought six copies of his new hardcover, they were all checked out. I picked up a collection of his short stories. He was good at those, too.

On the walk back home, I saw them coming out of a Hardee's. He had his arm around her. They were laughing. I was ready to fight now. Just walk right up to him and punch him in the fucking chops. He'd be the one sitting down on his butt this time, not me. And I'd remind her that she still owed me an apartment cleaning.

Good ole Michele and good ole Bill. That's the thing I've never understood about girls. Hard to imagine a guy more full of himself than Bill. But she thought obviously he was just fine and dandy. Otherwise she wouldn't let him have his arm around her. He was going to sleep with her and then he was going to tell everybody. I wondered how she'd react if I told her.

But I couldn't. Much as I wanted to go over there and tell her what was really going on, I couldn't make my legs move in that direction. Because I could live with my self-image as a geek, a loser, a boy-man but I could never live with myself as a snitch.

A few days later I signed up for computer classes at the community college. I gave up my room on the rent-due day and moved back home. The folks were glad to have me. I was being responsible. Dad said his buddy Mike could get me on at his supermarket and so he had.

What I did for the next few nights, after bagging groceries till nine o'clock, was glut myself on the past. I still had boxes of old *Fangorias* and *Filmfaxes* in my old closet and I hauled them out and spread them on the bed and just disappeared into my yesterdays, back to the time when there was no doubt that I was going to Hollywood, no doubt that I'd be working for Roger Corman, no doubt that someday I'd be doing my own films and no doubt they'd be damned good ones.

But my time machine sprung a leak. I'd get all caught up in being sixteen again and grooving on *Star Wars* and *Planet of the Apes* and *Alien* but then the poison gas of now would seep in through those leaks. And I'd start thinking about Michele and Bill and Spence and how my future seemed settled now—computer courses and a lifelong job in some dusty little computer store in a strip mall somewhere—and then I'd be back to the here and now. And not liking it at all.

On a rainy Friday night, my mom knocked on my door and said, Spence is downstairs for you, honey.

I hadn't told my folks about the falling out Spence and I had had.

I just said OK and went down to see him. He was talking to my dad. Dad was telling him how happy they were about my taking those computer courses.

I grabbed my jacket and we went out. I hadn't so much as nodded at Spence. In fact, we didn't say a word until we were in his old Dodge Dart and heading down the street.

How you been? he said.

Pretty good.

Your dad seems real happy about you being in computer classes.

Yeah.

You don't sound so happy, though.

What's this all about, Spence?

What's what all about?

What's what all about? What do you think it's all about? You took Bill's side on this whole thing. Now you come over to my house.

He didn't say anything for a while. We just drove. Headlights and neon lights and street lights glowed like water-colors in the rain. Girls looked sweet and young and strong running into cafes and theaters to get out of the downpour. His radio faded in and out. Every couple minutes he'd slam a fist on the dash and the radio would be all right again for a few minutes. The car smelled of gasoline and mildewed car seats.

He's getting really weird.

Who is?

Who is? Who do you think is, Jason? Bill is.

Weird about what?

About her. Michele.

Weird how?

He's really hung up with Michele. He won't tell me what it is but somethin's really buggin' him.

I'm supposed to feel bad about it?

I'm just telling you is all.

Why? Why would I give a shit?

He glanced over at me. I shoulda stuck up for you with Bill. The night he knocked you down, I mean. I'm sorry.

You really pissed me off.

Yeah, I know. And I'm sorry. I really am. I—I just can't handle being around Bill anymore. This whole thing with Michele. She's all he talks about and she won't let him do nothin'. He says it's like bein' in sixth grade again.

I wasn't up for just driving around. I'd done enough cruising in my high school years. I said, You seen that new Wes Craven flick?

Huh-uh.

There'll be a late show. We could still make it.

So you're not still pissed?

Sure I'm still pissed. But I want to see the Wes Craven and you're the only person I know who's got a car.

I don't blame you for still bein' pissed.

I don't blame me for still bein' pissed, either.

I didn't hear from Spence till nearly a week later. After the Craven flick, which was damned good, he started talking about other things we could do but I just told him I was busy. Sometimes, friendships, even long ones, just end. One thing happens and you realize that the friendship was never as strong as you'd thought. Or maybe you just realize that you're one cold, unforgiving prick. Whichever it was, I wasn't up for seeing Spence or Bill or Michele for a long time. Maybe never.

I went my glum way to computer classes and my even glummer way to the supermarket.

◆ ◆ ◆

He was in the supermarket parking lot waiting for me when I got off work. I walked over to his car. It was a warm, smoky October night. Big ass harvest moon. I wanted to be a kid again in my Halloween costume. I could barely—just quite—remember what it had been like to go trick or treating before the days when perverts and sadists hid stick pins and razor blades in candy apples.

I walked over to the driver's side of his car. I wanted to walk home. October nights like this were my favorites.

Hey, he said.

Hey.

You doin' anything special?

Yeah. Nicole Kidman called. She wants to go get a pizza with me. She said she'll pay for it. And the motel room afterward.

Remember to bring a condom.

She's got me covered there, too. She bought a big box of them.

We just looked at each other across an unbreachable chasm of time and pain. He'd been a part of my boyhood. But I wasn't a boy anymore. Not a man yet, to be sure. But not a boy, either.

He's pretty fucked up.

We talking about Bill?

Yeah. Had the day off. Drinking beers with whiskey chasers.

Good. We need to drink more. Make sure we're winos before we hit twenty-five.

I think maybe we should go over to Michele's place.

Why?

He stared at the passing cars. When he looked back at me, he said, You better get in, Jason. This shit could be real bad.

It was one of the little Silverstream trailers that are about as big as an SUV. Except, given its condition, this one should have been called Ruststream. It sat between two large oak trees on a corner where a huge two-story house had been torn down the summer before. The rest of the neighborhood blazed with laughter and throbbing car engines and rap music and folks of both the black and white persuasion filling porches and sidewalks, most of them trying to look and sound like bad asses. Her trailer was a good quarter block from its nearest neighbor.

Bill's motorcycle leaned against one of the trees. No lights, no sound coming from the trailer.

Maybe he's getting the job done, Spence said.

Maybe, I said.

The door was open half an inch. I opened it wide and stuck my head in.

What the fuck you think you're doin'?

I couldn't see him at first, couldn't see anything except vague furniture shapes. Smells of whiskey and cigarettes. A cat in the gloom, crying now.

Get out of here, Jason.

Where's Michele?

Where you think she is, asshole?

I wanna talk to her.

I told you once, Jason. Get out of here. I knocked you on your ass once. And I can do it again.

No, you can't.

Two steps led up to the trailer floor. I was about to set my right foot on the second step when he came at me. My mind had time to register that he was wearing jeans, no shirt, no socks, and he had a whiskey bottle in his hand.

He tackled me and drove me all the way to the ground. He meant to hit me with the whiskey bottle but I had the advantage of being sober. He smelled of puke and booze and sex and greasy food, maybe a hamburger.

As the bottle arced downward, I rolled to the right, moving slowly enough to slam my fist hard into the side of Bill's head. The punch dazed him but not enough to keep him from trying to get me again with the bottle. This time I didn't have time to move away from it. All I could do was grab the wrist and slow the bottle as it descended. It connected but not hard enough to knock me out. Or to stop me from landing another punch on the same side of his head as before. This one knocked him loose from me. His straddling legs loosened enough to let me buck him off. He went over backwards. He was drunk enough to be confused by all this happening so quickly. Now it was my turn to straddle him. I just wanted to make his face bloody. I hit him until my hands started to hurt and then I stood up, grabbed him by an arm and started dragging him to his motorcycle.

Go get his stuff from inside, OK? I said to Spence.

He nodded and ran over to the trailer. He didn't need to go inside. Michele was in the doorway, dropping Bill's shoes, socks, shirt and wallet one by one into Spence's hands. She wore a white terrycloth robe. She had a cigarette going. You stay with me for a while, Jason? she said.

Sure.

By now, Bill was on his motorcycle, roaring it to raucous life. Spence handed him his belongings.

Spence said, Looks like her nose is busted, man. You do that?

Shut the fuck up, Spence, Bill said. Then he made his bike louder than I'd ever heard it before. Bill glared at Spence for a long time and said, I don't know what I ever saw in a pussy like you, Spence. Don't call me anymore.

You beat her up, man. You don't have to worry about me callin' you.

He roared away, grass and dirt churning from beneath his back wheel. He got all the way down the block before I said anything. I'll just walk home later.

Wait'll you see her, Jason. He beat the shit out of her.

He walked back to the street and drove away.

The light was on in the front part of the trailer now. She was gone from the door. When I sat down at the small table across from her, she pushed a cold can of Bud my way. I thanked her and gunned an ounce or two. My head hurt from where he got me with the bottle. She'd fixed up her trailer just the right way—so that you forgot you were in a trailer.

Her delicate nose didn't look broken, as Spence had said, but it was badly bruised. She had a black eye, a bloody, swollen mouth and her left cheek was bruised.

Maybe you should go to an ER, I said.

I'll survive. She made an effort to laugh. I let him sleep with me but that wasn't enough for him.

What the hell else did he want?

Well, he slept with me but I wouldn't take my bra or my blouse off. I said I had my reasons and I wanted him to respect them. In some weird way, I'd started to like him. Maybe I was just lonely. I never could pick men for shit. You should've seen some of the losers I went out with in LA. My girl friends always used to laugh and say that if there was a serial killer on the dance floor, he'd be the one I end up with for the night.

So you made love and—

We made love. I mean, it wasn't the first time. The last couple weeks, we'd been sleeping together. And he tried real hard to deal with me not taking my top off. I wouldn't let him touch my breasts. She smiled with bloody teeth. My scream queen breasts. She shook her head. Or tried. She was halfway through turning her head to the left when she stopped. She had a bad headache, too, apparently. It was building up. His thing about my breasts. And tonight, afterwards, he just went crazy. Said if I really loved him I'd be completely nude for him. I liked him. But not enough to trust him. You know, with my secret.

She lighted a cigarette with a red plastic lighter. I'd never seen her smoke before. She looked around a bit and then back at me and said, It's why I left LA.

What is?

I don't have breasts any more. I had this really bad kind of breast cancer. I had to have both of them removed. She exhaled through bloody lips. So how would that be? A scream queen known for her breasts she doesn't have any more? I went to Eugene, Oregon to get the diagnosis. I kind've suspected I had breast cancer. I didn't want anybody in LA to know. I paid cash, gave a fake name, they didn't have any idea who I was. I had the double mastectomy there, too. I had some money saved and I used it to disappear. I just couldn't've handled all the publicity. All the bullshit about how my breasts inspiring all these young boys—and then not having them anymore. You know how the tabloids are. And then do a couple weepy interviews on TV. So I've just been traveling around. And I'll be doing more traveling tomorrow. Because I know Bill will call some reporter or tabloid or somebody like that. I just don't want to face it.

She said, C'mere, OK?

I stood up and walked over to her. My knees trembled. I didn't know why.

She took my right hand and guided it to her chest and then slid it inside the terrycloth so that I could feel the scarring from the mastectomy. I wanted to jerk my hand away. I'd never felt anything like that before. But then a tenderness came over me and I let my hand linger and then she eased my hand out of her robe and kissed my fingers, as if she were grateful.

Then she started sobbing and it was pretty bad and I said everything I knew to say but it didn't do any good so I steered her into bed and just lay with her there in the darkness and we held hands and she talked about it all, everything from the day she first felt the tiny lump on the underside of her left breast to being so afraid she'd die from the anesthetic—she'd had an uncle who died while being put under, died right there on the table—and how she went through depression so bad she lost twenty-five pounds in three months and how that then turned around and become the opposite kind of eating disorder, this relentless urge to gorge, which she was battling now.

In the morning, I helped her load her car. She didn't have all that much. I told her I'd pay the rent off with the money she gave me and return the key. She kissed me then for the first and only time—the kind of kiss your sister would give you—and then she was gone.

The story hit one of the supermarket papers three weeks later. She'd been right. The whole thing dealt with the irony of a girl who'd been made into a scream queen at least partly because of her beautiful breasts—and then losing them to cancer. A minister somewhere said that it was God's wrath, exploiting your body for filthy Hollywood money, and then getting your just desserts. You know how God's people like to talk.

As for me . . . tomorrow I'm flying to LA. My dad has a friend out there who owns a video company that produces training films for various companies. Not exactly Paramount pictures, or even Roger Corman. But a start. My folks even gave me five thousand dollars as seed money. They're pretty sure that in a year I'll be back here. And maybe they're right . . .

It's funny about Michele. I watch her old videos all the time. That's how I prefer to remember her. It's not because of her breasts. It's because of that lovely girly radiance that was in her eyes and her smile back in those days.

I still watch them and I'm sure Spence does, too. He got a job in Chicago and moved there a couple months back. Bill joined the Army. I wonder if he still watches them.

But most of all I wonder if Michele ever watches them. Probably not.

Not now, anyway. But maybe someday.

RIFF

JUST BEFORE DAWN I WAKE UP AND LISTEN TO THE hushed sounds from the room next to mine. When I hear these particular sounds at this particular time on a cancer floor in a hospital—three or four rushed whispering voices; faint squeaks of gurney wheels; and then elevator doors opening down the hall, eight floors down to the basement and the morgue—I know what's happened.

Charlie Grady died. I'd see him a couple times a day on my little walks up and down the hall. The nurses don't make me walk. I do it on my own.

I sort of knew Charlie wasn't going to hang on much longer. His wife was talking to a hospice woman but I figured Charlie wouldn't make it even that long. He was a nice old guy, real estate rich, never asking me the standard questions I get about my so-called fame. In fact, he said right out one day that he didn't care much for jazz. And he hoped that didn't offend me. His kind of money can give you that kind of confidence. He didn't give a damn if it offended me or not.

His wife is a weeper. She came twice a day to see him—his lung cancer and his eighty pounds overweight were shaping up to bring on one massive heart attack—and she never left but she was wailing. I sure don't blame her. She loves her man. But that doesn't make it any easier to take when you're in the room next door and trying to deal with your own problems. Health-wise, I mean. And every-other-wise, for that matter.

I have a 7:00 AM visitor, right after the doc making his rounds leaves my room. Guy named Larry Donnelly. Kind of a fix-it guy for jazz folk. Very serious jazz cat, Larry is. Really got into it in the slam where he served ten years for torching a building with a janitor still in it. Larry had no idea, of course. I called Larry a couple of days ago, asked him to stop up. He hesitates in the doorway now. Some people get like that about cancer. Scared. Like it's a plague you can pick up. "C'mon in, Larry."

◆ ◆ ◆

He's only there ten minutes. And is kind've junkie-twitchy all the time. Can probably feel the cancer working its way through his veins as he stands there trembling. Then he's gone.

I fall back asleep and wake up for a second time. This time it's the nurse with the rattling breakfast cart. They keep telling me to eat but my appetite has gone with all the rest of it. I'm in pretty much the same shape as Charlie Grady was. Except mine's in the pancreas. I'm hoping I'm as lucky as Charlie. A heart attack like that, you're one lucky man. And so are your loved ones. Quick and clean. Instead of hanging on.

Hanging on.

That's what I've done with my wife Karen the last five years. Met her in a jazz club in Chicago. She was a singer, then. Not much of one.

But she had the Look. That slender body, that melancholy face, the dark eyes, the tumbling dark hair. She was from Omaha but she made you think international. Paris in spring, where I gigged with Brubeck. And London in autumn, where I gigged with Miles. Milan, baking in the summer while we were working on my live album. I dumped wife number four for her, just as I'd dumped all the old ones for new ones. I never said I was proud of myself. But you get on the road, you're six, seven months out from seeing the wife and the kiddies, you're just naturally going to fall in love with somebody else.

What I didn't know that night in Chicago was that it was payback time. I'm sitting in the back of this tiny, drafty club and people are coming up asking for my autograph and if she isn't singing they ask me did I dig playing with Brubeck, was Miles as much of a diva prick as people said, was my label ever going to do a box set of my music— and hey, that was one fine article in *Time*, "The Legend of The Saddest Sax in Jazz History: Mike Thorne." It was actually the usual thing, that *Time* piece, how I'd managed to survive and prosper in a music world dominated by rock and rap, and how I was the Chet Baker of my time—handsome, media friendly and probably the best sax man of the past two decades. Thank God, the article concluded, that I never got hooked on junk the way poor Chet had. You read about Chet, man, and you want to cut your wrists.

So I'm sitting there trying to be nice to the people who come up but I'm paying more and more serious attention to this singer Karen Miller. The clarity of her beauty is astonishing.

Between her sets, I ask her over to my table for a drink. I can see how flustered she is. Mike Thorne, fifty-three-year-old jazz legend, asking twenty-two-year-old nobody to have a drink with him.

I get to play the cool dude that night. I'm properly humble when she's flattering me, I'm properly appreciative when we talk about her own performance, and I'm properly matter-of-fact when I drop some big jazz names I'm meeting later that night for drinks. What I am really is so smitten I'm like I was at the tenth grade dance when I could never quite work up nerve enough to ask Marietta Courtney to dance slow with me.

But that wasn't what was really going on at all. Subtext they call it. You know, where it seems like you're really saying this but you're really saying that, just below the surface.

What I was really doing was setting myself up for payback. For every time I'd ever cheated on a woman, for every promise I'd broken to my three daughters, for every heartbreak I'd caused—old numero uno was about to get his. Maybe this Karen Miller from Omaha couldn't sing worth a damn. But she sure knew how to lie, cheat, steal, betray and humiliate you.

If there is a Green Beret unit of heartbreakers and ballbusters, Karen Leigh Miller of Omaha, Nebraska was Commander-in-Chief.

◆ ◆ ◆

Thirty-eight years I play clubs. When I'm in my prime I'm hitting Letterman and Leno and guest playing on albums by big rock stars who want the cachet of having a jazz star on their CD. They don't know diddly about jazz but they think it sounds cool to the reviewers.

This is when I start collecting jazz memorabilia. I'm in places where Satchmo and Charlie Parker and Gerry Mulligan and people like that have played and so I start buying up things they left behind in the clubs and that the club owners might otherwise throw out in a box in the back.

This is also the time I get the critics on my back for playing Vegas. Just once, for God's sake. I don't have a right to make a fucking living? I can't take the scorn. A serious jazz musician playing Vegas as the opening act for some jiggle-titted TV star who thinks she can sing?

Karen digs it, of course. Me being in Vegas. While I'm on stage, she's sitting at a table out front with Cameron Diaz and Bruce Willis, who are in town shooting a picture together. Your regular jazz clubs—the kind I usually play in—you don't get Cameron Diaz and Bruce Willis, let me tell you.

Sam Caine is with them, too. Sam is my agent and manager. I met him twenty years ago when he was just one of the many hungry young men you see running up and down the halls of William Morris in search of clients who might have stumbled and fallen and would appreciate the hungry young man who helped pick them up.

Sam was then the assistant to my agent. By the time I decide to do a lot of my own booking, Sam is a full-fledged agent who is just about to open up a small shop of his own. He wants clients, I'm sick of big agencies. I handle most of the small gigs, he books the big ones. He's a failed actor, our Sam. You always hear about how many beautiful failed wanna-be actresses there are in Hollywood. There are an equal number of beautiful failed wanna-be actors.

Sam has no interest in jazz. He's a club lizard. If you can't hustle chicks while it's being played, Sam doesn't want to hear it. But he's funny and shrewd and gets me bookings I couldn't get for myself.

The years go by, my CDs aren't selling the way they used to, Letterman and Leno's people don't return Sam's calls, and you know what? By now, I don't care. I'm married to Karen.

The fourth year of our marriage, I learn three things.

1) Karen has spent most of the nearly two million dollars that was for my retirement. You should see our house, our cars, her clothes. It sounds like a joke but two million isn't what it used to be. My accountant keeps saying you gotta do something about this, Mike. But I never do. I'm scared she'll leave me. That started the second year, the way she'd get whatever she wanted by saying, just kind of off-handed, "I've gotta be honest, Mike. Sometimes, I wonder if we did the right

thing." And of course I'd give in and say, sure, baby, buy whatever you want. She went right straight through my money.

2) I find a note that she threw away in the tiny basket next to her dressing table—you could land a fighter jet on that table; an aircraft carrier should be so lucky to have that room—and right away I see what it says. And right away I recognize the handwriting. Now, I know she's had little nights when she's strayed. A couple of her boys got so hot for her they even broke the rules and called the house for her. I listened in on the extension. The first couple of times, I literally rush to the john and throw up. Now I know what I put all those women through. This time somebody else is holding the gun. But I don't confront her. It's the same with the money she spends. If I confront her, she'll leave me. But this time it's different. This time it's Sam and in the note he talks about how much they're in love. I do a lot of throwing up for several days running. And that's not so unheard of, you know. They say when Sinatra caught Ava Gardner cheating on him, he started puking around the clock, lost his voice, and ended up trying to kill himself.

3) I start losing weight. My skin color changes. Nothing drastic. But there's a peculiar faint yellow tone. The maid—of course we have a maid—she's the first one to say anything. She says I should see a doctor right away. All I can think of though is Karen and Sam. It was only a week ago that I found the note. The maid is insistent; and then Karen starts in on me about how I'm looking all of a sudden. I go to the doctor, there are so many tests I lose count at twelve, and the diagnosis is pancreatic cancer. Now I'm in the hospital. I hear Karen and the lady from the hospital in the hall the other day. "A cancer like this," the hospice lady says, "it never takes long, Mrs. Thorne."

◆ ◆ ◆

Karen says, "You really look good in those pajamas, Mike."

"Thanks for getting them for me, honey."

Night. You know how it is, night in a hospital. You can always tell the rooms where death has no dominion. There's laughter and maybe grandkids and a lot of plans about what's going to happen when the patient finally gets out of here. But the other rooms—there's a whispery quality and a tension and long terrible aching silences and both sides prepare themselves for the flap flap flap of houseslippers that come down the hall in the middle of the night. An elderly obscene gent who puts his gnarled papery hand in yours and leads you into a world you cannot fathom.

Sam says, "You sound a lot better than you did last night."

"Yeah, I thought I'd go dancing later."

Karen laughs, leans over and gives me a little kiss. They're on opposite sides of my bed. "Oh, honey, it's so good you've kept your sense of humor."

Sam looks at his watch. "Well, guess I'll push off, Mike. But I'll be back tomorrow."

They've been here fifteen minutes. Talk about strained conversations.

What he's going to do, of course, is go downstairs and wait for her. She'll stay another ten, maybe fifteen minutes and then leave.

I notice the strain on Sam's face. The strain isn't entirely because of the situation with Karen. He's lost his three biggest clients this year. The sniffling sounds he makes—nobody wants a coke head for an agent. Sam's deep in debt. Deep.

"Take care, Mike," he says and leaves the room.

"He's such a good friend to you," Karen says after he leaves.

"Loyal," I said. "Nobody more loyal than Sam."

I say that staring right into those elegant violet eyes of hers. She looks uncomfortable. "Yes, loyal."

The tone sounds. Visiting hours will be over in ten minutes.

As she bends over to me for her goodnight kiss, I see a moment of distaste in her eyes. I got a glimpse of myself this morning. I'm a lurid dirty yellow color. Even my eyes have a yellow tint to them. I've lost twenty-six pounds in just under seven weeks.

"You're all I think about, babe," she says.

"Yeah," I said. "You're all I think about, too."

"You're such a good husband," she says. And the tears come right on time. FedEx delivers them. You can order them in pints, quarters or gallons. "Such a good husband."

Fondling her hand. "And you're such a good wife."

The tone rings again and she says, "I'll see you tomorrow night. I thought I'd run up the coast tomorrow. See Shirley."

The good friend "Shirley" she's been talking about for three years. I've never met "Shirley" because she doesn't exist.

She gives me a peck on the cheek and then gives me another look at those pure glistening tears you order from FedEx. And then she goes.

◆ ◆ ◆

Larry calls just after nine. He knows better than to say anything meaningful. He just says, "Just wanted to say it was good seeing you today, Mike. Guess I'll have me a beer and watch the news."

"Sure wish I could have a beer," I say. "Guess I'll just have to settle for the news."

It's the fifth story on the ten o'clock news. "The home of jazz legend Mike Thorne was destroyed by fire tonight. First estimate is that everything was destroyed, including his collection of jazz memorabilia said to be worth between two and three million dollars."

Good job, Larry.

Karen and Sam would've sold the memorabilia first. The collection would've brought more like four instead of the three the anchorman said. The house was worth another million-and-a-half by now, with all the improvements she put in it. Insurance money is sweet.

But I canceled the policy last week. No insurance on the house, no insurance on my memorabilia.

◆ ◆ ◆

I wake up near dawn again. Sweet Ruth Andrews this time. Two doors down. Breast cancer. The gurney, the whispers, the elevator to the morgue downstairs.

I lie in darkness, waiting my turn.

SUCH A GOOD GIRL

NICOLE

NICOLE SANDERS WENT TO THE NURSE'S OFFICE DUR-
ing third hour and put on a pretty good imitation of a genteel
seventeen-year-old girl down with the flu, genteel meaning a
quiet, pretty girl who was still a virgin, had never tried drugs in any
form, and read Cousin Bette for relaxation.

Of course, it helped that she was a good student (usually, a four
point average), and generally perceived as a reliable girl. Nobody on
the staff of Woodrow Wilson High School would suspect her of faking
flu so she could get off from school. She had a near-perfect attendance
record. She just wasn't the kind to lie.

But lie she did.

In the parking lot, she climbed into the sensible little forest green
Toyota Gran had bought her for her seventeenth birthday last month.
Gran was her best family friend now. Dad was off in California with
his new wife. And Mom . . .

"I sure hate to see you come down with this stuff," the nurse said sweetly.

She headed home. This late in the morning, the expressway traffic was heavy. The sometimes foggy March rain didn't help, either.

Home was a nice Tudor in a small, upscale suburb of nice Tudors and nice Spanish styles and nice multi-level moderns. Mom had gotten the house in the divorce settlement. Dad made a lot of money at his law firm and he'd inherited quite a bit when his father died several years earlier.

Nicole didn't stop at her house. She went down to the end of the block and parked behind a stand of pin oaks that was part of a small park-like area.

The cop-show phrase for what she was doing was "stakeout." She'd heard her mother call in sick this morning—she was a far better actress than Nicole and had put on a breathtaking performance—and now Nicole wanted to see what her mother did all day. As she'd passed by the house, she'd seen her mother's car in the drive. So Mom hadn't gone anywhere. Yet. And if Mom did go somewhere, Nicole had a terrible feeling that she knew where it would be . . .

MITCH

"I really think Mamet sold out. You know, when he went out to La-La-Land."

It was a good thing she had a lovely pair of breasts because otherwise Mitchell Carey would have kicked her ass out of the apartment as soon as he got done screwing her last night.

He'd picked her up at a cast party. A small theater group had put on an ancient Mamet one-act. It was the sort of theater group that attracted the worst kind of pretentious wannabes and the worst kind of cruising idle rich, the rich seeing theater groups (correctly) as being ripe with sex, drugs and just about any kind of octopus-like emotional entanglement a man or woman could want. It was from the idle rich, a few of whom were Mitch's customers, that he'd heard about the play; so, having made the club scene earlier in the evening, having played his role as the handsome, fortyish Jay Gatsby to the disco and angel dust crowd, he decided to pop in on the theater folk. He'd stayed only long enough to meet Paula and woo her back to his den, whereupon he'd defiled her with great desperate pleasure. He hadn't merely screwed her, he'd ravished her and it had been wonderful. Three times they'd made love before heating up the remnants of a Domino's pizza lurking in his refrigerator. Then they'd found a great old Lawrence Tierney B-movie flick on a cable channel, *San Quentin*, and only after it was over and they were back in bed again with the lights out, only then did she start talking about herself (age 39, born in Trenton, New Jersey, three husbands, worked as a street mime and part of a comedy group ala Second City, had in fact come here to Chicago to get into Second City but so far no luck, look at Jim Belushi, she said, only reason a no-talent like him ever got in was because of his brother and everybody knew it) but by then he'd put a finger in his ear and switched the HEARING button to Off. By the time she got to voicing her plans to audition for the revival of Cat on a Hot Tin Roof at the Ivanhoe ("I lose a little weight, and wear violet contact lenses like Liz Taylor, and learn how to talk Southern, I think I'd make a great Maggie 'The Cat,' don't you?") he was blissfully asleep.

But now it was morning and she was standing naked at the sink in the bathroom while he was toweling off from his shower. And she was talking about how Mamet had sold out. Like Mamet would really give a shit about her opinion.

Then he noticed the time on the face of his Rolex that he'd set down on the tiny hutch next to the towel closet. He bought the best, man. Noticed the time and remembered his appointment. He had a customer he needed to meet at eleven-thirty. And it was now a quarter to eleven.

"I've got to hurry," he said. "I just remembered an appointment."

She was putting on her lipstick. She had remarkable lips. "I hope we're going to do this again," she said, still drawing the blood tube across her mouth.

"Absolutely."

She glanced at him skeptically in the mirror. "For real?"

"For real."

"I hate bullshit promises. I'd rather have you say you won't be calling again than, you know, stringing me along."

"I'm not stringing you along."

"We did this Cole Porter show in Denver, you know? And anyway there was this guy and that's all he ever did. We spent one night humping like bunnies and the rest of the run, he'd call me to make a date and then call me back to break it. I guess I should be happy he at least *called* to tell me he was standing me up."

"You've sure had an interesting life."

She glanced at him in the mirror again to make sure that he wasn't putting her on. "Really?"

"Really."

She seemed satisfied. "You know, I wouldn't mind blowing you before we trundle off."

"That's all right. I really am late."

He could never figure out why he felt so good at night with them in the bed and so bad—and so sad—with them in the morning when they were getting ready to go.

What he needed was some kind of new kick. Ennui was the word he wanted. Ennui was what he was suffering from. He made a nice living, he got all the ass a reasonable man could want, and yet he was a little bored. Something new was what he needed.

But there wasn't any time for navel-contemplation this morning. Had to hurry. He had an eleven-forty-five customer.

KATE

Thank God she'd been smart enough to take her watch along yesterday. Over noon, she'd hocked it. Place not far from the office where she worked in Lincoln Park. Guy with a glass eye and bad BO appraising both the watch and Kate herself. The watch he didn't have any problem with. Knew the exact market value. What he could pay out, what he could take in. The exact market value of the woman standing in front of him was another matter. Tall, elegant, beautiful in a nervous, vulnerable way. But going fast. Probably no more than forty-three, forty-four or so but going fast. He seemed to know why, too. Four-hundred, she got. Four-hundred.

Their house is shrinking. That's how she thinks of it. The last time after coming out of rehab and being a good little girl, the last time she fell off she hocked the TV, the stereo, the good china and the good silver. She'd had a good run. This was in the summer, Nicole visiting her father and his teenage-bride (Gwen is twenty-three, actually) for a month. Kate started hitting the clubs again, feeling good and young again. Sleeping around a little (always safe sex, of course), even developing a quick crush or two on younger men, the kind who used to be all over her, even when she was married, giving her ultra-conservative ex-husband one more reason to treat her like a whore. She could still remember the night a year into their marriage, that she'd told him about this little habit she had, which was where a lot of her household budget was going, and how he looked so dashed and doomed. It was almost comic, the way he looked right then, so shattered but self-righteous, too, as if it was impossible that anybody he'd even associate with could possibly be a junkie. A beautiful girl, the daughter of a powerful state senator, a Radcliffe grad, a suburban siren of stunning seductiveness, a coke head? There ensued eleven years—she had to give him that, he hung in there for eleven years—of one rehab program after another, trendy clinics and experimental programs all over the country. She'd gone as long as a year-and-a-half clean and sober, as they say. So much hope, so much anger, so much fear, so much despair, so much failure, hope-anger-fear-despair-failure, the same cycle over and over again. He never quite believed that she couldn't help herself. At least that was how she saw it. He never quite believed that she truly *tried* to kick once and for all. Poor sweet Nicole, she believed. That's why she was losing weight all the time and going into these terrible depressions (she'd been twelve when she took her first Prozac) and staying in her room practically every weekend when her mother was using. She could have joined her father in LA with his new bride but she feared for her mother, feared that if she went to California, her mother would die somehow. So she stayed. "You're such a good girl," her mother was always saying. Kate looked pretty good. The bones were the secret. She had good bones. Killer cheeks and a mouth that was erotic and just a wee bit petulant. Not enough to put men off. Just enough to intrigue. And the bod, even twelve pounds lighter than it should have been, the bod was good, too.

Four-hundred dollars in her purse and a day free of Mr. Cosgrove, her boss at the public relations agency, an egomaniacal twit who was always broadly hinting that she should go with him on one of his business trips east.

And on top of that, she would soon be seeing her old buddy Mitch Carrey.

Life was beautiful. Life was good.

NICOLE

In the daylight hours, the jazz clubs and the art galleries and the odd little shops of Lincoln Park lost some of their nocturnal allure. A wild wailing sax sounded better carried on the wings of neon than on the gritty breezes of daytime. And crumbling brick facades had no romance to offer even the dullest of tourists.

Nicole followed her mother to a restaurant called The Left Banke, the intentional misspelling too clever by half. Good student Nicole knew that the original Left Bank in Paris, home to the cubists and the impressionists, not to mention Ernest Hemingway and Gertrude Stein, had probably been pretentious but at least had spared its tourists coy restaurant names.

Mom was driving the four-year-old Buick. The last time she'd gone off, she'd been forced to sell the Mercedes-Benz station wagon to make house payments. Nicole never told her father any of these things. She got tired of his sanctimony. Her mother suffered enough. At the meetings Nicole attended a few years ago, she learned that she was probably what the social workers called an enabler; i.e., she helped her mother keep up her habit. But what was the choice? What would happen to her mother if Nicole didn't help her? Easy enough for them to say let your mother hit bottom and find her own way back up. But what if the bottom was death? How could Nicole live with herself? She had tried everything to get her mother to stop. A year ago, she'd even cut her own wrists and been rushed to the hospital and put in the psychiatric clinic for three days of observation. Now, she was working on her own last, desperate plan, a way to force her mother to turn herself back into rehab and this time—Oh please God, please God, let it work for her this time—start on a life without cocaine. But first she had to find one thing out . . .

Her mother didn't get out of the Buick.

Just sat inside as the light rain started.

Slick new cars disgorged slick new people running in their Armani suits through the rain, laughing and swearing as they reached the canopied entrance.

And her mother just sat inside the Buick.

He drove an old red MG, the steering column on the right side. He wore a tweed jacket in honor of the MG. He even had a pipe stuck jauntily in the corner of his mouth. He looked like a soap opera's impression of a sensitive British novelist: dark, shaggy hair, and an angular face handsome but with a hint of cruelty in the eyes and mouth. He parked next to her mother and then quickly got out of the MG and hopped into the driver's side of the Buick.

KATE

"You look tired, Mrs. Sanders," Mitch said when he got in the Buick and looked over at her.

"I have a pusher who calls me 'Mrs. Sanders,'" Kate said, a touch of desperation in her voice. "Is my life fucked up or what?"

"You know," Mitch said, "this makes the third time I've had to warn you. And right now, with the rain and all, I'm in a pissy enough mood to just open this door and walk back to my car and not sell you anything at all."

"Oh, God," Kate said, genuinely scared. "I forgot. I used the P word, didn't I?"

"Yes, you did."

And he had indeed warned her before. About the P word. P for Pusher. He'd explained his circumstances. What he was: Mitchell Aaron Carey. What he hoped to be, with his looks and all, was an actor. And he'd tried hard for several years, too. All the humiliating auditions. All the even more humiliating little jobs around the various theaters (he'd actually scrubbed toilets at the Astor one weekend). Now he was just taking it easy. Doing "favors" for upscale people afraid of or put off by the usual array of street people who dealt drugs. How many pushers could give you twenty minutes on Aristotle's theory of drama? How many pushers had ever had a two-line part in a Woody Allen picture? How many pushers had Chagall prints hanging on their walls? He was no pusher. He was just an actor temporarily between gigs making a little jack on the side, and being very, very civilized about it.

"God, I'm sorry. I really am."

He smiled. "I guess I really don't feel like going back out into the rain right now."

"I brought the money."

"You're kind've strung out, huh?"

"Yeah. Yeah."

He was torturing her a little for having called him a pusher. "You thinking of maybe doing a line right here?"

"You wouldn't mind?"

He smiled again. "You're a good looking woman, Kate."

"Thank you." But it wasn't compliments she wanted. It was the stuff.

"In fact, I've been thinking about you a lot lately."

"You have?"

"Yeah," he said, and reached in the pocket of his stylish leather car coat. He took the stuff out and showed it to her. "Yeah. I've been thinking about you quite a bit lately."

NICOLE

She followed him home. Watched him park. Watched him go up to his apartment. Then went into the vestibule and checked his name on the mailbox. The only male name on the four mailboxes.

She didn't feel quite ready for it yet. Tomorrow. She'd sleep on it. Sleep on it and think it through and kind of rough out how she'd approach him. Tomorrow was Saturday. No school. Tomorrow would be better.

When she walked in the house, her mother was dusting the living room and actually humming a song.

Nicole got tears in her eyes. This was her mother of long ago, before she'd discovered cocaine at a Los Angeles party ten years ago. She'd been there with her husband, visiting his relatives, and they'd ended up at a party in Malibu and she'd been drunk and up for just about anything—the party showing her just how much of her youth and adventurousness she'd had to give up as the wife of a neurosurgeon and so unbeknownst to Ken she'd tried it—and now she was happy only when she was stoned.

Dusting. And whistling. With the wonderful scent of a pot roast floating out of the kitchen.

She was Mom again. Nicole couldn't help herself. She flew to her and took her in her arms and suddenly they were both crying without a single word having been said, just holding each other. And then Mom said, "You're such a good girl, Nicole. And I love you so much."

◆ ◆ ◆

Nicole didn't sleep well. She kept waking up and thinking about what she was going to say to Mitch Carey.

Her plan was simple. She would tell him that if he continued to sell her mother cocaine, she would turn him over to the police. She believed—hoped, was the more precise word—that if her mother was cut off from Mitch's supply, then she'd panic and turn herself back to rehab. And this time it would work. This time it *had* to work. Absolutely had to.

Carey would be pissed but what could he do? He certainly didn't want to go to jail.

Mom made pancakes for breakfast. Blueberry pancakes. The kind she'd made back when Nicole was a little girl, and Mom and Dad were happy.

"I guess I'll go study at the library," she said, after finishing breakfast and putting the dishes in the dishwasher. "I'm going to do some more cleaning," Mom said. Then grinned. "It's kind of fun being a Stepford wife again. Now all I need is a Stepford husband."

Ninety-three minutes later, Nicole pulled her car into a slot behind Carey's apartment house. The interior stairs of the place smelled of rubber and paint. A new runner had been put on the steps and new paint on the walls. Whoever managed this place, they took care of it.

Carey answered the door out of breath and with a white nubby towel wrapped around his neck. He wore a tight white T-shirt and blue running shorts. A Stairmaster stood in the background. Classical music played. Carey had a strong, tight body.

"Yes?"

"I'm Nicole. Kate Sanders's daughter."

He looked surprised. "Is everything all right? Nothing happened to Kate did it?"

"No," Nicole said. "It's just that I'm thinking of turning you over to the police."

This time, he looked even more surprised. He grabbed her by the wrist and pulled her inside. "Hey, we don't have to invite the neighbors in on this, do we?" His nod indicated the three other apartment doors on this floor.

The apartment was impressive in a cold and calculated way. The furnishings were chrome and black leather, with a white and black tile floor and walls painted a brilliant flat white. The only touches of color belonged to the modernistic paintings on the walls. Nicole knew even less about painting than she did about classical music. This was the kind of room that intimidated her with her own ignorance.

Carey had quickly regained his composure. The panic and anger were gone from his eyes. He said, "Care for some wine?"

"No, thanks."

She had let two boys get their hands down her pants and play with her sex. At a ninth grade slumber party she had taken three drags on a joint. And she had looked at a couple of porno videos her mom and dad used to play when they thought she was upstairs asleep. This was the extent of her licentiousness. Drinking wine at this time of day was out of the question. Or any time of day. Wine always made her dizzy, and usually made her sick.

"Why don't you sit down over there on the couch and let me shut the machine off?"

He clipped off the Stairmaster and then wiped his face and neck again with the towel. He took the matching chair across from the couch. He sat on the edge. He kept pulling on both ends of the towel, biceps shaping as he did so. She knew this was for her benefit.

He said. "So you turn me over to the police, Nicole, and then what?"

"Then she gets so scared without her supply that she decides to try rehab again."

"I see."

"And this time she'll make it."

"So that's the plan, huh?" There was just a hint of a smirk on his mouth.

"That's the plan. I don't want you to sell her any more cocaine."

"What do I tell her when she calls?"

"Just tell her that you're not in the business any more. That you're scared of the police or something like that."

He looked at her and smiled. "If I ask you a question, will you answer it honestly?"

"If you'll turn down the music. It's pretty loud."

He was up and at the CD player in seconds. "Not a Debussy fan, eh?"

"Maybe some other time."

When he was seated again, he said, "Have you ever seen her happy when she wasn't doing coke?"

"Of course I have."

"I realize you think you're being honest. But think hard for a moment. And be honest with yourself."

She saw what he was getting at. Her mother was miserable when she was clean and sober. That, Nicole had to admit. She'd look at her mother and she'd look miserable. Tense, lost, angry, anxious. And late at night, she'd hear her mother sob. And there was almost never a smile. Or any expression of joy. Her life was simply a matter of not using cocaine. And she did not share the pride or the pleasure that others seemed to take in her not doing this.

His phone rang. "Think about it, kiddo." He reached over to a glass end table and picked up the phone. And said. "Hi. I've got company." He laughed. "Actually, yes, it is somebody you know. Your daughter."

Then, "I take it you haven't told her." Pause. "Then that'll be my pleasure, I guess." Pause. "I'll call you in a while."

After hanging up, he said, "She said she hadn't had time to tell you yet. She wanted to wait for the right moment, I guess."

"Tell me what?"

"She's taking in a boarder."

"A what?"

"You know, a roomer."

"Who?"

He grinned. "Me. I'm going to be living with you for a while."

MITCH

In the first week, Nicole took all her meals in her room. She barely spoke to her mother, and she wouldn't speak to him at all. She spent several Friday and Saturday nights staying over at her friends' houses.

Mitch enjoyed the setup. He was tired of all the artistes and pretenders he'd hung out with the past ten years. It was enjoyable to get up in the morning and have a home-cooked meal and then spend a few hours "blocking out" a novel. That's what he called it, blocking out. Taking notes and filling up lined pages with blue ballpoint ink. Such and so would happen in Chapter Six, such and so would happen in Chapter Ten and so on. He liked to think he was editing a film, moving this scene from here to here. The writing itself, after all this preparation, was bound to be simple. Or so he told himself. Of course, in ten years, he'd actually never written a word of text. But what the hell. That really would be the easy part.

He stayed in a basement room that was fixed up for guests.

He had his own bathroom and shower and TV set. He even had his own entrance, right on the side. His MG fit nicely into the third stall of the garage. He walked around the neighborhood on the sunny days. It was like being in a sitcom, all the neighbors tending their lawns and waving to him, the sounds of friendly dogs and driveway basketball, the aromas of backyard cookouts and fresh hung laundry on outdoor lines.

This was the change he needed. No doubt about it. He had business to tend to but that took two, three hours at most a day. Had to keep his hungry little junkies hungry, and had to resupply his own stash with his own wholesaler. He always liked to tell people he was in retail, and so he was. This was the change he needed. A new kind of lifestyle. He felt invigorated, young.

He went easy on the sex, mostly for the sake of Nicole. If she found her mother in bed with him, she'd freak. Absolutely freak. She was a very pious little thing, sweet Nicole. Kate said she got the self-righteousness from her father. She said that was one reason she was so glad their marriage was over, so she didn't have him in her face all the time dispersing rules with a ferocity that would have put Moses to shame.

One rainy Saturday night, with Nicole sleeping over at a friend's house, he nailed her. She was as hungry for sex as she was cocaine. She was damned good: knowing, patient, clever and seemingly tireless. At one point, he rolled off the bed and lay on the floor laughing and screaming "Call 911! I can't take it any more!" And then she'd started laughing, too, and jumped off the bed, landing right on top of him. They spent an hour on the floor violating every silky hot orifice in her body.

He kept her coked up, and she kept him sexed up. At first, the first three-four weeks, they were discreet. Wouldn't want little Nicole to find out now, would we? They waited until she was gone before they did anything. There were a lot of nooners, Kate rushing home from the office for a line or two of coke and a ripping good time in the sack.

One night, when Nicole was upstairs in her room doing homework, they decided to do it in his room in the basement. It was like high school, the sneaking around, Nicole the stern repressed Midwestern parent, and them the fuck-happy teenagers. She didn't catch them. The next night and the next night and the next night and the next night, they did the same thing, Nicole working on her homework and them humping in the basement. God, it was great, and the danger made it just that much more delicious.

One Saturday afternoon, she caught them.

Nicole had come home early from the library, tired from a long day's studying. They didn't hear her. They were having too much fun in Kate's bedroom. But Nicole heard them. She flung the door open and stalked into the bedroom and went over to him and grabbed him by the long, dark hair. A handful came off in her grip. She pushed him off the bed and to the floor and shrieked, "I want you out of here! And I mean right now!"

Humiliated, enraged, Kate flew from the bed and slapped her daughter hard several times across the face, hard enough to draw blood.

Nicole spat at her, silver spittle hanging comically on the end of Kate's classical nose, and then stormed out of the bedroom, and out the house.

She didn't come home that night.

Kate started calling all her friends. None had seen her. Mitch said that she was just punishing Kate, trying to scare her. Everything would be fine. He cooed, he cajoled, he caressed, and he finally got Kate back in bed. But the little bitch had spoiled his evening for him. Kate just wasn't there for him that night. Oh, they had sex all right, but there was none of her usual passion or ingenuity. It was like screwing a hooker who was having an off night. The little bitch really pissed him off. He was enjoying his suburban sojourn. He didn't want it ruined by all these mother-daughter politics.

She didn't come home until Monday after school. By then, even stoked up on coke, Kate was a nervous mess. Pacing. Biting her nails. Jumping every time the phone rang.

The little bitch.

She pulled in just as dusk was making it a better world. She sat in her car in the garage a long time. Kate wanted to go out there. Mitch wouldn't let her. "That's what she wants you to do."

"I've been such a terrible mother to her, Mitch. I really have." She was begging him to let her go out to the garage. But by now, Mitch was genuinely resentful of the little prig. She resented him because he'd usurped her place as head of the family. Without him here, Nicole would be giving the orders. That's how it was in some junkie homes. The older kid took over and became the parent while the parent became a pathetic child. A power thing. Nicole had enjoyed the power. Now Mitch had the power. And he wasn't about to give it up.

She finally came in an hour later. She didn't say anything. Didn't even look at them. She just went straight up to her room and quietly closed her door. Kate spent the night fluttering around Nicole's door like a moth around a summer night's streetlight. But it did no good. Nicole wouldn't acknowledge her in any way.

Kate wouldn't come down to the basement, not this night or the next or the next. Kate pleaded with Nicole to speak to her. But Nicole came in the door at night and went straight to her room and reappeared only the next morning, in time to go to school. She wouldn't even say goodbye.

Mitch took it for a week, feeling helpless and sorry for himself. He did not like being at the mercy of the little bitch. She was spoiling his time with middle America. But Mitch, failed artist, failed husband, failed father, failed son, was nothing if not ingenious.

Mitch had a plan.

NICOLE

She finally gave in, of course. Nicole.

Mitch was out somewhere. Mom was sitting in the kitchen. Drinking coffee. She looked great. The coke was killing her but it was a trade off. While she was dying, Kate looked better than she had in a long time, and was in a much better mood, too. Nicole poured herself a cup from Mr. Coffee and then came over and sat down at the kitchen table. The sunlight was bright and lazy in the air.

Neither of them said anything for a time. For this uneasy moment, they were strangers.

"You been all right, Nicole?"

"Yes. You?"

"This would be a very happy time for me if my daughter and I were getting along."

"Are you in love with him?"

Kate smiled. "God, no."

"But you sleep with him, anyway?"

"I *enjoy* him, honey. And part of that enjoyment is sex."

"And the drugs."

"Have you noticed how much happier I am? I mean, until you and I had our falling out?"

Nicole nodded.

"Have you noticed how much better I look?"

"I know what you're going to say, Mom. But you're wrong. The coke may make you feel better right now but it'll kill you eventually."

"Maybe that's not the worst thing, Nicole. To die, I mean. I enjoy the high, hon. I don't know how else to say it. When I'm high. I'm fine. And when I have my own pusher living right in my own home—" She smiled. "A junkie's dream."

"You shouldn't call yourself that, Mom."

"Well, that's what I am."

"You don't have to be."

"I'll never go back to another rehab program, Nicole. I don't want to be one of those zombies who just hangs on her whole life, trying to put off taking another line of coke. It's not a way to live. Especially since Mitch is right under my own roof."

"He doesn't care about you, Mom."

"And I don't care about him. Except that he keeps me happy with his drugs, and satisfied with his sex. You're old enough to understand that, Nicole."

"So I just live here with you?"

"You'll be leaving for college in California in four months. Then you won't have to worry about it any more." Then, "Don't you want me to be happy, Nicole?"

"You know I do."

"Then let me live the way I want to, hon. Then you can go away to college and not have to worry about me anymore."

"Oh, right. I go away to college and then I magically never worry about you anymore? It doesn't work that way, Mom. In case you hadn't noticed."

"Just be civil to him. That's all I ask. He doesn't like the way you and I are carrying on. Just be civil so he can enjoy himself while he's here."

Nicole carried her cup to the sink, washed it out, put it in the washer.

Then she went over and slid her arms around her mother and they hugged each other and they both cried and Kate said. "I just want to be happy and feel good for a little while, honey. That's all."

Nicole held her and kissed her. Tears filled her eyes.

A few minutes later, she was in her car and headed to the library. She had things to do.

◆ ◆ ◆

Two nights later, the three of them ate dinner together at the long, mahogany table in the dining room. Candlelight, of course. Lasagna with fresh peaches and Caesar salad, Nicole's favorite meal, lovingly prepared by Kate after work. Dinner was late, but the food was delicious.

"How was school today?" Mitch said.

Nicole looked at her mother. Her mother looked frightened.

"Mitch, I'm going to try and get along with you for Mom's sake, all right? But don't pretend you're my father. Or that you're interested in my life. All right? I mean, that's really a pain in the ass."

Mitch laughed. "I hate to disappoint you. But I'm not old enough to be your father, Nicole. I'm only fourteen years older than you are."

"I thought you said you were thirty-nine," Kate said.

He patted her hand. "I only said that to make you feel more comfortable. I'm thirty-two."

"Maybe you're lying to make Nicole feel more comfortable," Kate said, not entirely pleased by this sudden turn in the conversation.

Mitch smiled. "Yes. Maybe I am."

◆ ◆ ◆

And so it went. One week, two weeks. A family. That's what Kate pretended was happening, anyway. That the three of them were somehow bonding. Watching her like this made Nicole so sad she couldn't even cry. She'd just sit stunned for hours staring out the window of her bedroom at the dusk birds sailing down the salmon pink sky, arcing black shapes against the dying days, beings whose freedom Nicole could only envy.

MITCH

It was during Mitch's fourth week in the house that he cut Kate off. Unbeknownst to both Nicole and Kate, this was the plan he'd been working on for the past few weeks. He wanted to dominate his circumstances completely. And there was only one way to do that.

One afternoon, late, Kate came home from work tense and showing signs of needing her friend the white powder. Long day at work, the boss on her case, two of her coworkers in particularly grumpy moods. She related all this as she stripped out of her clothes and lay down on the bed with Mitch. Ordinarily, Mitch would have been right there with the coke. But not today.

When he didn't offer, she said, "I could really use a little boost, Mitch." That was her coy name for it. "Boost."

"You do for me, I do for you."

Her head had been on his naked chest. Now she rolled away from him and looked at his face. "Is something wrong?"

"You do for me, I do for you."

"I don't know what you're talking about." She was already getting a little shaky. "Please, Mitch, I don't mind playing games, but give me a little boost first, all right?"

He leaned over on an elbow and looked at her. "This is a good time for you, isn't it, Kate?"

"Yes. You know it is, Mitch."

"Me here. You getting a 'boost' whenever you need it. And the sex isn't bad, either."

"The sex is great."

"And you don't want it to end, do you?"

A flutter of fear in her eyes and her voice. "Don't want it to end? What're you talking about, Mitch? Why would it end?"

He hesitated. Went into one of his Acting 101 routines. Looked down at the nubby bedspread, looked up at her briefly, then looked down at the nubby bedspread again. Troubled young man. Searching for the right words. Pure ham. But most of the ladies loved it. He said, in barely a whisper. "I'm going to ask you to do me a favor and you're going to get all pissed off and self-righteous and probably throw me out."

"I'd never throw you out, Mitch. God, I wouldn't, I wouldn't."

Impish grin. "That's because I haven't asked you my favor yet."

"Just ask me, Mitch. Just ask me."

So he asked her.

"Oh, Mitch." she said. "I should've known you were pulling one of your jokes on me. Get me all scared the way you did."

"It isn't a joke, Kate."

"C'mon, now, Mitch. I know how you like to put me on."

"No put on, Kate. I'm very serious."

"But you *can't* be serious."

But then she saw that he was serious.

And she got all pissed off and self-righteous and demanded that he leave the house right now. And for good.

A number of the neighbors commented on the screeching, dish-throwing, foul-mouthed argument that ensued within the walls of the Sanders place but that could be heard as far as half a block away. It went on like this, grand-opera style, for at least an hour. The neighbors hadn't heard arguments like that since the good doctor, her ex-husband, had moved out. Things must be going badly with her live-in.

Things must be going very badly.

NICOLE

When Nicole got home that night, she found her mother at the kitchen table, her head down on her hands. Something was terribly wrong. She used to sense that when she was a little girl and her dad was still living at home. She'd come home after school in the echoes of one of their arguments and her stomach would knot up and she'd feel alone and scared, scared that one of them might have killed the other, and she would start to shake and cry and say little prayers over and over again that everything would be all right.

A half-filled bottle of J&B scotch sat on the table in front of her. One glass. No ice.

Kate looked up at her wildly in the wan glow of the kitchen stove light. She was inching back toward her bag-woman demeanor, the hair wild and ratty, the eyes sunk deep and rimmed with black circles, the mouth slack with sparkling spittle collected in the corners. She'd been at work today. How had she accomplished all this just since work?

She was sitting in her bra and panties, with her long, lovely legs crossed. She was swinging her right foot to a rhythm only she could hear.

Nicole sat across from her. "Where's Mitch?"

"You're late."

"I was over at Sherry's."

"You should've called."

"I want to know what's going on."

"Nothing's going on."

"Bullshit, Mom. Bullshit."

Kate sighed. "I kicked him out."

"Why?"

"Because he's an asshole."

"That isn't an answer, Mom."

"It is for me. I kicked him out because he's an asshole. That sums it up pretty damned well, I think."

"You're shaking all over. He didn't give you a boost?"

"Screw his boost. I don't need his boost."

Mitch's words came back to her. About how happy her mother had been when everything was going well between her and Mitch. How he'd get all the boosts she wanted. How she kept herself looking, great. How she was productive and happy. This was already like the old days. It was scary and sad. And not for the first time in her life did Nicole think of getting the gun out of her mother's dresser drawer and putting it in her mouth and killing herself. Many, many nights during the divorce, she'd thought of doing this.

"You want me to fix you something to eat?" Kate said. Her words, her manner put a melancholy smile on Nicole's face. "Oh, yeah, Mom, you're in great shape to cook. One more drink of scotch and you'll pass out."

"And that's just what intend to do, too. And don't you try to stop me."

Nicole sat there with her and watched her take one more drink. A good, big one. All the while muttering about how much better her life would be now that the asshole was out of it.

Nicole managed to get her to the downstairs john before she started throwing up. Then she managed to get her upstairs and in bed. Kate started snoring immediately. Nicole clipped the light off and went back to the kitchen. She fixed herself a tuna sandwich on toast and had a few chips and a diet Pepsi. She cleaned up the kitchen and went to bed. But she didn't sleep. She wondered what had gone wrong with Mitch and her mother.

The deterioration was pretty fast. Nicole could remember a time when it took her mother five or six days to get to the screaming, stomach-clutching, glass-smashing state in need of a boost.

This time, she made it in two days. She didn't go to work either one: the first day, she didn't even get out of bed.

Nicole missed another day of school.

She got in her car and drove over to a section where she was sure she could find plenty of drugs. She'd taken three hundred out of the ATM machine. She wasn't sure how much drugs cost but she figured that three hundred would be enough to buy something.

The trouble was that the street people scared her. She was always seeing TV news stories about car-jackings. Even with her doors locked, she didn't feel safe. She cruised the black streets but the angry curiosity of the faces—spoiled little white girl from the suburbs, what the fuck she doin' down here, fuckin' bitch—soon pushed her back onto the expressway.

She would have to convince her mother to go into the detox program run by one of the local hospitals.

But by the time she got back home, she found her mother drunk and belligerent. And the moment she brought up detox, her mother went into one of her violent frenzies.

Nicole stayed in her room all night.

The next morning, she called in sick to school and went to see Mitch.

He was using his Stairmaster again. Blue running shorts, white T-shirt. He didn't bother playing the suave host this time. He invited her in. He kept working out on the machine.

"Let me guess why you're here," he said. His tone was sardonic.

"You were right."

"I was? About what?" He was sweating and panting a little bit.

"My mother was very happy while you were there. The happiest I've seen her in a long, long time."

He smiled icily. "And you want me to come back."

"Yes."

He looked at her. "She tell you why I left?"

"No. Just that you'd had a fight. I thought maybe you'd tell me."

"I don't think so."

"I'd better let your mother tell you."

"I'm a big girl, Mitch. I can take it."

He smiled. "You go ask your mother."

"I want you to come back, Mitch. I'm sorry if I acted like a bitch. You made her happy."

He came off the machine so quickly, she was hardly aware of him at first. Sliding his arms around her back and waist, finding her mouth with his tongue, easing her against the wall so that she could feel his groin pressing against her.

She pushed against him but he was too strong. She tried bringing her knee up but he knew how to block it.

Finally, she bit his tongue. He fell back from her, cursing, dabbing his tongue with the tip of his finger. Then he laughed. "I knew you were a tough one, Nicole." He held up his finger. "Blood."

She walked to the door. Jerked it open. Walked out into the hallway. Slammed the door behind her.

◆ ◆ ◆

When she came in the back door, she saw several empty glasses smashed on the floor. Mom had been on a rampage again, the need getting overwhelming.

She went upstairs. Sobbing sounds came from the large bedroom.

A weariness came over her. It was odd to be this young and yet be so worn out. She felt as if she were ninety. On the way over, she'd thought about Mitch grabbing her and kissing her. Then she'd thought about the argument Mitch and Mom had had. She had a pretty good idea now what it had been about.

She stood outside the door a long moment and listened to her mother cry. Only a few days ago, Mom had looked young and vital again. And was busy and productive. True, there were peaks and valleys in her mood and addiction level, but on balance life was good and happy again.

You couldn't beat having a live-in pusher, she thought. She went into the bedroom. Kate peeked at her from behind a hand that lay against her face. "Go away. I don't want you to see me like this."

"I need to talk to you a minute, Mom."

"I can't talk now, honey. I'm sick. My whole body. Sick. You go downstairs or something."

"I think I know what you and Mitch were arguing about." She sat down on the bed. Took her mother's hand. Held it to her own face. She could feel warm tears on the hand.

"I want to thank you, Mom."

"For what, hon?"

"For not asking me to do it."

Kate didn't say anything.

Nicole said, "He wanted me to sleep with him, didn't he?"

Kate didn't say anything.

"That's what you had the argument about, wasn't it?"

Kate didn't say anything.

"If I agreed to sleep with him, then he'd stay and keep you in drugs. That way, when he got bored with you, he'd sleep with me."

"He isn't a bad person, sweetie. He just looks at sex different from how we do."

"He's a creep. He took advantage of you and now he wants to take advantage of me." She kissed her mother's hand. "Thanks for not asking me to do it."

"I knew how you'd feel about it, honey."

"I appreciate it." She gently put her Mom's hand back on the bed and said, "Why don't I make you a little soup?"

"I don't know if I could hold it down."

"At least, let's give it a try." She hesitated. "Then I want to talk to you some more about rehab, Mom. You can't go on like this."

Kate looked beyond exhaustion. Something had died in her. The gleaming eyes, the happy voice of a few days ago were gone. "Maybe that's what I need. Rehab, I mean." She spoke in a dazed voice, staring tearily out the window. "Maybe I should quit fighting it."

"Why don't you take a little nap? I'll bring the soup up in a half hour or so."

Kate held her arms out. Nicole slid into her sleep-warm embrace.

Nicole was watching the MTV Top Ten countdown. Eight of the songs were rap, with sneering black guys pushing their faces into the camera. Nicole was too romantic for rap. She liked the ballads, especially by the black girl groups, who were as romantic as the boys were unromantic.

She yawned. She was exhausted and looking forward to bed. Three hours ago, she'd served her mother chicken soup and a glass of skim milk. She'd tucked her into bed and turned on the electric blanket. When Kate was in withdrawal, she got the chills bad.

She was just about to click off the TV with the remote when the gunshot exploded and echoed.

Her first impression was that something had blown up. Stove. Or water heater. Something like that.

But in the next moment, she realized what had really happened. Gunshot. The gun from Mom's drawer. Upstairs. Mom.

Fear blinded her.

She took the steps two at a time, tripping on the last of the stairway, grabbing the banister to keep from falling over.

Mom Mom Mom, she kept thinking.

The master bedroom was empty.

The smaller bedroom was empty.

She ran into the bathroom.

Her mother, completely naked, vomit covering her chest and stomach, her head twisted drunkenly to see Nicole, sat on the edge of the bathtub, a gun in her right hand. The top of her head was dusted with plaster from the hole in the ceiling that the bullet had made. A half-full bottle of J&B lay at her feet.

Nicole could never remember her this far gone. She stared at Nicole but with no recognition whatsoever showing in her eyes. Huge goosebumps covered her arms and legs. "No more fucking detox, kiddo," she said to no one in particular. "No more fucking detox."

She raised the gun to her temple. Or tried to. The movement was jerky and imprecise and gave Nicole plenty of time to grab her mother's wrist and ease the gun from her hand.

Then her mother began sobbing. She slipped to the floor, reeking of her own vomit and urine, wild-eyed and aggrieved beyond Nicole's imagining, slumped trembling and dryheaving and crying on the pink bathroom rug.

Nicole knelt next to her mother but it did no good. Kate wrenched herself away. "I fucking hate you, you little snotty bitch! You want to put me back in rehab! I fucking hate you!"

Nicole tried several times to console her mother but finally gave up. Her mother had slipped into a fetal position and started muttering to herself in a language and cadence only she could understand. If even she could comprehend it.

Only a few days ago, this had been a happy woman.

Nicole slipped quietly from the bathroom, and went and made a phone call.

They were in the kitchen. Nicole and her mother. At the table. Drinking coffee. This was six hours after the shower incident. Kate had showered, eaten half a sandwich, and begun drinking black coffee as fast as Mr. Coffee could turn it out.

And, most important of all, Mitch had given her a boost.

Nicole had called Mitch. He'd agreed to come over. He'd brought a large suitcase. He'd agreed to try it again, with Kate and all, for a few days.

Mitch was upstairs now, in the master bedroom, waiting for Nicole.

"You don't have to do this, you know," Kate said. "You really don't."

"It was *my* decision, mother."

"I mean, you know how appreciative I am. And he is very good in bed, honey. And he promised me he'd be very, very gentle and take his time. You could do a lot worse, your first time."

"I'd better get up there. He's waiting."

"He's really not a bad guy, hon. He's really not." Then, "What're you going to wear?"

"Just my pajamas, I guess."

"Too bad you never liked sleeping gowns."

"I like sloppy old pajamas, Mom. They're comfortable to sleep in."

"You're so pretty." Kate touched her daughter's cheek. "And you're such a good girl."

Nicole looked upstairs. "Well, I'd better go."

She was just leaving the kitchen when her mother said, "You really don't have to do this, you know."

He was in bed. Propped up against the headboard. No shirt. Glass of wine. Cigarette going in the ashtray. A PBS concert of some kind on the tube. This was a very nicely appointed bedroom.

He smiled at her. "You looked scared, Nicole. I'm not the boogeyman. I'm really not."

"I'm not sure what I'm supposed to do."

He raised his wineglass. "Well, first of all, I want you to chill out a little. You know what I mean? Relax. Believe it or not, you just might enjoy this. Kate tells me you're a virgin. Is that true?"

"More or less."

"Oh-oh. Was there something you never told your mother?" The smile firmly in place.

"I've never gone all the way, if that makes me a virgin."

"Well, that certainly makes you a virgin in my book." He patted the bed next to him. "Why don't you come over and sit down next to me. I want you to like me, Nicole. I really do. We could have a very nice relationship. We really could."

"The three of us, you mean?"

"Sure, the three of us. Or just the two of us—and me—*and* the three of us. You and I would have one relationship, Kate and I would have another relationship. You see what I mean? And maybe sometime— He paused.

"Maybe sometime what?"

"Oh, we'll talk about it later, maybe. For now, pour yourself some wine and sit down here and let's get to know each other a little better. All right?"

He was gentle.

A couple of times, she even found herself if not exactly enjoying it then not exactly not enjoying it.

She'd had all these preconceptions. That it would hurt a lot. That there would be a good deal of blood. That she would feel deeply changed by the experience.

None of these things happened to her.

They made love twice. They started on a third time but then he asked her gently if she'd mind doing him. The doing scared her more than the actual intercourse. She hated doing him and when she sensed he was going to come, she jerked him out of her mouth. She felt angry that he came all over her mother's bedspread.

He lay back and pulled her down to him, holding her. He lit a cigarette.

"So, do you hate me?"

"I don't want to talk about it."

"I tried to be gentle."

"You were gentle."

"I tried to be nice."

"You were nice."

"I was hoping you'd feel a little better about me, you know, after we'd done it and everything."

She said nothing.

"You hear what I said, Nicole?"

"I heard."

"So, do you feel any better about me?"

She said nothing.

"Guess you don't want to talk, huh?"

"I'd like to go to my own room now."

"Sure, if that's what you'd like." Then, "You know what I'd like?"

"What?"

"You remember when I said 'maybe sometime.'"

"Yes, I remember."

"Well, what I was thinking about was the three of us getting together all at the same time."

"My mom?"

"Yes."

"And me?"

"Uh-huh."

"Having sex with you?"

"It could be a lot of fun. I mean, I admit is sounds a little over-the-top at first. But when you think about it, it isn't all that raunchy. I mean I'm sure it's been done before."

She stood up. She felt sick.

It would probably happen, what he was talking about. Somehow they'd be able to convince her to get involved in it. Somehow.

"I'm going now."

"Just think about it, Nicole, all right? What I was talking about?"

She slipped out of the dark bedroom and went into her own bedroom.

In about half an hour, her mother came in. The bedroom was all shadow and silver moonlight. Nicole was under the covers.

"Nicole?"

No answer.

Her Mom came over and knealt next to the bed. "Did it go all right?" Nicole decided to answer, "Yes."

"Was he nice?"

"Yes."

"He didn't hurt you or anything?"

"No." Then, "Could we talk in the morning, Mom? I'm real tired."

She lay there for an hour trying to get to sleep. But all she could think of was what he'd suggested, about the three of them getting together.

She slept until late into the dark night. They woke her with their noises. Her first impression was thet he was hurting Mom but then she realized it was just Mom's wild enjoyment she was hearing. Mom would go along with it when the time came. Not at first. Not without some convincing. But eventually, she'd go along.

She'd go along.

And so would Nicole.

Three different neighbors report the screams. People on the nice, quiet, respectable block are up from their beds and out the door, arriving in pajamas and nightgowns and robes and slippers just about the time the first patrol car reaches the Sanders' driveway.

A heavyset cop knocks on the front door of the Sanders's home, pauses, and then knocks again.

This is when the side door of the house, the one that opens on the driveway, eases open and Nicole appears.

None of the neighbors have ever seen Nicole look like this. Hair unkempt, pajamas torn and blood-soaked, hands filthy with blood. Blood everywhere. Even in her hair. Even on her feet. Blood. No mistaking what it is. Blood. She stands in the headlights of the police car, moths and gnats and mosquitoes all around the headlights (big motor throbbing unevenly, needing points and plugs), and that is where the neighbors get their first good look at the knife she used. Butcher knife. Long wooden handle. Good but not great steel. A knife she just grabbed from the silverware drawer before going upstairs.

A second prowl car. This one dispersing two cops. Man and woman. The man starts dealing with the crowd. Pushing them back. The woman goes directly to Nicole.

"I need to know your name, miss, and what happened here."

But Nicole is long gone.

The first cop comes down the steps. Says something to the female officer and then goes in the side door.

"What's your name, miss?" the female cop asks in a soft voice. "I want to help you. I really do."

The crowd has grown greatly in a few minutes. Two different TV stations are here now, one in a large van, the other in a muddy Plymouth station wagon.

The first cop is back from inside. Goes to the other male cop. "It's a mess in there. A man and woman. The woman looks like the girl there. She stabbed the hell out of them. It's a frigging mess."

A few people in the crowd are close enough to hear this. A whisper like an undulating snake works its way through the crowd. Shock and sadness and yet a glee and excitement, too. The shock for the pitiful young girl standing blood-soaked in the headlights, her mind obviously gone; and yet glee and excitement, too. Every day life is so—everyday. No denying the excitement here. And didn't Kate Sanders think she was at least a little bit better than everybody else? And exactly who was that man who'd moved in a while ago? And now look at Nicole. Poor, poor Nicole.

The reporter from the van, having heard what the cop found inside, now gets his cameraman to follow him around as he gets statements from various neighbors.

"Well, Kate, the mother, she and her husband split up a few years ago."

"They were very quiet people, really, though I think everybody knew that Kate had a quite a few personal problems."

The cameraman angles his machine up the driveway, letting his lens linger on the lovely, crazed, blood-splattered girl standing in the headlights, Ophelia of the suburbs, which will make great fucking TV, just this lone shot of the lone heart-breaking crazy fucking girl.

And (voice over) a neighbor lady saying into the microphone: "It's just so hard to believe. She was such a good girl; such a good girl."

PARDS

1

BROMLEY ALWAYS LIKED IT WHEN PEOPLE ASKED HIM what he did for a living because then he could tell them he was a writer. He didn't mention his day job, which was being the only forty-nine-year-old bag "boy" at DeSoto's Supermarket; no, he just told them about his writing, and then showed them a copy of the one and only paperback novel he'd ever sold, a western called *Gun Fury*, which had been published by a company called Triton. He never mentioned that Triton had declared bankruptcy right after *Gun Fury* appeared, nor did he mention that Triton had been one of the worst publishers in history. Bromley's listeners didn't need to know that.

2

"Never seen anything like these before," the new mailman said on one of Bromley's days off (he usually worked weekends, which most of the teenagers refused to do, and so Sam DeSoto gave him two days off in the middle of the week). Bromley was sitting on the front porch of the aged Victorian apartment house where he lived, reading William Nolan's biography of Max Brand and sipping on a Diet Pepsi. In addition to losing his hair, Bromley had lately started to gain weight, one of the Chicano kids at the store even calling him "Fat Ass" one day, the little bastard, and so now it was Diet Pepsi instead of the regular stuff.

So Bromley was in the shade of the sunny porch, Mrs. Hanrahan's soap opera blaring through the lacy curtains, when the mailman said, "What exactly are they, anyway?"

"Fanzines."

"Fanzines?"

"Yeah, magazines that western fans publish themselves. There're fanzifies for people who like the old pulp magazines and fanzines for people who liked the old Saturday serials and fanzines for people who like the old western stars."

The mailman, who was just old enough to remember, said, "Like Gene and Roy?"

"Exactly. Like Gene and Roy."

"So do you put one out yourself, I mean being a writer and all?"

"No; but I write for a lot of them."

"Yeah? Which ones?"

"The ones about the old cowboy stars." Bromley wanted to tell him about his dream he had sometimes; standing in this movie lobby in 1948 with all these great lobby cards showing Wild Bill Elliott and The Durango Kid (God, there was no getting around it; guys who wore masks were just great) and Gabby Hayes and Jane Frazee and Tim Holt and The Three Mesquiteers, and how down on one end there was this table overflowing with pulp magazines, *The Pecos Kid Western* and *Frontier Stories* and *Thrilling Western Stories*; and then another table with an old 1946 table model radio with the sounds of "Bobby Benson and The B Bar B Riders" coming out of it; and yet another table with nothing but Big Little Books; and there was a church-like holiness in the air and Bromley was caught up in it, tears nearly streaming down his face; WAS NOT THIS HEAVEN? And he had this crazy urge to eat Cheerios, just the way Tonto did; or Ralston Purina, just like Tom Mix; or maybe even Pep, the way Superman was always telling him to.

"Those'd be the ones I'd be interested in, the cowboys, I mean," the mailman said. Then he shrugged and handed Bromley his mail. "You're really an interesting guy, Ken, you know that?"

3

He'd been married once, Bromley had, in the early sixties, already working at DeSoto's, to a pretty but dumb woman whom his mother did not like at all ("I don't see why you have to move out when you've got so much room here, especially since your father died, and anyway twenty-two is too young to get married, she's just looking for an easy ride if you ask me"), a waitress who seemed to know what all her customers made per hour at this-or-that factory, at this-or-that delivery service. "Four bucks an hour, Ken, you really should look into that." But somehow he never got around to it. Just down the block from DeSoto's was the city's largest used bookstore and he spent most of his lunch hours in there. The air was holy, the dusty air of Ace Doubles and Gold Medal books, of *All-Story Weekly* and *Star Western* and *Adventure*, the cocoon of paperbacks and magazines in which he'd spent his boyhood, never much caring that he didn't have many friends, that he was virtually invisible at school, or that the violent arguments of his parents caused him to shake uncontrollably for long periods of time behind his too-thin bedroom door. No, there were always the Saturday afternoon movies, or his books and magazines to escape into.

One night—this was a year or so into their marriage, the night one of those perfect late spring evenings shot through with fireflies and the scent of apple blossoms—right there in the same wedding bed Bromley would sleep in the rest of his life, right there in Mrs. Hanrahan's apartment house where he would live the rest of his life, his wife said, "I need to be honest with you."

"Huh?"

"I—did something."

"Did something?"

He was smoking a Lucky with the sheet just half on him and listening to the night birds at the window screen, and she was lying next to him in just her underwear.

"You know that Jimmy I told you about?"

"Uh, I guess so." She was always telling him about somebody.

"You know. He makes six-thirty-two an hour out at Rockwell."

"I guess."

"And I let him feel my breasts. He has the red Olds convertible, remember, with the white leather interior?"

"Oh. Yeah. Jimmy."

"Well the other day he wanted to know if I wanted a ride home after the dinner rush."

"Oh."

God, now he knew what was coming.

"I knew I shouldn't have said yes but he kept pushing the subject. You know how guys get."

"Yeah, I guess I do."

"Well, anyway, I let him give me a ride home."

"Was this Thursday?"

"Yeah. Thursday."

"When you were late?"

She hesitated. "Yeah, when I was late."

"I see."

Neither of them said anything for a long time. He finished his cigarette and then just lay with his hands on his chest, in his boxer shorts which she was always asking him not to wear ("You're a young man, Ken, you shouldn't wear things like that").

Then she said, "But he didn't take me straight home."

"I see."

"I mean I told him to. But he didn't. He wouldn't listen to anything I said. He just kept driving out along the river road. He just kept saying isn't it pretty at dusk like this, with the sunlight real coppery on the river like this? I had to admit that it was."

"Did you let him do anything to you?"

"I let him French kiss me."

"Oh. I see."

"But I didn't let him put his hand inside my bra."

He said nothing. He wondered if his heart would stop beating. Just *boom* like that and he would no longer be alive.

"And I didn't let him touch me down there."

He said nothing.

"He tried, Ken, but I wouldn't let him."

The tears came abruptly and without warning. There in the darkness he shook so hard—just the way he used to shake when his parents screamed at each other—that the whole bed shook. His wedding bed.

She leaned over and kissed him then, and it was a tender and pure kiss, he recognized it as such, and she said, "You're more like my brother or something, Ken. I didn't want it to turn out this way but it did anyway. I mean you never want to go dancing or take me out to dinner or make love or—" She smiled there in the darkness. "You're more interested in your book collection than you are me, Ken. And you know that's the truth."

Later on after a long time of not talking, just lying there, her sometimes taking drags from his cigarette, sometimes not, she leaned over and kissed him and put her hand down there and got him hard, and then they made love with a purity and tenderness that broke his heart because he knew this would be the last time, the very last time, and when it was over and they were just lying there again, she started crying too, soft girl tears there in the darkness, her a girl as he was still a boy, and then just before she fell asleep she said—her only bitter comment during the whole night—"Well, your mother will be relieved anyway. Just don't move back in with her. I care about you too much to see that happen. OK?"

The next day she was packed and gone. Three months later he got proceeding papers from a lawyer in Milwaukee and six months after that he was divorced. Throughout the first year, she wrote him postcards fairly frequently. She mentioned different restaurants she worked at and she mentioned how hot Milwaukee was in the summer and then how cold it was in the winter and then one card she said she was getting married to a guy with a real good job (she didn't mention his name nor did she mention how much he made an hour) and then abruptly the cards stopped except, inexplicably, two Christmases later when she sent him a Christmas card with the snapshot of an infant girl inside. Her first child.

He stayed on at DeSoto's of course, spending his lunch hours at the used bookstore, and he did not move back in with his mother.

4

The odd thing was, Bromley learned about Rex Stone's moving not through one of the fanzines but when somebody at DeSoto's

(Laughlin, the smirky guy in the meat department) mentioned that Stone was moving to Center City, a mere eighty miles from the city here. "That fuckin' cowboy guy, you know, the one when we were kids, the one who could make his horse dance up on his hind legs?" Bromley could scarcely believe it. Sure, he'd known that Rex Stone (a.k.a. Walter Sipkins) had been born in this area but who could have guessed that after fifteen years of being a star at Republic (he'd starred in the studio's very last B-westem, despite the fact that most film books mistakenly attributed this distinction to Allan "Rocky" Lane)—after fifteen years in movies and ten more in TV (usually in supporting roles but meaty ones), who could have guessed Stone would move back to where he'd come from?

About a month after Laughlin gave Bromley the word, the local paper ran a big photo of Stone in full singing-cowboy getup holding up a sweet little crippled girl in his arms. The caption read: "Cowboy Star spends sunset years helping others" and the story went on to detail how active Stone had become with Center City civic events. Retired now, he "planned to devote his life to helping all the little 'buckaroos and buckarettes' who need him."

Bromley couldn't believe it. Rex Stone. Only eighty miles from here. Rex Stone. The man he'd always measured himself against. Sure, Bromley liked Hoppy and Roy and Gene and Monte and Lash and Sunset but none of them had compared to Rex because, despite the fact that Rex sang a lot of sappy songs and could make his horse Stormy dance along at the same time, Rex was a *man*. The jaw and the eyes and the big hands and the deep voice told you that. He was a man not in the way of a Saturday afternoon hero but rather in the rough and somewhat mysterious way of, say, Robert Mitchum. That was why, back in the forties and fifties, Rex Stone had not only had a huge kids' following, he'd also managed to snag a major following of young women. (TV people had later tried to cast him as a he-man in a short-lived adventure series called *Bush Pilot* but the series had been on ZIV, and when ZIV went down—the other networks inevitably pushing it out—so did Rex's series).

And now, admittedly paunchier, gray-haired, and jowly, Rex Stone lived only eighty miles away.

5

"Is Mr. Stone there, please?"

"Who the hell is this?" The voice was female and old and accusatory.

Bromley did the only thing he could. He gulped. "Uh, my name is Bromley."

"Who?"

"Bromley."

"Spell it."

"Huh?"

"You deaf? I said spell it."

"B-r-o-m-1-e-y."

"Bromley."

"Yes."

"So just what the hell do you want?"

"I, uh, I'd like to speak to Mr. Stone."

"He's busy."

And with that, she hung up.

6

Six days later:

Dear Rex Stone,

I know that you're probably too busy to answer all your fan mail so let me assure you that while I'm a long time admirer of yours, this letter has to do with a professional matter.

As a published western author (GUN FURY, Triton Books, 1967 and hundreds of articles in western and popular culture magazines), I'd like to interview you for a forthcoming book about western stars of the forties and fifties called: INTO THE SUNSET (Leisure Books).

You may have noticed by my return address that I don't live very far from you. I'd very much like to come up for a day soon, bring my tape recorder, and spend several hours with you discussing your career.

I phoned several days ago but a woman answered and we seemed to have been disconnected or something.

I'd very much like to meet you and help bring your millions of fans up to date on your life. I know that you never attend any of the "Golden Oldie" shows that Gene and Roy and Lash and the others sometimes go to so this would be a particular treat for everybody who has followed your career.

Please let me know your answer at your earliest convenience.

Sincerely yours,
Ken Bromley

7

"Who?"

"Rex Stone."

"Rex Stone. Don't you remember, I used to see all his movies?"

"Movies. Hah. Complete waste of time as far as I'm concerned."

And in fact, that had been his mother's opinion all the time Bromley had been growing up, and it was her opinion even now that she was eighty-seven years old and living in a nursing home thanks to the insurance her husband had left her.

But even in a nursing home, she had control of him. She was sort of like the Scarab in one of the old Republic chapter plays. All-knowing. All-seeing. Plus, she had him trained. He always checked with her on anything major, and certainly buying a Trailways ticket was major, even if it was only for eighty miles, even if it was only for a day. She was convinced that she was about to die of a heart attack at any moment and so she wanted him on call twenty-four hours a day. If he wasn't at DeSoto's then he'd better by God be in his apartment. And she certainly didn't like the idea of a trip to Center City.

"Why would you waste your money on him? He doesn't even make movies anymore."

"I want to write an article about him."

"Phoo. Article. They don't even pay you for those things. They only paid you $500 for a whole book. Talk about getting cheated. Why, I read that there Stephen King makes twenty million a year. It was right in *People*."

"It'll only be for a day, Mom. That's all."

"A day? You know how long it takes you to die of a heart attack?" She very impressively snapped her fingers. The sound was of twigs snapping.

They were on the veranda, late afternoon. She had a cigarette going and she was sipping a glass of beer. She'd raised enough hell with the nursing home people that they gave into her once every day. One cigarette. One glass of beer.

"I really want to go, Mom. It's real important to me." How he hated his voice. His groveling. His begging, really. He was fifty, and nearly bald, and two or three of the clubs he belonged to gave him "senior rates."

And here he was pleading with this shriveled up little woman wound inside a black shawl despite the eighty-eight degrees.

"He have a phone?"

"Yes."

"You make sure you leave me that number."

"All right, Mom."

"It's all a waste of time if you ask me."

He leaned over and kissed her cheek. "I love you, Mom." She snorted smoke through her nostrils and said, "You're more like your father every day."

He knew she didn't mean that as a compliment.

8

"Who?"

"Rex Stone."

"Guess I must be a little young to remember him or something."

"He was really popular."

"Yeah, I imagine."

Bromley caught the kid's sarcasm, of course. Twerp was maybe sixteen or seventeen and had an arm's length of blue tattoos (Bromley's mother had always insisted that a tattoo was a sure sign of the lower classes) and one tiny silver earring (which marked him as a lot less than manly, even if a lot of young men did wear them).

Bromley would've sat with somebody else but this was the 8:30 AM Trailways that went to the state capital and so it was packed with lots of old ladies in big summery hats and so there was no place else to sit. This was the last empty seat and the kid had come with it.

"He set an attendance record at the Denver rodeo," Bromley said.

"Oh."

"And in 1949 he came in right behind Roy Rogers as the biggest box office draw."

"1949, huh?" The kid shrugged and looked out the bus window.

Bromley put his head back and closed his eyes. The bus engine made the whole bus tremble. The smell of diesel fuel reminded Bromley of boyhood summers, walking down to the Templar Theater to see all the new Saturday matinee movies. It was easy to recall the smell of theater popcorn, too, and the way the sunlight blinded you when you emerged onto the sidewalk six hours later, and the way summer dusk fell, the birds somehow sad in the summer trees, and the girls you saw sometimes, always a little older than you and always blonde in a showgirl sort of way, and how they made you ache and how vivid and perfect they remained in your daydreams the whole hot school vacation. Not even after Dr. Fitzsimmons had convinced his mother it was just muscle cramps and not polio at all would she let Bromley go to the movies again. Not until the following summer.

After twenty miles, Bromley opened his eyes again. Next to him, the kid had this earplug in and his whole body was kind of sit-dancing to the music snaking from the transistor in his lap to the plug in his ear.

The way the kid moved around there, moving and grooving he thought it was called, struck Bromley as downright obscene.

Bromley closed his eyes again, and thought of the summer he got those funny aches in his legs and his mother went crazy and said he had polio for sure and lit candles to the Blessed Mother all summer and wouldn't let Bromley go to any movie theaters. She said that this was the number one place for catching polio germs and then she showed him a newspaper photo of a poor little kid inside an iron lung, a photo she always seemed to have handy.

The kid got off way before Center City, and Bromley had the rest of the trip to enjoy by himself. He'd been holding in gas for a long time and it was a pure pleasure to let it go.

9

"Here you go."

"You sure this is the right address?"

"Center Grove, right here."

"But it's a trailer park."

"That's right. Center Grove Trailer Park. See that sign over there?"

Bromley looked and there it was sure enough: green letters on white background, CENTER GROVE TRAILER PARK.

"Huh," Bromley said, "I'll be damned. A trailer park." Somehow he couldn't imagine Rex Stone living in a trailer. He had an odd thought: Did his horse Stormy live with him in there, too?

He paid the cabbie six bucks, six sweaty ones that had been deep in his summer pocket, and got out, lugging his big old Webcor recorder along with him.

The place was dusty, hot and Midwestern, a high sloping hill covered with long, modern trailers of the sort that put on the airs of a real house. Lying east and west, bracketing all the metal homes gleaming in the sunlight, were pastures, black and white dairy cows grazing, and distantly a farmer on a green John Deere raising plumes of dust as he did some tilling. A red Piper Cub circled lazily over head, like a papier mâché bird.

Each trailer had an address. Just like a house. He supposed he was being a snob, he after all lived in an apartment house, he after all lived in a three room apartment, but he couldn't help it. People who lived in trailers . . .

And then he remembered: his mother of course. "People who live in trailers are hillbillies." She'd never offered any proof of this. That was not her way. She'd simply stated it so many times growing up that he'd come to believe it. At least a part of him had.

Hillbillies.

He found the trailer he was looking for. It was an Airstream, one of those silver jobs, and it looked to be a block long and it looked to be almost sinfully tidy as to shell and surrounding lawn. Indeed, bright chipper summer flowers had been planted all along the perimeter of the place. He wondered what his mother would make of that.

He went up and knocked and then there *he* was.

It was a strange feeling.

Here you'd spent all your life with an image of somebody fixed in your mind and then when you meet him—

Well, for him, Rex Stone would always be this tall, handsome, slender cuss in the literal white hat astride Stormy. His western clothes would have a discreet number of spangles, his hips would ride a pair of six guns always ready to impose justice on the lawless, and he'd just generally be—

—well, heroic. There was no other word for it. Heroic.

What he would not be was a) this old guy with a beer belly, wearing a t-shirt that said I'M AN OLD FART AND PROUD OF IT, b) this bald guy wearing a pair of lime green golf pants or c) this fat guy with a beer gut that looked a lot worse than Bromley's own.

"You Bromley?"

"Uh, yes."

"I'm Stone."

At least he had a strong grip. In fact, Bromley even winced a little.

Stone hadn't quite shut the door behind him. He said, "Be right back."

Not even inviting Bromley in or anything.

Bromley stood there listening to the noises of the trailer park: an obstinate lawn mower somewhere distant; a baby crying; a couple arguing and slamming more doors than you'd think a trailer could possibly hold; and a radio playing an aching country western ballad about heartbreak.

Bromley came back out. He carried two folded-up lawn chairs and a six pack of Hamms beer.

He didn't say anything, just nodded for Bromley to follow. On the opposite end of the trailer as an overhang. Some tiles had been laid down to make a small patio. Here Stone flicked the chairs into proper position—his motions were young and powerful, belying his old fart appearance—and then he sat himself down and nodded for Bromley to do likewise.

"Beer?"

"Thanks," Bromley said. Actually, he didn't care much for alcohol but he wanted to be polite.

"That's an old one, isn't it?"

Bromley looked at his tape recorder. Indeed it was. A Webcor, a big heavy box with heads for reel-to-reel tape up top. Twenty-five years ago a friend of his had desperately needed money for some now forgotten reason. Bromley had paid him fifty dollars.

"It still works well, though. Just because it's old doesn't mean it can't do the job."

Stone laughed a slick Hollywood laugh and winked with great dramatic luridness. "That's what I tell the ladies about myself." Then he leaned forward and with a big powerful hand slapped the arm of Bromley's lawn chair. "Just because I'm old doesn't mean I can't do the job."

Bromley laughed, knowing he was expected to.

Stone seemed to relax some then, sitting back and sipping his beer. He studied Bromley for awhile and said, "Sorry, my friend."

"Sorry?"

"Sure. For being this old fart. You know, the way my t-shirt says."

"Well, heck, I—"

"Sure you did."

"I did?"

"Of course. You grew up seeing my movies and you've got this picture of me fixed in your head—this strong, handsome young man—and then you see me—" He shrugged. "I'm an old fart."

"No, you're not. You're—"

Stone waved a hand. "It doesn't bother me, son. It really doesn't. I mean, everybody gets old. Gene did and Roy did and Lash did—and now it's my turn."

Bromley wasn't sure why but he sort of liked it how Stone had called him "son." Made Bromley feel young somehow; as if most of his life (that great golden potential of youth) were still ahead of him and not mostly behind him.

"So you want to wind that puppy up?"

"That puppy?"

"The recorder. That big ole B-52 Webcor."

"Oh. Right. The recorder."

"And I'll tell you how it all started. And how it all ended."

"Yeah. Sure. Great."

So he wound that puppy up and Rex Stone started talking.

10

See, he'd never had any intention of being a movie star. He'd just been visiting in Los Angeles that day in 1934 when he was drinking a malt and having a ham sandwich in this drugstore when he happened to notice that, out on the sunny street, a group of people were standing there watching some kind of accident. Being naturally curious, and being from the Midwest and wanting to bring back all the great stories he could, he went outside to see what was going on, only it wasn't an accident, it was a movie, a bank robbery get-away was being staged, complete with a heartstoppingly beautiful actress holding a tommy-gun and dangling an extra-long cigarette from her creamy red lips, and a fat bald little director who not only wore honest-to-God jodphurs but also carried a bullhorn and wore, if you could believe it, a monocle over his right eye.

That's how it started, how Presnell, that was the director, saw him standing there on the edge of the crowd, and between shots came over and started talking to him, and then had this very fetching young girl come over and take down his name and the address where he was staying, and four days—literally four days later—he was playing a six-line role in a western and singing as part of the cowboy singers who backed up the tone-deaf star.

Not that the rest of it came easy. It wasn't overnight or anything. By Stone's estimate he appeared in forty-seven movies (at least twenty of which came from Monogram, for God's sake) before it finally happened. One day Herbert Yates of Republic looked at sagging box office receipts for his westerns and then decided to give the singing cowboy movies one last try. Yates had been under the impression that singing cowboys had bit the dust about the time television started imposing itself on the American scene. Well, as usual, Herb's gut proved savvy: The Rex Stone pictures, eighteen of them in all, were the biggest-grossing Republic pictures of the era, and came in right behind Roy and Gene in overall grosses. Rex Stone was a star, at least in those small American burgs where the Fourth of July was still a big deal and where men, at least on occasion, still held doors for ladies.

As for Rex personally, he was not only a favorite with the kids, he was also a favorite with the starlets, as Louella Parsons, then the country's premiere gossip columnist, noted with great delight. Rex was a big handsome lug and don't think he didn't take advantage of it. In one year he was hit with three fists (from jealous husbands), one champagne bottle (from a jealous fiancée) and two paternity suits. It was about then that he started marrying, a practice he kept up until the Rex Stone pictures started losing money and old Herb finally quit turning out westerns. Some movie historians had him marrying seven times; Rex himself claimed a mere five brides, though he did admit that there was one quickie Mexican marriage that might/ might not have been legal. Anyway, the marriages didn't exactly help his popularity. Roy and Gene scrupulously kept their private parts in their pants; Rex seemed to be flaunting his and in those areas of the country where the Fourth of July still meant something, and where men still opened doors for ladies, his rambunctious behavior with starlets hurt him, and hurt him badly.

Then came the fifties and all those failed TV pilots and TV series. He started looking heavier and older, and then he started flying to Italy where westerns were being turned out faster than pizzas, and where Rex Stone, even with something of a gut and something of a balding head, was still a big deal. Meanwhile, he kept on marrying, two brides between 1955 and 1959.

By now, the marriages were no longer scandals, they were jokes, the stuff of talk show repartee, and Rex Stone was pretty much finished.

Nobody heard from or about him. Various organizations such as The Cowboy Hall of Fame, which tried to keep members up on news of all the old film stars, did their best to track him down but even when he got the letters, he just tossed them away. He didn't want to go on the rodeo circuit and be this sad old chunky guy on this big golden Palomino waving his white Stetson to a crowd of kids who had no idea who he was. He did not want to cut ribbons at supermarket grand openings, he did not want to be surrounded by dozens of sad grotesque aging fans (no offense, Mr. Bromley) at "nostalgia" conventions, he did not want to be featured in every other fanzine about old western stars, and brag in print about how good movies had been back then and what shit (relatively speaking) they were today.

So for the past twenty obscure years, what he'd been doing was just moving around the country in his Airstream and living in all the places he'd always wanted to live (North Carolina for the beauty and the fishing; Arizona for the climate; New Hampshire for the beautiful autumns and New England sense of tradition and heritage).

11

"Do you ever miss any of them?"

"Any of who?"

"You know, your wives."

"Oh."

"I mean, now that you're older and settled, isn't there one of them it would be nice to have along?"

At this point, Stone started glancing over his shoulder at the rear window.

Bromley hadn't noticed before, but despite the machine noise the air conditioning unit made, the back window was open about halfway. Bromley wondered why.

"Not really, I guess."

"You ever hear from any of them?"

"Uh, not really."

Then, unable to stop himself from asking this gushy question, Bromley said, "Wanda Mallory, was she as beautiful in person as she was on the screen?"

"She was a bitch and a gold-digger."

The thing was, Rex Stone hadn't said this. He'd just been sitting there holding his beer, with his mouth closed, and then out came the words.

Except the voice wasn't anything like Rex's at all. It was a crone's voice, a harsh cranky old lady's voice, and it had come wafting from the open back window.

Seeing how baffled Bromley looked, Stone said, "Why don't you try and get some sleep, Mother?" He was addressing the partially open rear window.

"You tell him what a little conniver she was. What a little conniver they all were."

"Did you take your medication this morning, Mother?"

"Don't try to change the subject. You tell him the truth about those little harlots."

"Yes, Mother."

"And I mean it."

"Yes, Mother."

"All that money you wasted on them."

"Yes, Mother."

"And I always had the smallest room. The very smallest room."

"Yes, Mother."

And then there was silence and Rex Stone just sat there sort of slumped over in his chair, whipped, beaten, this old man who looked as if some young guy had just delivered a killer blow to his solar plexus. He looked sad and embarrassed, and he even looked a little dazed and confused. Bromley had no idea what to say.

The voice had reminded him a little of the mother's voice in *Psycho* whenever she got mad at Norman. Or actually (God forgive him) of his own mother's voice.

After awhile, still not looking Bromley straight in the eyes, Rex Stone said, "Why don't we hike on up to the rec room? It's a real nice place." One thing: he was whispering his words.

Then he looked nervously up at the open rear window and then he started making these big pantomime gestures that said Follow Me.

Obviously Rex Stone, cowboy star, singer of lush romantic juke-box ballads, wooer and winner of untold gorgeous starlets, was scared shitless of his mom.

12

Ping.

"Every one of them?"

Pong.

"Every single god damn one of them."

Ping.

"But how?"

Pong.

"Because she got me by the throat the day I was born, and she hasn't let go since."

Ping.

They had been in the recreation hall for twenty minutes. It was a big and presently empty room shady and cool on this hot day, with two billiard tables, a jukebox, a candy machine, a Coke machine, a sign that said I'M A SQUARE DANCER AND PROUD OF IT, and the Ping-Pong table on which Bromley and Rex Stone had been play-ing for the past ten minutes. Stone was good at it; Bromley not.

"Hell, they even started whispering I was queer," Stone said. "Just married all these women to make things look good, you know, the way some of the actors did but hell, I like girls, not boys."

"So you loved every one?"

"Every single one."

"And your mother broke up each marriage?"

"Every single god damn one."

"You couldn't get rid of her?"

"Hell, I tried, don't think I didn't, but about the time my bride and would move into our new place, my mother would come up with some new ailment and force me to let her move in."

"Is that what she meant by always having the smallest room?"

"Yup."

"So she's pretty much lived with you all your life?"

"All my life, ever since my father died anyway, when I was eighteen."

"And your wives—"

"They'd just get fed up with how she controlled me and then they'd—"

"—leave. They'd leave you. Right?" Bromley said, thinking of his own wife, and how much she'd resented his mother.

"That's exactly what they'd do. Leave."

Ping.

Pong.

Pause.

The game went on.

And then Rex Stone said it, "You aren't going to put all this stuff about my mom in your article are you, son?"

There was a definite pleading tone in his voice and eyes now.

"No, I'd never do that, Mr. Stone."

"When the hell you going to start calling me Rex?" said the old man at the other end of the pool table.

Bromley smiled self-consciously. "All right—Rex."

"You think you got enough?"

"Yes; yes, I do." Bromley said, and he did, more than enough for a good article about Rex Stone. The fanzine readers would love it.

"You play pool?" Stone said.

"Better than I play Ping-Pong."

"Good. Then let's try a game."

They were each chalking their cues when the black phone on the west wall rang.

Rex glanced at it with genuine alarm.

He shook his head and walked over to it. "Yes?"

He looked back at Bromley and shook his head. "All right, Mother, so you found me. Now what?"

Now he turned to the wall and muffled his voice, as if he didn't want Bromley to hear a word of it.

"You know how embarrassing this is?"

Pause.

"I'll go to the drug store tonight. Not right now, Mother."

Pause.

"I get pretty sick of you telling me that I don't take good care of you, Mother."

"All right." And then a huge, sad sigh.

Rex Stone hung up and turned back to the phone. "Maybe I'd better go check on her," he said. "Maybe she really is sick this time. You mind?"

"No, Rex, that's fine."

So they left the recreation hall and went back to the trailer. Nobody, not the little kids, not the mothers pushing strollers, seemed to pay any attention to Rex at all.

Bromley wanted to say: hey, this is *Rex Stone* for shit's sake! Rex Stone!

On the way back, Rex told him a couple of stories about Lash LaRue and Tim Holt but Bromley could tell that Rex was still embarrassed about his mother's phone call.

Bromley said, "I'll have to be leaving in twenty minutes. There's only one more bus back to town today."

"I've really enjoyed this, son."

"So have I." And then Bromley decided to ask him. Rex would probably just say no, that it was a dumb idea, but what could it hurt to ask.

"Rex?"

"Yup."

"How would you feel about getting dressed up in your cowboy duds and having me take your photo?"

"Ah, hell, son, I don't know about that."

"It'd really go great with this article. Your fans would really appreciate it."

"You think they would?"

"I know they would. They'd love it."

So Rex Stone chewed it over for awhile and then shrugged and said, "How about just standing next to the Airstream?"

"That'd be great."

When they got back to the trailer, Rex started whispering again. "Why don't you wait out here, son. I'll go inside and change my clothes and then come back out. All right?"

"Fine."

So while Rex went inside, Bromley went over and got his Polaroid all ready.

Rex didn't come out in five minutes. Rex didn't come out in ten minutes. Rex didn't come out in fifteen minutes.

Bromley could hear it all, oh not all the words exactly, but certainly he heard the tone of voice. She was chewing on him in a steady stream of rancor that managed to stun and depress even Bromley, who wasn't even directly involved.

Every few minutes, he'd hear Rex say, "All right, Mother," in this really sad, resigned way.

And then it ended all of a sudden and the trailer door opened and there stood Rex Stone in his cowboy costume, the big white hat, the fancy cowboy clothes with spangles and fringes, the big six-guns slung low on his hips, and his trustworthy guitar dangling from his right hand.

Bromley hadn't realized till this moment just how old Rex Stone was.

How the whole face sagged into jowls.

How the whole gut swelled over the gunbelt. How the hands were liver-spotted and trembling. "I sure feel silly in this get-up, son," Rex said.

"But you look great."

"You sure about that?"

"I'm sure about that, Rex." Bromley waved his hand a little and said, "How about a step or two to the right, just to the side of the door."

And it was at that exact moment that the trailer door opened and out stepped a little kewpie-doll of a woman, no more than four-eight, four-nine, no more than eighty pounds, no more than two or three hundred years old, buried inside of some kind of gaudy pink K-Mart wrapper, her feet swathed in matching pink fluffy slippers that went *thwap, thwap, thwap* as she came down the stairs and took her place next to her son.

"I forgot to tell you," Rex Stone said, "Mom asked if she could be in the picture, too."

13

He tried for the next six weeks to write the article. Every few days, Rex would call and say, "Just wanted to see how it was going, son," and would then say, "You, uh, haven't mentioned my mom or anything in it, have you?" and Bromley would say, uh, no, Rex, I, uh, haven't.

But for some reason he couldn't write the piece.

Every time he started it, it was just too bleak. Here was a guy who'd been in a very real prison all his life. (Not unlike Bromley.) Here was a guy who kept trying to break away and break away but couldn't. (Not unlike Bromley.) Here was a guy who had obviously wanted to spend his life with beautiful women but whose mother just didn't like the idea. (Not unlike Bromley.)

So how could you write a piece about a guy who'd been a hero to Bromley's whole generation . . . and tell the glum truth?

Because it was a pretty pathetic story.

14

Rex called two days after Bromley mailed him the article. "Son," he said.

"Yes?"

"I—"

And then he made a familiar sound. "You know what that is, son?"

"You're blowing your nose?"

"Right. And you know why?"

"Why?"

"Because your article made me cry. And not cry for sad, son. Cry for happy."

"I'm glad you like it, Rex."

"I don't like it, son. I love it."

"I wasn't sure how you'd feel about it. I mean, I took certain liber-ties and I—"

"Son, you done good. You done real, real good."

15

The day the fanzine arrived, Bromley sat down in his recliner and started reading it, the way he did with all his own articles.

He turned back the cover and flipped through the pages till he saw the picture of Rex.

He'd stuck to the older photos. He certainly hadn't used the one with Rex's mother in it.

And then he read the caption under the photo of a young Rex as the cowboy star: "Here's a heartwarming article about cowboy film giant Rex Stone and how he's spent his life living on a horse ranch in Montana, sharing his bountiful life with his beautiful wife and three children."

Just the kind of life Bromley had always wished for himself.

A wife and three children.

Just the kind of life his generation would have expected Rex Stone to live.

16

"You haven't called me for a long time."

"I called you the night before last, Mother," Bromley said.

"I could be dead for all you care."

"Yes, Mother."

"Lying here on the floor while you're out running around."

"Yes, Mother."

And then he thought of Rex Stone's ranch in Montana, Rex and his beautiful starlet wife and their three perfectly behaved children.

He'd go visit Rex there someday soon.

Very soon.

That's just what he'd do. "Are you listening to me?"

"Yes," Bromley said. "Yes, Mother, I always listen to you."

Someday very soon now.

Ed Gorman has been a full time writer for nearly 30 years. His first novel, *Rough Cut*, was published in 1985, and since then he has published dozens more. He has won nearly every major award—the Shamus, the Anthony—for "Best Critical Work"—the Spur, and the International Fiction Writer's Award. He's twice been nominated for the Edgar. He was awarded The Eye for lifetime achievement by the Private Eye Writers Association in 2011.

Jon Breen of *Ellery Queen* magazine noted: "Ed Gorman has the same infallible readability as writers like Lawrence Block, Max Allan Collins, Donald E. Westlake, Ed McBain, and John D. MacDonald."

Kirkus called Ed Gorman "One of the most original crime writers around."

The Oxford Book of Short Stories noted that his work "provides fresh ideas, characters and approaches."

Gorman's novels *The Poker Club* and *The Haunted* have both been filmed.

CPSIA information can be obtained
at www.ICGtesting.com
Printed in the USA
FFOW02n0402250416
23503FF